# The College of Corn

by

## Kunyang He

**Harvard Square Editions**
**New York**
**2017**

*The College of Corn*
copyright © 2017 Kunyang He

ISBN 978-1-941861-43-1
Printed in the United States of America
Published in the United States by
Harvard Square Editions
www.harvardsquareeditions

Part One

1

"The Chinese are coming," a Chinese man standing at a bus stop whispered to a young Chinese woman, probably his girlfriend, now squinting under bright sunlight in the direction the man was pointing. A crimson bus stopped across the street. The pneumatic door let off steam as it slid open, coughing off passengers with sleepy bones and bleary eyes adjusting to the scorching overexposure to the Midwest. They had arrived in an Illinois university town. At last, this was the United States of America.

From the coach's storage area, the driver was unloading the luggage. Passengers flung super-sized suitcases and overfilled duffel bags onto their shoulders, and began fumbling in briefcases, purses and wallets, fishing and feeling for maps, receipts, scraps of paper with words that they squinted at to decipher. Zippers wheezed open and closed, one of which broke off in an untimely manner, a piece of metal launching into the air, followed by a squeak of surprise, then a string of laughter.

A few freshmen arriving for the first time were dressed fashion-consciously despite the sultry weather. They were startled by squirrels lingering around pestering the humans for food, while sophisticated juniors, disillusioned seniors, and two careworn graduate students looked as if they could not care less about the natural beauty and the swathing serenity on the campus during the last few days of the summer vacation. Some of them even hated this place. They hated the windy climate, the food, the spread-out campus tiring their legs with its classrooms and dorms built insensible to space and distance, and the seemingly borderless, besieging corn fields, and for some of them, what they hated most were newcomers.

The bus left right away. It would drive six miles until it got onto Interstate 57, a highway linking Missouri and Illinois that parallels the old Illinois Central rail line for much of its route: a shortcut for travelers headed from the South (Memphis, New Orleans, etc.) to Illinois. Then it would follow Interstate 57 to Chicago, bypassing a few counties like Ford, Iroquois, Kankakee, Will and after two hours' drive, it would land on Canal Street in Chicago. There were buses like this driving back and forth three times a day between C_University and the roaring metropolis.

I was trying to cross the campus intersected by cement paths from the west where there was a small post office, when two new Chinese students came up to me. "Excuse me, sir. Do you happen to know where the International Student Centre is?" They spoke in English as they were uncertain of my nationality and might have mistaken me for Korean, Japanese, or just an American.

They reminded me of my first year in the United States, jaunty, fresh and over-polite, which I would never be able to pull off again. Back then I was twenty-six, now I am thirty-two.

I was a doctoral student in the art history department, since on finishing a master's degree in graphic design, I couldn't get myself a full-time job. However, my case was by no means very bad or even worthy of complaint. On the contrary, the concept of the job market had changed from a place to seek a stable adult life to an arena for dogfights.

Smug about getting into the college of corn, I was determined to find peace and beauty in long forgotten artworks. There were students who had stayed in the department for twelve years until nobody dared ask them about when they would be ready to defend their dissertations or just leave. I thought I could do that, too. My university was a big state university, famous for engineering, accounting, financial planning, actuarial and a few other majors worthy of the astoundingly high tuition and promising rosy career outlooks. It attracted international students from all over the world, and not least from China.

My mother originally protested my decision to stay on in the United States rather than going back to China, but my father soon upheld it. "I have talked with your mother; she is fine," he said on the phone with his usual air of solemnity and finality.

Incidentally, my father, who was quite an interesting figure, had retired from a Chinese state-owned coal mining company. He used to be the general manager, appointed by the authoritarian government thanks to his aptitude for coming up with witty epigrams for blue-collar workers and a well-shaped face. Since he believed that he was successful in every possible way except being artistic, his only son had to attend every art class the family could afford and that my hometown city could offer — calligraphy, life drawing, painting, piano, even martial arts. They were overwhelming and bewildering to a teenager with average intelligence, a pale face and a weak stomach. Eventually, I turned out a mediocre painter with the taste of a king.

Being a typical mediocre artist and a philistine of culture, the man who knows about what he should, and makes sure that it has no effect on him, I spent most of my time chasing after hysterical girls rather than practising my craft. In the last six years, my heart had been broken three times, and the fourth relationship, as the girl had moved to Iowa, had been in a state of tepid lingering, with a tenuous connection sustained by a few phone calls initiated mainly by me.

Having walked thirty minutes in the scorching sunlight, I arrived at the center of campus. The hardback edition of *The Newspaper Designer's Handbook*, with which I had frolicked in a grove on the west side of the campus, started to weigh me down.

Unlike the dewy-eyed squirrels who lived off campus, their high-strung, campus-centric relatives scuttled across the lawns, chasing one another, flying among tree branches, sparing no time to lament their automobile-flattened peers stuck on the tarmac. There was a squad of these rodent daredevils rallied near a cafe, ambushing customers, and then skirmishing among themselves. The cafe manager used to be a librarian at the university. Having inherited his father's business and the same old-time smile, he was now busy behind his own counter. Beside him stood a pierced and sulky undergraduate. When I slipped in, a TV screen was loudly broadcasting a program in which a florid middle-aged man was talking fanatically about eradicating identity fraud with regard to the current presidential election. I stood shivering in the air-conditioned foyer adjacent to the counter while I had a moment of respite from the torrid weather outside.

The undergraduate greeted me. "Still on campus?"

"Yeah, have some work to do," I said.

"Good, good," he nodded, sucking his lower lip, "then how can I help you? Coffee?"

"Medium, please," I said.

His eyes fixed on me, making me feel like I must have said something inappropriate. But the frozen look on his face lasted only for a fraction of a second. Then he said, "why don't you take a seat, and I'll bring the coffee to you."

I was bemused. For one, his assumption that I was taking a coffee for here was unconscionable. Secondly, since when had this joint changed into a restaurant, and did this mean that I had to tip him? And thirdly, was he...?

"Alright," I said meekly, turning to the room dotted with empty stools and round tables looking like giant mushrooms.

I seated myself and put down the chunky book on the table. Having nothing to do, I began to finger through it. The book was rated as a four-out-of-five-star book by fifty-three reviewers on Amazon.com, so it was supposed to be a reliable book. I would not have bought it but for a young Chinese woman whose English name was Rachel. She wanted me to read it. She was a doctoral student in the communication department. We had been friends for three years and had many common interests. The discrepancy that kept us from being the loves of each other's lives was that she seemed to have a clear vision of her life and a fabulous passion to realize it, while I epitomized the very lack of those qualities. She'd started up a Chinese newspaper two years earlier, the first Chinese newspaper at the university, and I had been volunteering as a graphic designer, her protégé, ever since. Recently, she had become unsatisfied with my shoddy work. Prompting me to buy a book was only part of her project to ameliorate the editorial office.

The undergraduate came up, set down the coffee in front of me with his multiply-ringed fingers. Then, he pulled up a mushroom and sat down.

"My name is J. J.," he said, holding out the other hand.

"Hi, what's up?" I asked. Discomfort grew in my sternum.

"I know you work for the Chinese newspaper," he said, "can you do me a favor?"

I was relieved. I adjusted myself, my butt negotiating a few square-inches of space on the chair, and I said, "What can I do for you?"

Then he took out a thumb-drive from his back pocket. "Here are some of my writing samples. You are hiring, aren't you?"

"Yes, we are."

"Great. I should have sent them to the email address, but I figured no one was gonna read it."

"Well— " The accusation was well deserved, and I was about to fudge my next remark, when he said, "It's OK. I mean it would be great if you could do me this favor." He said, "Anyway, the coffee is on the house." He stood up and flashed me a grin.

I left the cafe holding the thumb-drive and clutching the book under my arm. I went through the Student Union building and stepped onto the quad lawn, flanked by the new computer science buildings that towered over the old, diminishing structures still accommodating the liberal arts. The sun was beating down more harshly on the inner campus area, as this was sparsely planted with trees except for a few church spires topped by gilt crosses soaring blindly into the blue.

I alighted on a walkway dappled with the shadow of two enormous oaks whose bright-colored and exuberant foliage fronted Gregory Hall. The flagged floor was hot and grainy. I glanced back before I slipped into the vestibule. The campus looked arid, depleted of life but full of mechanical energy.

## 2

"Leave the door open," Rachel said.

An air conditioner was humming at the end of the office, not producing as much cool air as noise.

"I saw a lot of Chinese coming today," I said, stepping in.

It was a small office, crammed with furniture. There were four heavy desks, three antique desktop computers, three steel-made bookshelves and a fold-up couch Rachel had moved in from her own apartment, all packed in a room of about seventy square feet. Though it had a built-in air-conditioner, the real cooling relied on a quaint wooden fan that hung over the center of the ceiling.

"What are they?" she asked in exasperation, as if I made her lose track of something on the computer monitor, set too close to her chest.

"I guess students?"

"Young? Old? Urban? Country?"

"Young and old. I can't tell if they are rich or poor. If they are poor, they spend practically everything on their clothes."

"Come, come, potential subscribers," she said cheerlessly.

Rachel had a pert face, an average stature, and was now wearing a pair of tight jeans topped by a plain, grey T-shirt. The philosophy here was to make the attire disappear in the presence of a fine body. She was one of those inspirational cases in which the heroine had completely transfigured herself from a chubby, plain-looking Chinese girl with a flabby waist, flimsy limbs, and a set of weak lungs into a figure absolutely photographable for, say, a medical billboard. She had debunked the myth with which her mom had been pestering her: You are weak because you were born a weak baby, and being weak is fine for a Chinese lady.

Now she went to the gym every day; from 6:00 p.m. to 8:00 p.m., she had to get on a treadmill, running, watching news channels, exercising her will power and imagining her dumpiness transferring into something pert and photographable.

"You got it?" she said to me after a long pause as if she had just recalled the cause of my absence.

"It's too big; it didn't fit in the mailbox." I lifted the book, weighing it in my hand.

"There are no rules these days," she said accusingly, "sometimes they don't deliver it because it's too big, sometimes because it's too long, sometimes you have to sign, sometimes they just dump it in the corridor and it gets stolen."

While talking, she craned her neck nearer to the monitor, straining her eyes. She snorted occasionally and, once in a while, growled at a grammar error or an ill-phrased sentence. The serious air on her face made her look even more adorable and reassuring. But I had been warned to keep my private enjoyment to myself, for she had declared twice that our relationship could never go beyond this newsroom.

The newspaper came out weekly on Thursdays. The contributors to the paper were volunteers, so the budget went for printing costs. We printed it in the printing center of the university, and stacked them on the wooden or plastic newsstands that dotted the campus. The paper was subsidized by the university, and an office room was provided after Rachel persuasively appealed to the college administration: it was a shame for this university with so many Chinese students not to have a Chinese newspaper.

For the first issue, she, the chief editor, wrote an erudite essay paraphrasing or parodying Hegel: "A newspaper is the quintessential representation of the unfolding of the absolute idea haunting a society." It was a foolish piece of writing. Very few people knew what that meant and fewer solitary souls read the paper. A Chinese restaurant advertised its menus for six months, and then, even though Rachel let the contract run over for another extra three months, the boss of the restaurant still wanted to terminate. And it was a shame that the boss should send his autistic son as the terminator, whereas Rachel had been very discreet so as to have an amicable settlement.

On top of running the newspaper, twice a week, she taught an undergraduate course on sociological theories. Aiming to make young students feel hateful of consumerism, she taught as if she was a missionary with a divine message. She would invite a sullen girl who had not grasped the ideas presented in class to her office, and talk at her for hours until the girl gave herself up, promising to re-write an essay to get on with the rest of the critical squad. Sometimes, to simply flaunt her power, she would downgrade a snooty, cynical student who was smart enough to write a fine piece but failed to do it with all his heart.

She also held the presidency of two student organizations. One was the Film for Social Change Club, and the other, the Asian Women's Resource Center. The latter was almost founded single-handedly by herself, and Rachel refused to affiliate it with the university's women's resource center because the latter was, she thought, too white. Every Friday night, a group of young women and a chubby boy who seemed to have nowhere else to go brought homemade cheese cake to the office. It was called, behind her back, the Man Hater Club. She knew it. God knows if she liked it.

"I am thinking of expanding," she said to me, turning away from the screen.

"Expanding what?" I asked, alarmed. "With what?" I added.

"Why? New pages," she said.

"How many pages do we have now?" I asked. "I think we should have new staff rather than more pages."

"You don't know how many pages we have?" she asked gravely.

"Why? I never count." I braced myself.

"Eight!"

"What do you have in mind?"

She swirled the chair around, drawing it up to me, eyes full of brightness and fresh hopes. While she started to pitch to me the new grand plan for the paper, I noticed a string of grey hair dancing at her temple. I was startled and then cringed. Suddenly I felt guilty. I was not as dedicated as I had made myself out to be. I knew I would eventually betray her or not be able to live up to her expectations. I would, like the Chinese restaurant advertizer, back off one day and disappear.

"What is this?" As I was not really listening, I was distracted by a cardboard box, unpacked and lying beside the monitor. I took a peek inside the box and there was a piece of jagged rock.

"Oh, that." She stopped. "Well, it came with this." She reached up to a rack and took down a file folder. She slid out a piece of rumpled paper and handed it to me.

It was a page torn out of a gossip magazine. An oversized, naked lady was lying on a nameless beach, and a red arrow scribbled on recklessly was pointing at her head. Over the head of the obese woman and at the end of the arrow, a line of scandalous red marker read: "Rachel is a bitch. When you die I will dance on your grave!"

"Oh, my..." I exclaimed. "Who did this?" I held the paper, my hand trembling.

"Considering the quality, I'm not really worried," she said, taking it back, and she filed it away. "And you don't worry about it either; I need you to write a thank you letter."

"Are you sure?" I asked.

She didn't answer my question. "Somebody just donated five hundred dollars to our account."

"What?" I raised my voice involuntarily as this came as a bigger surprise. "I mean, really?!"

## 3

Rachel had a theory: there are two types of bores living in their two kinds of imaginary worlds. The first strives for a utopia in which everyone will have an ideal life, so that they are bound to fail. The other strives for himself to have an enviable life, but never has the time and the intelligence to examine what is worthy of striving for. The first group is largely made up of impractical socialists, hot-headed activists, and some hard-ass professors who scream about socialism but had never done any manual work in their lives besides changing light bulbs. The other group is just a big crowd, which generously accommodates myriad precocious art students so eager to show the world their premature talent, young women born attractive, who are preoccupied with worldly nonsense, and also most rich people, who are not satisfied with just being rich but anxious to have their names associated with culture or politics.

She said she could not stand working with any of these types, so she ruled out most of the applicants who wanted to work for the paper. And this might be the reason, I privately thought, that she tolerated me. I was sufficiently disillusioned, but not to the extent of facetiousness. Pessimistic about personal achievement but still being one of the few well-dressed Chinese students in their thirties. Compared to me, those applicants, according to their cover letters, were either impractically pompous, raving about social change, or robotically pragmatic, listing their merits as if they were high-end technological devices that were just launched, sleek and gleaming, from a laboratory. So even though the work was now encroaching upon my studies and eating away at Rachel's health, we rarely had interviews, even after the former intern, one day, stormed out of the office.

And 'losers.' She had the habit of using this politically incorrect word after a disappointing round of interviews. Sometimes she meant the first type and sometimes the second.

I said to her, "If you have such high standards, you'll end up running the paper all by yourself. "Three is enough," was her answer and her kind of superstition. And she would add, "Three is a triangle, so it's stable. We perceive our universe to have three spatial dimensions. The threefold office of Christ as prophet, priest, and king. Three time's the charm. *The Three Musketeers.* Three means alive in Chinese Culture." And once she said, "Do you know Hegel's dialectic of Thesis + Antithesis = Synthesis creates three-ness from two-ness. Three is the noblest of all digits, as it is the only number to equal the sum of all the terms below it, so there must be something democratic about three."

My response was invariably: interesting.

And context was an interesting thing, too. The words that sounded portentous from a middle-aged pseudo-intellectual sounded perversely adorable from a young woman trying to build up her charisma and present her seriousness. Plus, she was an atheist, a rational spirit, so she might have to rely on philosophical, high-theory-minded madness to tide her over in the face of many an adversity in life, which might strike randomly and have no real, logical explanation.

When she used up all her procrastination strategies and finally admitted that having a perfect trio would be too good to be true, she agreed to invite two wait-listed undergraduates from the journalism department for a set of tentative interviews.


A meeting was set at two o'clock, the hottest hour of a day. Rachel had turned the air-conditioner off, for she was having a hard time hearing what the first student was talking about. The young woman was talkative, talking at a lightning speed in a high-pitched voice, dragging out her answers to every question, and always landing on a tangential anecdote.

She started off her introduction by emphasizing that she was a feminist, citing unlikely life experience as testimony. Her intonation went up and down like a professional raconteur, and her emotion oscillated between sulk and cheer like an actress'. I thought she was creating a fictional character, improvising imaginary scenes interspersed with climaxes and dramatic endings in order to compensate for her lack of real experience. Dishonesty should not be condemned too much in the case of an intimidated and aspiring girl, as F. Scott Fitzgerald once said in his *The Great Gatsby*. However, Rachel, never a fan of literature, thought she had caught out a fraud and confronted the young woman mercilessly with willful interrogation. There was a subtle moment when I felt I had to intercede, and another when a fight was in full bloom and I ran to intercept the second applicant in the corridor. This young woman was a beauty.

In the end, I stopped the interview, cut Rachel off in the middle of her speech, calling her name twice like an umpire reminding a prize fighter to keep off sensitive zones. They were both startled, and there was something helpless and melancholy in their eyes. The young woman acted as if she had not even begun to introduce herself or was just about to reveal her innermost thoughts. For Rachel's part, she stared at me, her face set, as if she had just been woken up from a nightmare.

"Thank you for coming." Rachel stood up, holding out her hand.

"Thank you for having me," said the girl reluctantly.

As she passed me seeing her off at the door, the girl asked, "Did I at least do OK?"

"You did well," I said. "You did very well, at least I think so."

It was five o'clock. The second student came in. She looked a little annoyed since she was supposed to be received forty some minutes earlier. Rachel apologized, and the girl made a good impression by accepting it amiably. The beauty was dressed in a sleeveless frock, white, patterned with dark blue spheres. She had an oval face, slightly pointed ears, hair tied up in the back. Though not wearing earrings, both piercings were conspicuous; she must have done her homework and thought jewelery was inappropriate for this interview.

"We can chat casually as a warm-up if you like," Rachel said as she was recovering.

"Sure, sure." The beauty nodded.

"How did you hear of us?" Rachel asked.

"How could I not hear of you? It's all over the campus." She smiled.

"Oh, what did you hear exactly? I mean, people talk about the paper?" Rachel was excited.

"It's a fair newspaper," she said, trailing off towards the end of the sentence.

Rachel's face clouded over.

"OK, then let's cut to the chase," she said.

The girl was unnerved by Rachel's sudden change of attitude. Of course she didn't know that Rachel had been putting a larger and larger piece of herself into the paper. As a result, the paper had become her own baby whether she realized it or not. Anyone who ever had known that the paper was run by only one and a half persons would be awed, and would admit immediately that it was a miracle. But the girl was right; the paper per se was just a fair newsletter, an eight-page tabloid at most, and without a single commercial sponsor.

"Did you hear of the murder, the femicide?" Rachel asked.

"Oh, yes, it's barbaric," the girl answered quickly.

"What kind of story would you write if you were asked to report on it?"

"Oh, well, it's complicated."

"What's so complicated? It's a murder, isn't it?"

"Right, it's a murder. But it is said that she might have done something to provoke it; off the record, she might have been cheating on him."

"Who?" Rachel asked coldly.

"The murderer."

"No, no, no, no, I want to know who said that?!" Rachel was swinging her head and then raised it with set eyes.

"Who said that? People. Ordinary people. I am by no means siding with them but…"

"Are they Chinese?" Rachel interrupted before the girl was finished, "off the record."

Now the girl looked much more than uneasy.

"I am sorry I interrupted you. Please, please continue," Rachel prompted.

"It's OK, I'm not siding with them anyway."

"Then how do you perceive the gossip you just mentioned?"

"The gossip? I think it's natural."

"What is natural? Would people feel the same way if the victim were the man instead of the women?" Rachel grilled.

"Well, I don't know, no, I don't think so," the girl said, much agitated. "Well, if the victim were the man, people would think the woman must have had no choice."

"That's right! Have you seen the logic that in either case the girl is portrayed as powerless and passive? No matter if she is the victim or the convict?"

"I don't know. Is that a question?" The girl looked confused, fidgeting on her chair, maybe thinking the whole thing was a mistake.

"Don't you?" Rachel prompted.

"I don't know, this is a little novel to me," she said, "the idea is a little novel. I have to think about it. But I think I would just report the fact, objectively."

"Objectively," Rachel repeated the word slowly to herself and scribbled something misogynistic down on a notebook in her lap, and then her fingers dovetailed like a miniature parapet, setting on the notebook she had unceremoniously closed.

4

The whole event, the altercation, the dismay of the young women, seemed to have no significance to Rachel. She bore the students no malice, and she hoped they didn't either, but if they did, she seemed not to care. As soon as the interview was finished, she suggested that we go to the gym, together; a rare proposal, which meant she was in a fairly good mood. And there was triumph in her voice, as if she had successfully beaten her enemies down; once again, she kept them at bay. No one would meddle with her paper, her editorial authority, nor most of all, her writing.

Rachel had a strict, childish attitude toward her writing. No one was allowed to read it when she was working on it, and not everyone should when it was done. But when you did, you ought to do it thoroughly and carefully. She resented being criticized even if she

allegedly welcomed it. She was obsessed with the right
use of the semicolon, the coma, the dash; when she put
in the last period, it was like a sacred seal. Nothing, not
even a typo, needed to be pointed out, and to do so
would mean being accused of being fussy.

One of Rachel's hats was self-appointed columnist
for the newspaper. Her essays were a mixture of
acrimonious cultural criticisms and scathing
indictments. Once she wrote one about the last
generation of the overseas Chinese students. It
epitomized her style.

There was a time when C_ university only had a
dozen Chinese students. They knew each other as
cronies. They went fishing together weekly, brought
their prey back to one of their apartments, turned it
into a slaughterhouse, and made a feast. Creatively,
they hid behind their culture and language, played
ignorant of social responsibilities and agnostic about
their own, and this country's, future. When accused,
they explained that they were once deprived children,
and now some of them even had hungry kids of their
own to feed. Now that they had given up everything
they cherished in order to fulfil the requirements of the
academic institution, they were entitled to do anything
not against the law. They were interested in nothing
public but would look askance at whoever talked
about the politics of their homeland in English. They
were as blind to the local community as a pack of
tourists on a six-year long vacation. They saw
themselves as elites but acted like a batch of mindless
gourmands. Some of them became scholars and

professors, who still remained lifeless, dull, rigid and prurient...

I didn't read it the first time I saw it because I didn't read the paper at all. Then a friend came to a meeting with the article. That was the first time I truly wished that nobody actually read the paper. For many a day, I was dogged by the dread that the office would be incinerated or ransacked, and that she, probably together with me, would be burnt in effigy or alive. This proved that I was shamefully thin-skinned. The pandemonium I anticipated didn't come, but Rachel was invited to a talk on the rise of China. The whole event was recorded. During the Q & A, a young man sprang a question on her, asking why she had it in for Chinese and the rise of China.

I remember she suddenly blossomed like a white peacock standing among grey grouses. She said, "If ordinary people's welfare and freedom can be so easily denied, then any miracle is possible. The Great Wall of China was the perfect symbol of this kind of miracle. China is rising like a blister. It has become the second largest economy in the world. But behind the glorious veil, villages were levelled; peasants were flushed out of their hometowns and turned into cheap wage labors; old ladies jumped off roofs to protect their houses from demolition; activists were put in jail; journalists got stabbed by both mobs and government agents. The middle class clung to their saving accounts as the only passport to paradise. The poor, demoralized, looked up to slave owners. A new generation was born, oblivious to history and morality. They grew much taller, much stronger and also much more ignorant. They believe in success and vanity. They are cynical, and from an early age, they became proficient at nothing but consuming, eating and traveling..." That was one of her speeches, and that was when it occurred to me that she was a woman politician, a career still not available back home.

In the latest issue of the paper, Rachel wrote: "I am a volunteer at the Asian Women's Resource Center. I often ask those battered Chinese women why they still stay in their relationships. Of course, kids need a father; some of the women are afraid that breaking-up could spur the man to kill them, and there is always the problem of money. But when I ask them why they chose the abusive men in the first place, they often fudge their answers implying that they felt the criminal really loved them, thought highly of them and treated them like a princess. In return, they are ready to sacrifice objectivity for being looked up to. As they had been neglected by society, their integrity and moral judgments were skewed by whomever offered them flattering compliments. Since they had lost the ability to tell what was right from what was wrong, they often made choices against their own interests. Most of the time, they were diligent helpers for those criminals. The women, with some technical training, were the perfect subjects for running cold-blooded, bureaucratic machines able to commit massacres."

She was not a feminist angel sent down on the earth to help her sisters. Most of the time, she refused to help at all. Just a few days ago, a woman called her on the phone, saying she had a graphic story about a despicable professor and a Chinese undergraduate. The woman pleaded with Rachel to disclose the dirty laundry. Rachel heard her out, nodding, whispering consent into the phone. She gasped intermittently with surprise. But in the end she said in earnest, "Thank you for calling us, but our space is very limited; I am sorry there is nothing we can do to help you in this case." At that time, I was chasing heartily after a *bluebottle* fly in the office, holding a menacing aerosol spray. She ordered me to quit the buffoonery, told me the story, and asked for my opinion. I asked her if it was reportable at all and what the consequences would be if the story came out.

"If it got out, someone would get fired," she said. "The two of us might get killed, though." She laughed.

"Then don't do it," I replied.

"It's impossible for some professors to control their penises."

"Chinese?" I asked. "Harassment? Pregnant? Rape?!" I was exhausting my imagination.

"She had a whole package. She should have gone to the police."

"Having an affair?"

"No! God! I can't believe you," she yelled. "He won't let her go! He has been stalking her and last night almost broke into her apartment."

"Was that the girl on the phone?" I asked.

"No, it's her friend," Rachel said. "The girl is having a nervous breakdown."

I put away the sprayer and sat down. "It could be a libel."

She didn't answer me. Her emotion was subsiding, and she looked over her notes. Then she filed them into a folder and put it away. At length she said, "I bet that caller has never read the paper."

She only had limited sympathy for the victims. For starters, she resented those who only picked out the most dramatic moment, the self-serving climax filled with their own foolishness, for their own convenience, leaving out the beginning and the middle. The female characters thus portrayed were bores spending most of their time wanting and doing nothing, waiting throughout the whole story for salvation. And she thought that melodramatic tragedies were distasteful. They were filled with tragic elements sown by the protagonist's sheer stupidity, vanity, lack of a proper education, blind passion, troubled childhood or bigoted parents. It was easy to feel for them, but would something educational come of it? It was simply not a subject for the paper, which was meant to civilize the readers!

"So there is nothing we can do about it?" I asked her.

"I guess not," she said, turning back to her desk. She wrote a few lines down for future reference: "Tragedies carried out by simpletons cease to be tragedies and become farces. The tragedy of the Chinese Civil War, the Chinese Cultural Revolution, the Great Leap Forward and the Great Famine causing millions of deaths, and today, an old Chinese professor harassing a young girl, without an enlightened narration, without serious reflections, are just boring tales, and one day would come back, and would come back eternally.

## 5

Though articles were the responsibility of the author and did not necessarily represent the opinions of the newspaper, some people just refused to understand the disclaimer. The latest issue of the paper which had been put on the stands in the English building, Psychology building, Lincoln hall and undergraduate library were all dumped into garbage cans in a flagrant manner. The way they were thrown there, uncovered, was meant to be seen. Someone had taken Rachel's article personally.

I was asked to do an investigation, which Rachel had already embarked on. I wanted to say that she really had it coming, but I chickened out. There was nothing to investigate. What could I do? Call the police? Report the affair to what authorities? Should I just put the papers back since most of them were unblemished? So I performed my duty most perfunctorily. I was the last person who wanted to get to the bottom of this. Mismanagement in the office was conspicuous. It was hard to say who was to blame for this vandalism. For example, two weeks earlier, I'd sincerely promised the young waiter, who could be a budding genius, in the coffee shop to give his writing sample to Rachel, and I forgot the whole conversation. Could I blame him if he was the vandal? He was entitled. If I'd been a lesser person, meaning younger, I might have done that, too. Maybe I should have stood up to Rachel about the external investigation and suggested an internal one. That would certainly be more fruitful.

After refilling the stands, I went to the coffee shop. I apologized to the young waiter, saying if he could forgive me and magnanimously give me another thumb-drive, I would be a better messenger this time. "Hey, man, you don't have to say sorry," he said. We exchanged email addresses, and I ruled him out as the perpetrator. It was a relief.

Then what was most unlikely happened. I had taken a book out from the main library. Dashing down a flight of stairs leading to an elevator, I almost ran into a woman flouncing out from behind a corner. As I was apologizing, I saw that she was the first applicant who had forged her identity and was confronted by Rachel the other day. Her face was all red, and the color went all the way down to her hands in which a stack of Corn-respondences, the newspaper, was choked in disarray.

"Oh, hi." I was the one who was more embarrassed. "How are you doing?" Instantly, I was thinking about what Rachel would do in this situation.

She didn't answer, but fixed on me with a threatening look in her eyes. Then, she jerked her body out of my way and flounced into the exit.

"What's this for?" I called to her as she was stealing a glance back at me. She stopped at the door.

"You deserve it," she braved.

"This is…" I was searching for the least aggressive accusation.

"Your boss is a bitch!"

I pointed at the papers and said, "That's her freedom of speech," I said, "you can't do this. Please put it back."

"Oh, what about my freedom of speech?!" she said. "Whoever controls the media has freedom of speech? Then this is my freedom of speech! I wish I had burnt it, and I will next time."

She ran away. Standing at the elevator, I turned what she had just said over in my thoughts. "In China, she'd be called a 'naughty girl'; here she could be a terrorist." So I decided to tell no one about it.

I thought the secret behind the vandalism was going to remain in the deep ocean of my heart only to be divulged when Rachel and I were both far beyond the sound and fury. However, Rachel devised a tempestuous way to catch the vandal, and swiftly mete out punishment that alerted me to the possibility that she might have tolerated *my* blasé behavior only because I was on the right side of the history.

There sat the naughty girl in Rachel's office. *How did she find out?* I thought, siding with the girl who had just stopped crying to sob. In the office, Rachel handed her a tissue, and the vandal dabbed her eyes. Rachel crossed her legs like a sadist. A piece of writing paper rested on her thighs wrapped in tight jeans. The girl burst out in even more tears and suddenly lost her balance on her chair. Rachel's firm hand seized her, keeping her from falling over and allowing her to regain her balance. Rachel was a tough teacher having had years of experience and proven skills at handling trouble makers. She was wont to say, "Office hours are a war zone; nobody really likes them, but you just have to cope with them." Helping students used to be a core value in education, gradually became a burden and a dark art. Senior teaching assistants would divulge esoteric secrets to rookies if they paid their due respect: you should neither be too strict nor too easy; too strict would get complaints from average students with above average levels of egoism; too easy would result in mockery and defiance from those who actually read what you assigned. There were TAs who would fail half of a class and bravely stand up for it, and those who dispensed A, A+, A++ as if they were fortune cookies. Both had strengths and weaknesses. Smart students waywardly signed up for Nazi-type TAs' classes to prove their superior intelligence. TAs who only gave out A and A+ attracted more and more lazy students. The bottom line was: if there was no student to shop a TA's class, the TA might lose their scholarship. Rachel was no doubt one of the toughest. Her line was: "It's just a middle-class institution; no one will die from getting a C, won't they?"

After a pause, Rachel resumed her remonstrance but with less indignation than graveness, "This is not China. This is totally unacceptable."

An hour earlier, she'd ordered the vandal to come to the office immediately, or she would report the case to the authorities, and whatever type the perpetrator was, being either the daughter of a China King or a drama queen herself, would be looking at an expulsion.

The girl nodded, still sobbing, and occasionally squinting at me. "An informant!" she seemed to say. I did not utter a single word until the girl left.

"God, it's an asylum, isn't it?!" Rachel cried out, sensing the girl had gone.

"How did you find out?" I asked.

"Was I too harsh on her?"

"At least you are consistent."

"What do you mean?" She stared at me.

"Are you really wondering if you were harsh enough?"

A confused, almost gawking look passed over her face.

"Do you think you pick on Chinese women because of self-hatred?" I said with a tentatively confrontational air.

She was burning up; my last remark got to her, "What was I supposed to do? Let her burn the office down?"

"Easy," I said, "I just meant in general." I caved. "How about... *Not everybody in this world has had the advantages that you've had.*"

She remained silent a second, and her silence wasn't like a sober reflection but more of a stubborn bullhorn.

I wanted to end the discussion, so I said, "I mean you don't need to distinguish your virtue by punishing the vices of your peers."

"Stop talking me into..." she retorted, "and they are not my peers. I can't deny that I happen to be a Chinese woman, but that's where the similarity ends."

"So you're telling me you have never treated them like dirt just because you assumed you knew what they were?"

"No, I didn't."

"I don't think so. I think you take it for granted if they meet your standards, and senselessly bash them if they fail to. You are a lesser human being when you deal with your peers."

"Would you please stop using that word?"

"I will, I will." I put up my hands, splaying my fingers, backing off, almost gored by the edge of a desk. There was no way I could win the fight, even if I had all the arguments in the world. The best I could hope for was her backing down without sacrificing her authoritative appearance. So I went to my desk. There was the thumb-drive plugged into my laptop, but I decided not to give it to her at the moment.

She picked up a letter on her desk from the donor of the five hundred dollars. "I think we should thank this mystery donor in person," she said suddenly.

"What donor? Oh." It was a gratuitous proposal, but I let her put it to me. "Yes, we should. Five hundred bucks is a lot of money," I added promptly.

"Could you do it please?" She turned to me with her saddened eyes. She was deflated and sighed tenderly. I looked at her face. Her beauty exasperated me. I succumbed to an impulse to do something to let this weak-kneed moment last.

"Absolutely," I said.

6

The undergraduate library was located at the center of C_University. It was a strange construction, for on the surface of the ground there were only two phone-booth-like entrances, but underneath them, a whole maze of labyrinthine tunnels and rooms beehived an acre of rather fertile land. It was so designed for sheltering people from sporadic tornadoes, notorious in the Midwest. Flanking the two entrances were two sculptures. Smoking was strictly prohibited in the library, so young smokers gathered around the sculptures as they didn't want to be seen smoking from all four directions. In spite of these not-so-distinguished features, it was the most patronized library in the university. The library, together with the university, was built in the middle of a seemingly endless stretch of corn fields. The idea was to seclude college students, mainly prospective engineers, from the vanity fair, so they could rigorously focus on their computers and crucibles. But the ascetic ideal was humanely adapted. As the library was located prominently at the center of the university, it was a good place for gatherings, coffee drinking, showing off new attire and hairdos, and also for people-watching. There were all types: undergraduates whose hairlines were receding, and doctoral students looking as young and zesty as cute little buttons.

I was wondering what this patron was like. She finally agreed to meet me after I insisted twice on thanking her in person in my emails. I sat in the hallway of the library waiting for the benefactor, watching students pass by. The hallway was like a catwalk featuring purchased individualism: fishnet stockings and sequined chemises versus tulle frocks and open-toed sandals, V-neck versus turtleneck, slim-fit jeans versus Chinese-lantern-like pants; sneakers like moonwalking contraptions; and geisha-like Asian girls in high heels, clownish fraternity boys wearing loose Greek-lettered tees and caps hand in hand with freckled sorority girls, Indians as lean as antelopes, and people as gay as in arty Hollywood movies.

*What do the rich look like?* I thought, *Are they tall? Are they as lean as the stereotype goes? Are they sulky, desperate, or as miserable and blasé as characters in Fellini's movies?* Her name was Alice. "Is she Chinese? Oh, she was at least able to read Chinese. Is she one of the nouveau riche?" There were a lot of nouveau riche kids at this university. This town was full of Chinese nouveau riche kids. They drove Mercedes and called them affordable since they had more expensive cars parked in their garages for nightlife. Their parents were either corrupt government officials or businessmen having amassed a great deal during the last thirty years when the gate of China opened ajar. They used to be poor, so they felt compelled to let their only child feel rich.

But I had a strong feeling that this Alice had nothing to do with them. For one thing, the prose she wrote in the email was grammatically flawless, and syntactically elegant.

> *Dear Alex*
>
> *Thank you for the flattering letter you wrote me. I am, however, by no means as kind and generous as you might reckon. What you said about me fits the description of a florid and opulent English gentleman, who reminds me of a Dickensian character. I am just a student, and appreciate the service the newspaper has been providing for the community. Don't worry about the money. You guys deserve it. Long live the Chinese newspaper!*
>
> *Sincerely*
> *Alice*

I had googled "Dickensian." So she must be a Charles Dickens fan, or at least she wanted to be 'reckoned' so. Either was good enough.

A librarian was pulling the curtains, revealing a barren garden from 50-feet deep in the ground like the bottom of an enormous well walled by grids of window panes. The noon sunlight diffused through the wall-like windows, shone on the pit, giving the students precious natural light for two hours a day. It was beautiful outside. Students and staff were coming and going. A lunch break had turned the outdoor cafe into an international bazaar, a cosmopolitan scene. C_university had been stealthily taking on more and more international students to balance its financial deficit. Chinese and Koreans were now part of the solution to the ubiquitous cutbacks in public education. If only the high tuition could save fine art, music and critical thinking from being whittled away. But these were non-concerns for the young and beautiful at this time of the day. They were more focussed on their chances of falling in love, say, in this library, this rosy, delicious afternoon.

A young woman turned up, dressed in grey yoga pants and a light purple T-shirt. "Hi, Alex." She called to me as if she already knew me. She wore her shoulder-length hair down, with a wave behind her ears suggesting a relaxed ponytail. She looked fairly athletic; her suntanned skin around her neck and collarbone had an American look that could rarely be pulled off by yellow skin. Her attractive, bony face harbored thin, long eyes that emitted a sweet, languid look.

"Are you Alice?" I stood up.

"Oh, yes, I go by Alice, alright." She stuttered, so I thought it must be a pseudonym that was not supposed to be used by strangers.

Her strong American accent made me hesitate over whether to initiate a handshake. Otherwise, in case she was a real Chinese, it could be safely dispensed with. She smelt faintly fragrant, yet not of perfume as much as of some upmarket shampoo. And if she was not actually ill, she must have been very nervous, for her hands were fidgeting, quivering in her pockets and she seemed as if she was trying to keep them under control.

"I just wanted to thank you in person for the donation you made," I said.

"Oh, you're welcome," she said.

Her voice was obligingly short-winded.

"Well, we just want you to know that we really, really appreciate it. Please drop by the office sometime. You know the website, so you must know where we are." I found myself winding up the conversation prematurely. "Last but not least, we'd like to give you two tickets to a student concert. It's nothing, but…"

"You are hiring, aren't you?" she asked suddenly.

"Oh, yes. We're always hiring. It's just…" I broke off, and then repeated, "well, yes, we are hiring." I thought it was courteous to let her lead for the moment.

"Gender and cinema studies," she said, putting her left hand lightly on her chest as if she was making a confession.

"Really? That's fantastic!" I said and regretted the word 'fantastic' at once, which must have made me sound like an idiot. Nervousness is infectious. So I added, "Well. How about I buy you a drink and let's talk about it."

"Thank you. But I just quit," she said.

"What?" I was confused, and then it came to me. "No, no, no, I mean coffee or tea or something! I don't mean alcohol; I don't drink alcohol either," I said and became conscious of my English.

She hesitated. "Then, alright," she said weakly, eyes veiled in doubt.

7

In the summer of 2013, teaching assistants, adjunct professors and quite a few tenured professors went on the longest and bitterest campus strike in the history of the university, asking for raising living wages for graduate students who were also teachers. They didn't get it. Instead, the following year, a *campanile* was built where the strikers had rallied, and an Asian woman known for her iron fist when it came to unionized labor assumed the university's presidency. These things were not supposed to be taken together, nor was the firing of a professor who had infuriated a wealthy Jewish donor by criticizing Israel's foreign policy. But the community sensed their relatedness. The bell tower had become the butt of many unkind jokes for its shear tallness with its two colossal brazen bells and a derelict garden at the bottom lacerated by a grass-thronged path.

Alice and I were in line at a coffee shop when she suggested we take our coffee up to the bell tower. She said she didn't relish the idea of sitting down since she had been sitting for days. By that time, she had relaxed and become all the more communicative.

While we took a shortcut to the site, she said, "I am sorry I was a little awkward in the library. I just don't like the ambience there, and I was afraid I would run into someone I really don't want to see."

"Don't mention it. Totally understand you," I said to her as we were strolling down the pavement dappled with sunlight. "I, myself, have a long list of enemies. But it's a small circle. We are stuck with each other, aren't we?"

She didn't reply; she grinned.

"Are you a doctoral student?" I asked, sipping the coffee in my hand.

"Yes. Cinema and gender studies," she said it for the second time.

"What class do you teach?" trying to bring up a common concern.

"Oh, I don't teach classes."

"Research assistant?"

"I am not an RA either. I came with a fellowship."

"Oh, I almost forget that one," I said, "because it's rare these days. Where did you go to school before?"

"I got my masters degree from Harvard."

"Oh, excellent. I mean, you are excellent."

She frowned and the conversation dried up. To cover the silence, I took out a pack of Sweet 'N Low from my trouser pocket, torn it open with my teeth and wiggled the sugary dust down into my coffee cup. It was a sunny day, yet it was very windy. The sugary dust refused to drop into the cup, but sprinkled on my neck and lips. I stole a glance at her. She grinned. There was something in her gait and the way she held her head and the cup that suggested a privileged upbringing. *It's all very good,* I thought, indulging the complacency of having her company. A year later, I would recollect that this was the best moment in the relationship.

"What do you do for the paper?" she asked.

I hesitated. "Let's see…it's a small team so we're not specialized. How about you send us a resume and a writing sample," I said obligingly, "I'll give them to my boss. She's a doctoral student in the communications department."

"What kind of writing do you prefer?"

"What kind? Any kind," I improvised. "The kind that best represents your style, I guess. You know, I am basically a technician, fixing computers and stuff, so…"

"OK. Thank you." She looked a little disappointed and stopped talking.

Then she started again with a change of the subject.

"I'm sorry. I spaced out. How is your coffee?" she said, leaning closer, turning her body a moderate angle toward me.

"I am Chinese, I was brought up drinking tea. But now I just can't get through a day without drinking at least four cups of coffee. It's bitter, dehydrating and expensive, but I have to have it. I feel I have a mental problem of sorts." I decided to stop to see if she was interested at all.

"What is it?"

"The psyche? I don't know. One of my friends, she's a psychiatrist. She said it's like sex, it's not just a pure body thing. You know? It's like if you messed up your brain then you would have sex problems. Am I boring you with my charlatanism?"

"Yes, but go on," she smiled.

I blushed, "Well, she said it is not the coffee per se that I drink. It's the idea. I'm drinking the idea." I rotated the coffee cup in my hand. "I know it's gonna hurt when I have stomach cancer, but I can't help it. Do you know what I mean?"

"I know," she said, still smiling.

"Really?" I was amused and said in affected sincerity, "Then please tell me what I meant."

"You mean you need a thing to materialize your anxiety," she said.

I had to shut up because that was pithy, and she continued, "and it's like the way Starbucks is advertising now. I don't relish being told that the coffee you buy actually makes a difference in Africa. It's bullshit."

I laughed.

"Sorry," she apologized.

"No, why? I like it. It's true," I said. "And that is exactly what I meant, if you messed up the idea you would have problems with the thing, even if the thing is still the thing."

"Well, not just that…" She strained her face; her lips pouted a little as if she had some serious matter to let out, but restrained. "But you don't want to hear about it."

"Oh, yes, please. Our conversation has been a disaster so far; I bet it couldn't be worse."

She laughed, a charming, little laugh.

"I really dislike people, I mean, OK, Chinese, sitting in a Starbucks, acting as if they were in a fashion show. You know what I mean?" She stared at me with her long, curly, attentive eyes.

"Kind of," I said.

"Come on. It's just coffee!" she was emboldened and blurted out and became even bolder. Now she seemed to be chastising an imagined audience before her eyes."An overpriced one if you care for my opinion." She added, "Where do you live?"

"What?" I was left open-mouthed by this incoherent question. "First street; First and Healey."

"Oh, you're lucky. I used to live in Lychee Town. A thousand or so Chinese live there. You chance upon three women with *anchor babies* in their bellies just crossing a street."

"You feel responsible for that?" I said, slightly annoyed.

"No, I just moved out," she said. "But they're scholars! Don't they have better things to do with their brains...?"

"I don't know," I said. "Maybe all the people in this world haven't ..."

"—had the advantages that we've had," she finished my words. "I know; that's why I moved out."

She stopped talking.

For my part, as much as her last remark surprised me, I was so complacent that she used 'we' instead 'I', which had just transformed this casual acquaintance into a friendship.


On reaching the tower, the school buildings gave way to a pastoral scene. The wind also picked up speed, lurched behind undergrowth, and then sprung out, launching a raid on a flower bed; topped up its energy and rushed up to us, did a hodgepodge job on our hair and clothes.

"Are we still going up?" I asked.

"Are you afraid?" She was excited, guiding me down the path toward the cast-iron stairs.

The narrow entrance was cordoned off with steel chains. A no-entry plate was clanking ominously in the high wind. She manoeuvred past the plate with a matter-of-course air and stepped on a stair of metal bars giving out a grating sound under her weight. Before I could say anything, she had legged a dozen steps up the spiral staircase. I was still of two minds about the trespassing when I thought of the strikers, and followed.

"You know. I don't want to bore you. But again, we really appreciate your donation. My boss wants me to give you the tickets to a Chinese music concert. It's tomorrow night. We are one of the co-sponsors. I hope you can make it," I said, panting, while we were climbing up.

"Chinese music concert?" She asked, panting, punctuated with a break in her footsteps.

"Off the record," I said, restraining my breath, "it's just a class of students. Don't expect too much. But I think it will be even more interesting, don't you?"

"Yes, I think so. Thank you so much."

"No, thank you," I said and found myself standing at the top of the stairs. "I don't think we can go any further."

Eighty meters above the ground with two giant bells hanging over my head, I attempted a look out from over a short brick parapet. The vertigo I felt was heightened by the gale, full-fledged now, howling through the eye of the tower, hosing at my face at full speed. I was still holding the coffee cup now as if it were an anchor.

"First time up?" she said, eyes closed, strands of her hair whipping out of her ponytail.

"I suppose there is something to see?" I asked.

Without answering my question, she asked instead, "What's the thing you said you were giving to me?"

"Oh, tickets. Two tickets to a music concert."

"What am I gonna do with them?" she said dreamily.

"Well, you can bring your boyfriend." And after a pause, I added, "I suppose you have one."

I felt the tickets in my pocket; they were still there. But I was afraid that if I took them out, the wind would take them away.

8

"Baa, baa, baa, baa, boom."

The last phrase of a piece of Chinese melody was disrupted by a pack of cheerful students' intruding on the auditorium during the musicians' practice. The amateur musicians put down their instruments, letting strings and mallets rest in peace. The students frozen at the door waited, their eyes roving over the auditorium, until a woman dressed in a black costume, a full-length linen frock, stood up, left the rest of the band on the stage, and walked up to them with an elegant, high-heeled gait.

The woman turned the students at the door away. They started to leave reluctantly, making deliberate loud noise in the corridor outside.

The woman walked back to the band, standing in front of the musicians who were straightening their backs and sitting on the edges of their chairs, as if they were a group of detained drunk drivers waiting to be questioned.

"Well," the woman said, "you did it. The last time was the best you have ever done in the last three months. All your hard work has paid off. I am so proud of you. If you could do the exact same thing tonight, you would be all stars."

The musicians were relieved. They laughed, cheered and shook hands. One of them started to clap and the others joined, clapping for the woman, their teacher, who was now fighting back her tears.

I was the only member of the audience to witness to this emotional rehearsal. As the band was dispersing I went up to the lady.

"Priscilla, Priscilla," I said admittedly, "I can't believe you did it again."

"They did it."

"Yes, but still. It's amazing. It's nothing like even a week ago."

"What did I tell you?" She smiled, dancing a little jig of frivolous footwork, her high heels making brisk clicking sounds on the parquet floor.

"Yes, it's absolutely amazing. You are amazing," I said as the last student waved bye-bye to us.

"Are we expecting a big audience tonight?" I asked.

"I don't know. The weather is fine," she said with a sly grin.

Priscilla was one of my lovely friends. She was also Rachel's friend, and how she and Rachel got to know each other was quite an interesting story. Priscilla was a doctoral student in the music department, and had a teaching scholarship that also required her to direct a Chinese ensemble: a one-credit course offered to students who may or may not have any experience in playing a Chinese musical instrument. She and Rachel were both invited to a Chinese New Year's gala hosted by the Chinese Students and Scholars Association or CSSA. The CSSA invited Rachel to report on the event, where Priscilla was invited to play — she could play any Chinese musical instrument: percussion, strings, wind, and it was a thrill to watch her switching from one instrument to another with such grace. But the whole ceremony turned out to be the backdrop for a beauty pageant, about which neither of them was informed in advance. Rachel was angry and wrote an article afterward claiming that the whole ceremony was a debauched and disgusting event, and particularly picked on Priscilla's performance for the butt of a scathing joke. Later, after Priscilla had proved her innocence and that she was not a lesser tigress herself by confronting Rachel twice at the office, demanding that Rachel publish an apology.

Rachel said, "God, that woman! We'd better make friends with that woman." They became friends, and their friendship went, over the years, from good to the best.

Eight o'clock. A crowd of spectators arrived at the auditorium. Most of them were the friends of the musicians, sent to take pictures. Among them was an elderly man, a professor. He was Priscilla's supervisor, allegedly the most powerful man in the field of World Music. Rachel had gotten in early and taken a seat in the first row. The band was filing onto the stage, sitting down. Stage lights rendered the stage effulgent, with the rest of the room gradually receding into darkness. Then the music started. It went quite smoothly at first. During the first piece, I even saw the supervisor tapping his varicose fingers on his knees. But some mishap sabotaged the third piece. A young man, who was playing an instrument with two strings, missed almost an entire phrase and this sent a flutter of jitters to the others. Though they regained their pace and rhythm quickly, the amateurs lost their composure, and carried on for the rest of the show as if they were a group of medical students operating an autopsy with extreme accuracy and seriousness. No matter how hard Priscilla tried, fidgeting in her seat, gesticulating, the band just refused to come to life again.

The lights came on. I saw the old man stand up before the first round of applause subsided, and slip away through a back door.

The audience rose and turned to the aisles. I was among the few who jostled our way against the current, dodged and sidled and finally got up to the stage. Rachel had gotten onto the stage already and was mingling with a small crowd. Priscilla was wearing a frozen smile and might have admitted to herself that the failure of an amateur performance was nothing to be worried about, was even politically correct. The young man who made the clumsy mistake was surrounded by his cohorts. They were patting his shoulders as he shook his head.

"Fancy grabbing a drink?" I called out to Priscilla, leaning on the pillar of the stage.

Rachel threw me a look and Priscilla nodded. "In a minute," she said.

I turned back, looking the moving crowd over, searching for Alice. She was not here.

An hour later, we huddled around a round table at a dim bar. "That was good, wasn't it?" I broke the silence.

"That's not the point," Priscilla said to me, still wearing heavy makeup, now ablaze under an orange lamp, "The point is... you know what the point is. Don't make me explain it to you. I have a headache."

I knew what her point was: she believed every student had the potential to be a great musician, and it was the teacher's responsibility to draw them out. She loved teaching, but she felt the university had been taking advantage of her. So whenever the middle-aged Chinese dean of her program scowled at her teaching style, or a visiting musicologist beamed persistently at her breasts, the unfair feeling would raid her all the harder. She had become grumpier over the years. Last year, having had a political epiphany, she decided that loving an underpaid job was a political weakness. She started to go to the Graduate Employees' Organization where Rachel was also an active member and very vocal about labor issues. As the vice-chair in the Asian Women's Resource Center, Priscilla had been using patience as a weapon to talk weak-minded women out of their abusive relationships. After a counselling session, she would walk two miles to her favorite Thai food restaurant to have a feast. These were the two ways to deal with her own frustration. As a result, her body started filling out, became first chubby, then a little too plump by the Chinese standards.

She was sitting with me and Rachel, savoring a cup of ice cream with chocolate syrup, flowing down through varicolored sweet toppings.

"Do you know the Confucius Institute?" Priscilla said to us, munching like a little raccoon.

"Yes, why?" Rachel was alarmed.

"The ensemble is closing down, or..." Priscilla said.

"They want to take it over?" Rachel asked.

"Oh, my God, how did you know that?" Priscilla exclaimed, "Yes, only if I write a proposal can I keep this job and start working for them."

"Will you?" Rachel asked gravely.

"Of course not!" Priscilla banged down her cup. "They are all bores."

"But how are you going to make ends meet without the scholarship?" I asked.

"Maybe it's time to make some sacrifices." She laughed, scraping the bottom of the cup.

"What's your plan?" Rachel said gravely.

"I don't know yet. Maybe take on two more babysitting jobs. It wouldn't make much of a difference," she said.

"How about asking your father to lend you some money?" I said. "You can give it back when you graduate."

"Speaking of my father," she finished off the cup, drawing her chair up closer, "my mom called me the other day. She said he beat her again. I said, why do you call me?! Call the police! Put the bastard in jail. Put the fucking capitalist in jail."

"How about spending his bloody money?" I said.

"Well, I will if I must," Priscilla said. "Don't you worry, Alex."

"Do you mind if I order a piece of a cake?" She waved her hand to a waiter.

"No, please, you are entitled," Rachel laughed.

I pulled my chair back, crossed my legs, shaking my head.

Priscilla put it to me, "Why are you so gloomy today?"

"I'm OK. Thank you for asking."

She turned to Rachel, "I am selling my costumes. Do you know anybody who would be interested?"

"You're selling your costumes?!" I exclaimed. "That'll look bizarre on stage. The nudity ensemble."

"Calm down," she said, laughing. "I am just selling the fancy ones. They can't tell the difference anyway." Then she laughed hysterically.

"Do you want me to lend you some money?" I said. "Don't be shy."

"Oh, dear Alex!" Priscilla put her hands on my face, "you are so cute! Please marry me."

9

The writing sample that Alice sent me had been printed out on three letter-sized sheets of paper, and was laid on one of the racks on a two-storey document holder that had the label *Applications* glued on it.

Two days later, it had been transported into the other rack, but Rachel had not said anything about it. I picked it up in her absence and ran through it for the third time. It was a fine piece of reporting on a local art exhibition. Her prose was exquisite but by no means showy. The event was well narrated and dramatically so. The interviews were introduced and quoted so that the writing was punctuated by lively quotes. The description of the exhibits was careful, but averted giving too many gratuitous details that might render the objects dead. If this was not acceptable, I doubted there'd ever be one that would be good enough for the newspaper. It could be that Rachel did not want a third person in the office. If that was the case, I couldn't stay either. How could I tolerate such anti-social, tyrannical behavior long term, especially when the possibility of seeing Alice every day working beside me was so palpable?

I had this grievance in the back of my mind for a few days until one Thursday. I was not supposed to work at the office on Thursdays because I had a language exchange partner, a 30-year-old white man, who agreed to meet once a week, me practicing English and him Chinese. We had a prolonged session that day because this was our last one, for he was graduating and soon would go to China to hunt for a job as an English tutor. But he didn't feel ready for it. He had to work because he was the incumbent to a large student loan, and his mother was a disabled widow living on food stamps. Our farewell in a parking lot turned out to be very sad and gloomy. And then Rachel called me up, demanding my immediate presence at the office. For the first time, I was really mad at her. Who did she think she was? Did the universe really revolve round her? Did her authoritarian altruism qualify her to push people around at will? And it really pissed me off when the emergency call was for nothing really *emergent*, just a mislaid laptop. I had it locked in my drawer, and she didn't have access to it, but so what?!

So I went up to the office, unlocked the drawer, reminded her that I was on my day off, and then, faced with her indifference to my complaint, I confronted her with the writing sample.

"May I ask you a question?" I said.

"What?"

"Have you read the writing sample I gave to you?"

"Oh," she acted as if something suddenly dawned on her. What a good actress?! She said, "I was just about to ask you some questions about her. Stay. Sit."

She turned her back on me, so I sat down like a disgruntled dog.

She told me that not only was she interested in Alice's writing, but it was the best writing sample she had ever read. She laughed about being intimidated by her, which could mean that she really had been intimidated by her. Then she asked me many questions: Where is she from? Is she a southerner or a northerner? And she specifically asked whether this Alice was a vain, ambitious type since she was so good on paper at such a young age. I answered them with some of my own inventions and occasionally retorted with phrases like "Define ambition", "so what" and "does it really matter?"

At last, she said she wanted to meet this Alice sometime, and I said, throwing a fit, "what about today?"

"Today?"

"Yes, today. She has been asking for an interview for a long time," I lied.

She sat in her authoritative armchair, a quizzical look on her face, as if the meaning of this whole afternoon was coming to her. She prolonged the eye contact for another second and nodded and granted me this request. Now I was responsible for the idiocy I had started. How could I call up Alice and ask her to come to the office? It was all Rachel's fault!

## 10

The next day brought the first meeting between Rachel and Alice.

I had handed Alice a cup of tea to help her digest a homemade cookie that Rachel had brought from the batch she had made for the Man Hater Club.

With all the anticipation and precaution, Rachel's first impression of Alice was that Alice was a real credit to her gender, age and race. Thirty minutes into the conversation, Rachel and Alice had already covered a lot of common ground: feminism, two recent books on Judith Butler, which smoothly led to an anecdote about a disorganized professor they'd both had classes with. This instant comradeship was also ascribed to their similar dress code and equality in physical attractiveness. It could be inferred from their talk that they were both excellent students now and back in China and Taiwan, and that they both were considered to be prodigies in writing and were incorrigible perfectionists. I had a betrayed feeling and feared that I had invited another Nazi woman into the office.

"Thank you for agreeing to see me at such short notice," Rachel said.

Alice put down the cup of tea. "Thank you for having me."

"I really want you to write for us," Rachel said cheerfully.

"I am so glad..." Alice seemed to be taken by surprise.

"Sure. As soon as possible. The office has only the two of us. We have been searching for the third Musketeer for a long, long time, haven't we?" Rachel smiled to me.

I pouted my lips and nodded.

"Just you two?" Alice exclaimed. "Why? There are a lot of Chinese students in this university. Have you ever advertised on the Chinese Students and Scholars Association's website? They have two thousand or some subscribers."

Rachel paused, then said lowering he voice, "Yes, they have."

"Seriously, the CSSA," Alice repeated passionately, "oh, well, not that any serious people really like them. They're so corrupt. But it's the biggest Chinese organization on campus. We can still take advantage of it."

I had done a little Facebook investigation on Alice since we met the first time. Under a garish banner of the CSSA's beauty pageant page, it was written: "Alice Tang, due to her charming personality, outstanding intelligence, talent, and witty answers to judges' questions, was crowned the runner up to Miss China at C_University."

Rachel had no idea about it. She put both of her feet down on the floor. "Well, we can talk about our publicity later. We do have a lot of things to catch up on," she said. "But to tip you off first, they don't like us either. Maybe because I once bashed their beauty pageant. The president has been holding it against us. Don't you think so, Alex?"

I saw Alice holding the tea cup up near to her mouth until the rim screened off almost half of her face that had gone from pink to the warm red of humiliation. She became uncontrollably nervous again.

I shrugged my shoulders, "Alice had a theory about Starbucks," I said to change the subject.

The subject was not picked up because Rachel said suddenly, "By the way, since you went to Harvard, what's the difference between private schools and public schools in the United States? Are the stereotypes true?"

This question seemed to have the right effect, Alice started to unwind in the chair, and soon opened a point-blank attack.

"Sometimes I feel this country is still ruled by a group of feudalists," Alice said.

"Sometimes I feel the same way," Rachel agreed congenially.

"God!" Alice exclaimed. "It's suffocating. Everybody is so self-important and so intimidated like they only care about filling up their resumes. The schools are only exacerbating social inequality, creating so-called elites who end up wide-eyed American lawyers, doctors, cowards! Intimidated cowards," she braced her back against the back of the chair theatrically as if she was reeling from her words.

Then Rachel followed with flank attacks.

They both agreed that the United States was falling apart and was downgrading to a polarized, class society. And they were like two embattled members of the intellectual underground, like those German philosophers exiled from the Third Reich during the

Second World War. After taking a look at me, they kindly admitted my membership to the club with their condescending smiles. They also agreed that only very few people were actually aware, and the masses lived complacently in short-sighted smugness.

The vehement tirade and the witty disparagement were followed by a moment of silent poignancy. And it was from this melancholy pit that the idea of building a cultural criticism frontier, starting from the newspaper, was brought up and agreed.

They exchanged phone numbers, and Rachel insisted on walking Alice out of the building.


"You like her?" I asked Rachel getting back to the office.

"I don't know." She sounded cheerless.

"But you seemed to really like each other."

"Did I?" Rachel seemed to be surprised by what I said.

"If you don't, then you are a..."

"I mean she is qualified. I won't let my personal taste come between her and the newspaper," she said, blushing, "it's all for the paper."

Part Two

## 11

Not to give the impression that Rachel and her newspaper were all that absorbed me that summer. On the contrary, I had it well compartmentalized. I had a real life on the side.

As soon as my long distance relationship had dried up, I had a new girlfriend. Her name was Nina. She was a first-year masters student in my department, and this was her first year in the United States. She was eight and a half years younger than me. Her father was an opulent coal mining businessman and a stickler for hard work and premarital virginity. Because of her belated juvenile rebellion, she had had quite a few boyfriends by the time I met her, and she told me she had had sex with all of them. She was rather literate in English literature and in red wines, and was brought up eating extremely spicy food in the west of China. I was from the south; my diet was bland. Once she concocted a soup for me, and it almost sent me to heaven.

She had a very good sense of humor, but was notorious for losing her way on the highway. I was sensitive about wasting time idling, so I admired her ability to fritter away a whole month without feeling any guilt. I was a movie buff; she said theatre made her feel both claustrophobia and agoraphobia. We made love once, and both of us considered it a failure and a mistake. She said frankly afterward, "As much as we love each other, our bodies hold the biological fact against us." And I thought she might have exaggerated her sexual experience. We didn't break up. Instead, we stayed up late talking and kissing, enjoying each other's company, cheering each other up when things went bad at school. She was hopeful she would eventually find her soul mate, while I was not. Yet everyone thought we were lovers. We took each other to gatherings, but when we were there, we acted as if we were very much available.

When you get to know someone, you start to see the person everywhere as if you just learned a new word and started to come across it all the time. I saw Alice at one of the parties that Nina brought me to.

It was a Saturday night. I had been a little disappointed since stepping into the living room. It was one of those typical gatherings filled with half-hearted Ph.D. students: younger ones huddling up, talking with each other about their dissertations and conferences, and those who had been around for a few years, whining, complaining about the weak arm of the union. I stood beside a senior student with silver lines in her hair, nodding and smiling as if she knew what criticism was.

Alice appeared in the doorway, wearing whitewashed jeans, a blue university hoody, and a pair of New Balance trainers. She was followed by a young, white, European man who was very, very angry with her. She saw me and gave me a wan smile, which made my heart flutter. I could tell the man was ticking her off. I faintly heard him from my seat on the sofa accusing her.

"I have never known anyone so selfish and stupid!" muttered the young man, gritting his teeth.

"What did I do?" She scowled and seemed to be confused.

"Selfish and stupid!" he scolded with a groaning voice. He seemed about to strangle her with an invisible rope.

"What did I do?" Alice was staring at him with blinking eyes, belching, inhaling and exhaling with a good deal of effort. So I realized that she was very drunk.

"What did you do up there?!" the man asked.

"What did I do? Nothing. Do I have to prove it? I can prove it. He can prove it." She was pointing to some person she was supposed to have been with earlier in one of the guest rooms.

Her boyfriend snatched her hand back furiously, and slung her body onto his arm like a marionette.

"You're hurting me!" she said.

"You are a piece of..." He stopped, seeing the hostess walking in their direction.

"Is she OK?" inquired the hostess.

"I am OK," Alice braced herself against the dizzying effect of the alcohol.

"She's OK," said the man and turned to Alice, "Are you OK?"

"I'm OK," she said with affected certainty.

"I hope you are OK," said the hostess half accusingly as if she wanted the man to control his impish child.

After the hostess left them, Alice teased, still drunk, "Are you jealous?"

"Jealous of what? You are amazing!"

Never had I seen a man so ready to explode.

"We were talking about literature. E.M. Forster. That guy is a real aficionado. I was about to introduce him to you," she said.

He lowered his head and then raised it again with an ugly simper at the corner of his mouth.

"That's enough, let's go home."

"But I'm not done with talking to Steven," she said.

"OK, I'll wait outside and you take your time talking to whoever you want. But don't be too late." He let her go and stormed out to a porch adjacent to the living room. He lit up a cigarette as Alice started to dodder among the guests. I walked up to her and kept her from falling over. Then, having changed his mind, the man stormed back into the living room, made an apology to me and kidnapped his girlfriend away. This time she didn't put up a bit of a fight.

Nina came up behind me from the other end of the room.

"What's the matter?"

Some of the students began whispering about the couple.

"I don't know her that well," I said to my girlfriend, deliberately letting a few others within earshot eavesdrop.

Then indistinctly I heard a young lady say: "I heard that she is from a very rich family."

The audience nodded understandingly.

## 12

"God, this party is boring!" Nina said, leaning on my shoulder. She whispered into my ear, "We shouldn't have come."

"Then, let's go home. It's nine thirty," I said.

"I don't want to go home either." She yawned and took out her smartphone, flipping on the touchscreen aimlessly.

"Cornerstone Fellowship? Junk mail!" she muttered to herself, "the second Annual Graduate Symposium on East Asia. What is this? Do you know what this is?"

I happened to know what it was.

"The next one? It's a...well, it's a sort of academic conference."

"Have you ever been to an academic conference?" She got excited. "What was it like?"

"It was like a bunch of egoists nit-picking each other's papers and telling tasteless inside jokes. You wouldn't like it."

Then she burst out, "Oh, there is a party at Fifth Street! My friends are all there."

"A bar?" I asked.

"It seems like someone's apartment." She shook my arm. "Let's go."

Fifteen minutes later, we turned up at the door of the designated apartment. I took a glance at my watch; It was ten, and I drew my sleeve down over it. I was tired. My first impression was that the party had been cancelled. There was only a young woman in the living room. She was sitting on a fat couch.

"You made it. I hope you didn't feel obliged," the hostess, wearing a white mask of make-up, said to Nina.

"Oh, you just saved my day," Nina said, hugging the hostess.

"Have a seat. Please be my guest." The hostess included me in a hearty nod.

I found an armchair in a corner. I slumped myself down and immediately I felt the steel springs from underneath the canvas cover goring me.

"Coffee? Juice? Tea? My mom brought me some tea from Taiwan," said the hostess obligingly.

"Then tea, please," Nina said.

"Oh, you like tea? I like tea. They've got some really good tea at the Japanese House. Have you ever been to the Japanese House? It has the authentic look. Have you ever been to Japan?" The last question was addressed to me.

"Not really, I am mainlander. It's not easy for us to get a visa to Japan."

This distasteful detail seemed to make the hostess uneasy. She raised her plucked eyebrows at me, and then swept to my date, and they looked at each other, laughing.

"He is a nerd," my girlfriend said.

"I had a lot of fun last time I was in Japan. You should go," the hostess said.

When the subject was exhausted, the hostess brought two cups of tea from the kitchen to the living room, set one down for me and the other for Nina, sitting with both hands folding on her knees. I said, "Thank you," and intentionally averted my eyes from her face, watching the water changing colors as the tea leaves unfold and sank down to the bottom.

"Do you watch Japanese movies? Or Manga?" she said from across the coffee table.

"I read a book by Murakami if that counts," I said. Why she was so obsessed with Japan?

"Who?" The hostess turned to Nina.

"Murakami. Norwegian Wood," she said.

"Oh, of course! Norwegian Wood," she exclaimed. "How rare to meet someone who cares for reading novels these days!" She seemed about to clap her hands. "I liked novels when I was a kid," she continued. "Let me show you something. Here's my personal collection! Come on," she said, prompting us to go to her bedroom.

I followed a few steps behind Nina, and stopped at the door, extending the courtesy of not intruding on a Chinese woman's privacy.

"Come on in!" she urged. "See that!" She pointed to a few paperbacks interposing a stack of textbooks on a makeshift bookcase formed by four, squarish, plastic boxes.

"Wow, you read a lot…" Nina said.

Suddenly, we heard heavy thumps coming from outside the apartment.

The door to the living room plunged open.

"Oh, Hi." A drunkard stood at the door, gripping the door knob, turning his head back and forth, fighting against his insobriety. He stunk of alcohol even from ten feet away. Then, the rest of the party poured in.

"I am sorry, but I have to get up early in the morning," I said to Nina and the hostess.

"Stay!" The drunkard pointed at me, exclaimed, "You must stay or we will force you to. Don't make us commit a crime."

"Stay! Stay! Stay!" the other students, now all in the living room, started to shout exultantly. Nina stared at me accusingly.

"Ok, alright, I'll stay," I doubled back, slumping down in the middle of the fat couch, sending two school girls momentarily into the stinking air, and then received their bodies squashing on me.

"Oh, Sorry! Sorry for shaking you up." The girls were giggling and laughing uncontrollably.

"Never mind. How…" I was about to introduce myself. The girl beside me had turned her head away because a young man strolled up, dangling a bottle of Jack Daniels in front of her. "You want some?"

"What is that?" she asked.

"Wine."

"What wine? I am not old enough to drink."

"Crap! You are shit." The young man brushed her off theatrically, and stuck the bottle in front of my face.

"I'm fine. I don't drink either," I said.

At this time, more young students came in, carrying two kegs of beer and big bags of snacks. They proposed a game of Truth-or-Dare which was rejected in favor of another supposedly more exciting game. The music was cranked up louder and louder. The guests formed a circle to cheer a girl on to drink directly from a bottle, until the crowd was broken up by a guy chasing after another guy, claiming that he had to kiss him on the mouth before midnight.

Nina, now wearing a pair of big plastic sunglasses, was drunk too. She was standing in a corner, using a red marker to smear bloody, vampire mouths on whomever happened to pass her by.

I could have simply walked out of the door at that point without anyone noticing. But I dimly suspected that some of the boys would do something very inappropriate to Nina. Without being a killjoy again, I strolled up to Nina, whispered into her ear, "Having a fun time now?"

She grabbed my chin and smudged my face with two big red strokes.

"Oh, hi," I introduced my new identity to her. "How do you like the party?" I said.

"I am terribly happy." Then she sighed. "Why don't you drink? You haven't had anything to drink, why?"

"I don't drink. I am alcohol intolerant," I said.

"Is that a kind of disease?"

"I don't know. I just invented it."

She smiled, and I smiled.

At one o'clock, a young woman in the living room broke down crying. She simply burst out and started to wail. The rest of the students were taken by surprise, and the boisterous party seized up momentarily as computer speakers played a melancholy song.

"What's going on?!"

"What happened?!"

The sobbing girl refused to answer. A few students had gathered around her offering consolation and padding on her shoulders.

I looked at Nina, standing next to me, for a clue.

"Her dad was jailed last week," she whispered to me.

The girl was led into the bedroom, stumbling along and still murmuring something under her breath. The door was shut and the party resumed immediately. Music had been recycled. Everybody was just as happy as they had been before the incident.

## 13

I distinctively avoided letting Rachel in on my personal life. First of all, I had never had a conversation with her about my dating a girl who was much younger than me. It was not that I looked up to Rachel's saintly, ascetic lifestyle or that I was ashamed of my sensuality and anchorlessness. It was just that American individualism had never been integrated into my character and, certainly not into hers. I was afraid that the discrepancy between our respective outlooks on what was appropriate when it came to private enjoyment would tear our business partnership apart. Or maybe I was afraid that she'd hit me with a reproach so vivid that my weak stomach wouldn't be able to digest it, as she usually did. But over time, I just assumed that she knew. It *was* a small circle.

And Priscilla was also aware, as she knowingly asked after my girlfriend, telling me that she had been tipped off by a friend. What a pretentious gal! She had no friend except Rachel. And she gaily and shamelessly asked if she could arrange a double date since she was dating an undergraduate who was just twenty-two years old! She must have thought that we had something in common. I told her, "I'm very busy."

And I was not lying. Rachel was most often not satisfied with my work, and my department was having an evaluation on its graduate students' research progress. The authorities seemed to know that one of the students was not studying artwork other than art gallery receptionists. As a result, we each had to write an article — a fictional work, essentially — to convince the authority that 'I' was not the black sheep, and was making good progress. It was a tiresome job. But as soon as I finished the article about my fictional progress, the good, old, artistic sense of achievement, the subjective awareness of my accomplishing a piece of intellectual work came back to me. It was the first time in a year that I had been in this celebratory mood since I quit painting. I wanted to ask Nina out. A double date might not be a bad idea after all.

So I called up Priscilla and suggested we could go see a documentary movie. A group of European scientists collided particles to reveal a new subparticle in reality that had long been presumed to exist in theory. Multiple Nobel prizes had been handed out. Government funds had been paid off. Scientists all over the world ran into each other, hugging and jumping around. And thanks to American movie makers, we commoners also had the luxury of sharing this awe-inspiring event. I told all this to Priscilla and expected her delightful acceptance. But she was a real portentous Hongkonger.

She said, "Oh, the documentary?" her voice was loaded with hesitation.

"What's the matter?" I asked, "it was your idea, wasn't it?"

"Yes, fine. Let's do it. I'll ask him to pick you up." She hung up the phone before I could say otherwise. I was upset. I was sick of being pushed around by haughty Chinese women. I decided that I would stand up to their whims and haughtiness from now on, or I would cut them off once for all, saying good riddance. I was determined.

Nina and I were talking about rich Chinese kids being a bad influence on other undergraduates. "What kind of parents would buy their kids luxury cars?" Nina was saying. Two minutes later, Priscilla's young boyfriend pulled up in front of my apartment. The boyfriend's name was Pim, and the car was a BMW sedan. Nina made a grimace of incredulity.

Priscilla sat in the front seat beside her young boyfriend. We scrambled in. The car seats felt compact, soft, and air-conditioned. The GPS lady was telling us to branch off a main road onto a narrow street.

To my annoyance, Priscilla had not said anything, not even a word of greeting to Nina.

*You must be kidding me*, I thought.

"I am sorry the radio is broken." Pim turned his chubby face around to the back seat.

"It's alright," Nina said.

"Have you guys heard of Nutrilite?" Pim asked in order to fill the silence.

I waited for the others to respond, and obviously everyone was waiting for me.

"It's the world's number one selling vitamin and dietary supplement," said Pim. "All my friends and I are in the business."

"Yes, I know the company," I said.

"No, it's a not a company, it's a brand, the company is Amway. Have you heard of them?" he asked me sternly.

"Yes, I suppose I have," I said.

"Well, I don't care about money," he said out of the blue, "but they've got some very interesting people there, inspiring people. Yesterday, I met a guy at one of their conferences. The man's speech made me cry. You all should have heard that speech. It was an experience that would change your life forever."

Priscilla didn't make a sound. Pim kept talking.

"What's your major, Pim?" asked my girlfriend.

"My major is philosophy."

"Oh, really?" she exclaimed. "And you still have time to run a business on the side?"

"I don't care about my studies very much," answered the undergraduate.

This seemed to finally goad his partner.

"Then, what do you care about?" said Priscilla scornfully.

The car made a sudden lurch; Nina nudged my elbow.

"My parents," said Pim. "They are getting old, and I haven't been able to be with them." Then he sank into a sort of melancholy as if a catastrophe had split his family apart.

We arrived at the Art Theatre on Green Street, and a long line of moviegoers was falling in behind a ticket booth.

"What a geeky town!" Priscilla muttered.

"The theatre only has three hundred seats," I said.

Priscilla was fidgeting. "Then what should we do?"

"We can still try," I said.

"What if there are no tickets left?" Priscilla asked.

I was very close to flying at her.

"I'm fine," said Nina.

"We can try," Pim said.

"But what if there are no tickets left for us?" Priscilla repeated.

"What's the worst-case scenario?" I said, holding my temper in check.

"It was a mistake to come today. It's a premiere. What a geeky town!" Priscilla was almost crying.

Pim started up the car again. We blew past the theatre, and then pulled into a parking lot.

"Do you guys want to see Godzilla instead?" Pim asked. "There's a new Godzilla movie at Carmike."

"What?" Priscilla shouted, turning her head in search of a clue.

"Godzilla! Godzilla!" Pim suddenly changed into a foreign accent. "It's a monster movie. The lizard-like sea monster from Japan. It's a Japanese sea monster at a new altitude in 3D animation."

Priscilla choked back some words and then said, "Who is this Japanese sea monster? If you want to watch a Japanese sea monster, please drive me home first."

"What's wrong with you?! Shit!" Pim muttered the last word.

"What did you say?" Priscilla stared at him, her eyes filled with fury.

"You heard me," Pim retorted.

Then Priscilla opened the door and stormed out of the vehicle. Pim pulled up the handbrake and followed her out while Nina and I sat in the back seat watching, bewildered, Nina's mouth agape in amazement.

In the parking lot, Priscilla and Pim were yelling at each other while Nina and I were spectating the fight through the windshield. Priscilla was standing under Pim's flat nose, shouting and shaking her head in a frenzy. Suddenly, she jerked her back around. On striding away, she was seized by his stumpy hand. Then she pointed her index finger at his face menacingly, almost poking his eyes, and then swiped his cheek with a whack. Pim stepped back; Priscilla stepped up and took out her cell phone, poking uncontrollably on the screen.

It turned out to be my phone she was calling. I didn't pick up.

"Sorry about this," I said to my girlfriend and got out of the car.

Priscilla and I met on the curb.

"I am sorry," Priscilla said.

"It's OK. I understand," I said. "Let's just go back."

"I really can't get into that car now," she said, "can you let him drive you back?"

"I can't just leave you here," I said.

I went back to the car, and negotiated between the curb and the vehicle. At length, we decided that Pim would drive Nina back, and I would escort Priscilla home. I didn't know that this would be the moment when Nina would decide to end our romance.

## 14

I was turning over in my mind the ugly look Nina had flashed me when we were parting. Priscilla didn't say a word on the way.

At the door of her apartment, I said, "Are you OK? Do you want me to come in?"

She hesitated, and then said, "Sure. Come in."

Her apartment was a scandalous mess. A mound of clothes piled on a couch was toppling down on the carpet, which must not have been vacuumed for months. The room was scattered with books, pamphlets, leaflets, pictures, magazines, a chequebook, and delivery boxes not yet unpacked, and empty ones that should have been thrown away. On the kitchen counter were unclosed books, baubles, filthy cutlery, and more food boxes, which took up the whole space. So I had to give up the idea of making some soothing tea.

"How's our guitar class?" I looked at an empty guitar bag lying on the floor, and it occurred to me that Priscilla still owed me an acoustic guitar course under her private tutelage. I had given her two hundred dollars up front and so far only had had one class.

"You still want to learn?" she called to me from the bedroom. "Or I can give your money back by the end of this month. I am a little hard up this month, and every month, you know."

"No, don't give it back to me. I still want to learn," I said, picturing myself strumming out a melody in some nightclub, stealing a young girl's heart.

"Is Pim living with you? I haven't been here for a while; what happened? What exploded?" I was checking if she was ready to talk about what had happened.

"No, of course not." She blundered out of her bedroom. "I can't stand him."

"You can't stand him? I thought you were together."

She tried to pass me a cigarette through the air. "Who said we are lovers. We have sex; that's all."

"How do you like it?" I asked.

"Oh, I'll let you know; I'll let you know," she said. "Where's the guitar?"

"This is your apartment," I said.

"Where did you put it last time?"

"It's been...how long? A year?"

Then she went for the kitchen and then the bedroom, opening closets, cabinets, and then slamming them closed.

"What are you doing?" I set the cigarette down on the ransacked coffee table.

"Do you really want to know about Pim?" She stopped behind the kitchen counter, putting her hands down on it, holding up her shoulders high, and closed her eyes as she took a deep breath.

"I don't mind," I said good-humouredly.

Then she walked back to the living room and squashed onto a couch and flung a strand of hair that had been bothering her back behind her ear. "He is a piece of shit!"

"Since forever?" I asked.

"First of all, this little shit calls me every two hours; ask me about everything. Should I go to a class? Should I go to the gym? Should I call my mother? My mom is having a fight with my daddy, is it her fault? Can we eat together? What does materialism mean in the class of Popular Culture 101? Why isn't Popular Film 101 about popular films at all?"

"Well, he's in his twenties," I said, "what do you expect..."

"Then I discovered that he was stalking me," she cut in angrily, "he staked out my apartment."

"Really? For what?" I asked in surprise.

"I didn't answer his call so he staked out my apartment."

"You caught him?" I was amused as the plot thickened.

"No. Why?"

"Then how did you know that? How do you know he staked out your apartment?"

"He chickened out and left at the last moment. But I swear to God, I smelt his cologne in the corridor."

"His what?"

"Cologne; it's Armani Aqua for Life. I knew it was him!"

"That's crazy."

"And this little piece of shit told his mom about us." She flew into another rage.

"You mean she didn't know about you?"

"Then that bitch called me and asked me why I am playing on his son's innocence?! I bet she thinks I'm a whore. Can you believe that? His son's innocence?"

She broke down, lurched backward, and loosened herself into the couch.

"This might sound cliché, but maybe that's what you should have expected when you started dating a teenager."

"We are not dating." She sat straight momentarily to clear up the concept.

"OK, took a teenager as a sexual partner."

"And you know what?"

"Calm down."

"He said he could not separate his body from his soul! He thinks of me as a whore too!" she yelled her last remark, crooking her index finger back, pointing it at her nose.

"Then why get involved in the first place?" I asked her.

She didn't answer. She stood up on her feet and stormed into the bathroom, leaving me in the living room pondering my own question.

Why they went out in the first place was that Priscilla thought younger people had a particular charm. They had not yet been contaminated by the cold calculation of real society. For her, youth had a sort of raw energy, perpetual enthusiasm, which had not yet been tamed and domesticated into a useful shape or means of any secular practice. And it was exactly this lively uselessness that she thought of as artistic, because art is supposed to be lively and useless. Since her love life and artistic life had both been stultified by a few sophisticated but, according to her, intrinsically diffident middle-aged men, she was made blind to the fact that the difference between a stultifying old man and a younger version was just time.

15

Rachel had always despised psychoanalysis. To her, psychologists were failed sociologists. Where there was a mental problem there was a social cause. As a result, she was rarely interested in other people's personal affairs and feelings. My psychoanalysis for her was: Rachel's mother was an unfulfilled woman because Rachel's grandpa was a prominent scientist in Mao's China, having set a high standard for personal achievement, who died leaving neither money nor happy family memories. When Rachel was a child, she often thought that the interminable quarrels between her mother and father were her fault. So she was strict about her own behavior, was a model student at school, and acted the role of an intermediary in the family. When all failed to cheer her mother up, she finally recognized that it was not her responsibility. A final touch of the take-it-or-leave-it dispassion was added to her high-strung temperament.

"How was your double date?" Rachel asked casually, breaking all the tacit rules of the office and my assumption that she never cared.

"How do you know?" Her sudden interest excited me since I could use someone sensible to talk to about the anecdote. So I instantly poured out, "It was a disaster. Priscilla lost her temper in a parking lot. I've never seen her like that. But I told her that's the price to pay for dating a kid."

She looked at me as if I were only twelve, and then self-importantly directed the subject in her favor. "Some of the post-socialist kids are just amazing," she said. "There was a boy in my lecture last night, must be a freshman, gawking at me like he was just born into this world."

While Priscilla and I were arguing over which of our dates was more politically justified and socially conventional, Rachel was giving a lecture to a group of politically-minded, unconventional undergraduates at a social event hosted by a Taiwanese students organization. She talked about the epidemic of plastic surgery destroying Korean women and now blitzing China. The talk was a big success. She really swept the crowd off their feet, giving them the food for thought she was aiming for. But she just could not tolerate one dissenter among the entire audience.

I paused for a second, let the subject go reluctantly, and then asked, "What did the *post-socialist* kid say?"

"Who cares what he said?" she was prepared. "What was very impressive was that he dared to give me sarcastic applause before I was even finished."

"Wow, and he didn't say anything?" I pictured a poor, jaunty freshman unknowingly giving Rachel a sarcastic applause, and privately rooted for him.

"He thought girls had the right to choose, you know, that kind of crap. And his girlfriend, sitting beside him, looked like a tired ghost, you know, that submissive kind of girl with eyebrows plucked, face covered with lipstick and white powder. I asked him why it was always the woman's obligation to look beautiful. He said he didn't know, but he still thought plastic surgery was OK..."

Before Rachel could finish her tirade, there was a knock on the door. As it was weak, shy, and tentative, Rachel pressed on with a few more words until the knock resumed.

Rachel raised her voice. "Come in."

The door opened, revealing an Asian girl in a pink plaid shirt and blue jeans.

"Hi." Her smile was sweet, and her teeth were so white that the shiny enamel made me feel self-consciously old and ugly.

"Hi, have you lost your way in the building?" said Rachel understandingly, "Don't blame yourself. This was originally built to study the IQ of rats."

The girl didn't get the joke. "No, I am looking for you. Do you remember me?" she said to Rachel.

"Oh!" Rachel exclaimed, "you were at the lecture last night."

"Right!" The girl cheered, still standing in the doorway, "I'm glad you remember me."

"How couldn't I? You were taking notes." Rachel nodded, smiling.

"Yes, I liked your talk very much. And I know you are from Guangzhou. I am from Guangzhou too." The girl stepped into the office. "And I know you were a student at South China Normal University. My mom also graduated from there."

"Really? What a coincidence." Rachel's voice trailed off as she didn't really fancy a college reunion.

The girl seated herself. Cartoon characters of humanoid pink piggies were embroidered on her pants where her kneecaps were showing through, and a smaller version of the same character reincarnated on her pink, jelly-like clogs.

"Professor, could you recommend some books for me?" the girl said earnestly, "I feel you are so knowledgeable."

"Well, first of all I'm not a professor," said Rachel.

"You're not?"

"No, far from it, I am a teaching assistant. Actually, I'm a graduate student. Do I look like a professor?"

"Wow," the girl exclaimed, "you are so knowledgeable! But still, can you recommend some books for me?"

Rachel hesitated. "What are you interested in? What fields?"

"What fields? Any field, or could you recommend a field or a course for me?" she said quickly, "I am interested in what you said last night about consumerism and feminism. I mean I agree that our generation is too much into consumerism. I want to know more about it."

The girl continued, not giving Rachel a chance to say anything, "And how do I improve my English?"

"Well, you can take a critical social theory class if you want to know more about consumerism, wait," Rachel paused, "are you a freshman?"

"Yes, I am."

"It has prerequisites. But you can take a class of British literature if you want to improve on your English," said Rachel. "I know the instructor; she is very willing to help international students."

The girl's eyes lit up. "Then I will, I will. I am so lucky I came to the lecture last night. Seriously, everyone is telling me that I should stay away from any course having anything to do with literature or theory."

"Who told you that? That's outrageous," Rachel said accusingly.

"All the sophomore, junior, senior Chinese students I met told me to stick to maths and statistics. They said because we are not native English speakers, we can't compete with Americans."

"You don't have to compete with anyone. You are not here to compete. Just follow your interests and work harder."

"Then I will, I will," the girl said heartily.

Their catechism diverged into more casual subjects: the girl had been naturalized; a bridge in their home city had been demolished due to its stark ugliness; and of course, America seen from a distance is so different from when it's seen close. It was a long conversation. At length Rachel had to stand up and cordially lead the girl out.

The girl kept coming back to the office afterward, and I kept running across her on campus. But over the time, she disappeared. At first, she waved at me from time to time in a corridor or from across a campus street. But after a few months, she stopped acknowledging me in public, and then probably avoided seeing me altogether. I was confused, but had no interest in finding out the reason. One day I casually mentioned this to Rachel. She told me the girl had failed to pass a midterm exam for the class of British literature due to her rambling writing style. And the girl tried to argue with the instructor and even threatened to sue her TA for being a racist. Her instructor backed down, allowed her to drop the class. Thus, started another rumor about the university not taking Chinese students seriously.

## 16

The office had a ghost staff member. Andy Lu was never committed to the newspaper, but once in a while, offered a hand as a 'commissioned' photographer. He majored in Electronic Engineering. However, what he really wanted to be, he revealed in his solemn claim, was an artist. He was a dedicated photographer for sure. He took his camera everywhere he went. Birds, architectures, landscape, streets, strangers, and various foods raw and cooked. Photography was the language he spoke, and he was so productive that people took notice of his work and reposted it on their Facebook pages.

Rachel thought his work pristine. It represented the taste and the image of the newspaper, which was supposed to be unpretentious and rooted in the local community. We had been publishing Andy's pictures for a year already, and even though there was rarely any money in it, he kept saying that it was a pleasure to work with us.

Once in a while, he would drop by the office in person, and talk senselessly in the way he thought a real artist should do. Being a keen advocate of keeping abreast with new photographic technology, he would bring his newly purchased photography gears with him. Whenever the industry put out, say, an underwater camera, a lens with an even wider angle, or a camera case providing multiple ways to customize his gear, he couldn't help but buy it.

Andy Lu breezed into the office, wearing a brown khaki vest with 15 pockets. Putting down his heavy camera case, he said, "How is everything going, guys?" His voice was wimpy and unassertive. He drew a chair under his rump.

"We're doing OK." Rachel stood up, turning and leaning on the edge of her desk. "How are you doing?"

"I am doing great!" He pulled his case closer to the chair as if someone was going to snatch it away. "I heard that the newspaper is going under." He meant it as a joke.

Rachel was annoyed and remained motionless.

"I mean I heard that you are running out of money," he corrected himself.

"Yes, yes, we're planning for the worst. But we're safe for a year," Rachel said tersely.

"Oh, then I must have gotten it wrong," Andy Lu said. "I thought you were closing down."

This really put Rachel off, "Don't you worry; we are OK for now; any new pictures?" Rachel asked.

"Yes, but I am into microscope photography these days, you know, photography through microscopes. It's an amazing world. You should see my pictures of flies and spiders. Then you'll know how fantastic the universe really is. Well, it's hard for me to explain in words how symmetrical and harmonious they are. You really have to see them. They must be God's creation. I mean they are the evidence of God."

This proved to be beyond Rachel's taste. "But you will still be taking pictures of the campus, won't you?"

Andy put his hands into his vest pockets and opened the vest up like a door, revealing his horizontally striped shirt. "Don't worry; I'll keep on the theme of campus life, but I'm getting more serious about art," he snapped, "plus, I have a lot of time this semester. My advisor is moving to Wisconsin, so I don't have to go to lab every day. You know what? Our department has hired a new dean. She thinks highly of me; she's given me three more classes to teach. One of them used to be my advisor's class. What an honor! She used to own a company; she was a successful businesswoman; she knows how to run a department better than my advisor ever did. Administrative skill is essential for any institution, for a department or for a newspaper." The last phrase was a challenge.

Rachel's tolerance was running thin. "I know you are a busy man. How can I help you today?"

Andy Lu's face set. The pockets in which his hands were hidden were like two puny wings that were about to take off. "Oh, I just want to check in with you guys, see if everything was still OK."

"Everything is OK," Rachel said. "Thank you for checking in."

"Good, good. Problem solved; every problem has a solution." Andy Lu lifted his case and set it on his lap. He continued, lowering his eyes as if he'd suddenly become shy. "Rachel, I am going to have a picnic tomorrow. I want to know if you could join me."

This caught Rachel off guard. In a moment of

dumbfounded confusion, she said, "Oh, OK, thank you."

"Great!" Andy exclaimed, as he just had nailed a date.

"I mean we have never had a social event, right, Alex?" Rachel directed the question to me invitingly.

I stood up. I had been shunned in the last fifteen minutes and was unceremoniously left out of the invitation. But I would not hold it against Andy Lu anymore, now that I was mad at Rachel. Why should I hold anything against him? He was a lonely man, an honest man, and was one of the tiny engines of academic capitalism. What he wanted was just to be thought above average, and in return he had been offering his blood and sweat and doing what he had been told to do. Compared to Rachel, he was a simple saint, a good proletariat in America. As we parted at the door of the office, I shook his hand in a comradely fashion.

"Good luck with your microscope photography, Andy," I said sincerely, standing at the door, seeing him marching away with his case in hand.

Rachel stared at me as I stepped back into the office. She asked, "What was that?"

"It's a date," I re-joined, "and you just accepted it."

"No, it's not a date. You must go with me," she said as if she was going to have an abortion.

"No, I will not go with you."

"Then I'll say I am sick."

"Then you'll be very, very rude and we may lose our photographer." Then, I teased, "When was the last time you went out on a date?"

"None of your business," she answered abruptly. But later, as she pleaded with me to go, she told me. "It was actually five years ago."

## 17

Andy Lu was not arbitrarily setting off a false alarm when he suspected that the paper was closing down. The paper was registered as a student organization. One of the requirements for setting up a student organization in C_ University was having at least five active and registered members. Originally there were Rachel, Andy, Priscilla, me and another friend of Rachel's who had graduated the year before. As Priscilla was also graduating and so was Rachel herself, the future of the paper was nothing but gloomy and precarious. We had to have another member to proceed with the re-registration. Rachel had been scheming to penetrate the bureaucracy. She asked me to sound out Alice about this situation, saying if Alice was interested, I should prompt her to make a decision. "Tell her we want her now," she ordered. But I put off calling her from the office because the tower-climbing event had made our relationship more than I wanted Rachel to know about. I made an excuse and went back to my apartment early that day.

I meant to call her when I got back. But I didn't. Of all the formalities or flirtatious opening lines, I could not dredge up a single one that would serve the course. It was fortunate that the ceiling light in the kitchen was on though. It had not been working for a month, and the landlord finally had sent for a handyman. I stood barefoot in the newly illuminated kitchen, contemplating a full-fledged though dead cockroach lying under the sink frozen in mid-convulsion. This apartment had survived a minor burglary, a major seepage of rain from the west windows, the impotence of the three quarters of the oven rings, and now verminous floorboards. It seemed impossible to find an ideal apartment, not to mention a decent landlord. I had been with four different landlords: an old lady, LSM Development, Campus Property Management, and Fourth Street Realty. They all had their scams, rules and hidden secrets. My first landlord was a very white woman, traditionally built, churchgoing, nice, but the energy bill of her wooden-board house would soar ridiculously high in the winter, which would inconveniently last half a year in the state of Illinois. So I moved to an efficient studio with LSM Development. The energy bill was controlled, but soon I had an out-of-control relationship with a girl. Then we decided to move together to a one-bedroom apartment, and LSM Development decided that I could not get my deposit money back because of, first, sanitary issues, and when I had proved that the accusation was preposterous, they simply stopped communicating with me so as to test out my civil litigation savvy. I sized up the litigation costs and gave up. Afterward, having lived together for a year with the girl, we broke up, and I moved out of the apartment, signed a contract in a hurry with the Fourth Street Realty, and started to live with three other young male students, one from China, one from Korea, and an American delivery man whose first name was Josh. Josh lived from hand to mouth. One day, Josh disappeared with a big plasma screen TV we'd paid for together and pawned it for two hundred dollars. Then the jittery Korean moved out, saying that this place was not safe anymore. Then the sheepish Chinese law student moved out. Then I moved out.

This was how I ended up now standing in this small, dingy studio looking out on a loud parking lot. Over time, it had become crowded with furniture. Every weekend, when cars rolled into monstrously built shopping outlets, coughing up people looting clothes, leather, jewelry, and furnishings, my schoolmates always invited me to go and would claim to have saved hundreds of dollars at the end of a day shopping. "If you can never stop buying, you can never stop working," I said. But I often went along to the malls anyway. Where else could I go in order to hang out with my dear, worldly friends? So I unwittingly bought a room of variegated trumperies. But I didn't really care about living in a shoddy, garish apartment, because when I was a child, I always had my own messy, garish room. Alas, I was such a happy, ruthless child, often chased after by my stentorian father with a punishing switch in hand. I would dash into my room and slam the door in his face. Once in the room, I was the lord. I could invent my own style of calligraphy, assemble my toy army soldiers, and masturbate to my imaginary lady who lived alone always half-naked in a purplish cloud.

I was supposed to call Alice, but procrastination set in. I wanted to find something to do in the apartment. I was standing in front of my bookshelf on which my books were neatly stacked. *Twelve Plays by Shakespeare* for eight dollars were arranged exactly as on the day they arrived. "What should I do?" I said to myself. "Study? Of course, but..." Study required a peaceful mind. "Call Nina?" I had called her up to apologize about the botched double date, and her voice told me that the next call ought to be initiated by her.

Outside the window, a tree and a light pole were standing side-by-side gangling against the background of a dimly lighted back street. The enveloping dark, sweet night had set in. I turned on the radio, trying to tune in to something. I caught a local station that blasted out rock music, and the National Public Radio was broadcasting plane crashes and army invasions I could not do anything about. So I turned it off.

Then I found myself calling Alice.

"Hi, is this Alice speaking?" I cleared my throat.

"Hello, the person you are calling is in the hospital," a female voice came through.

"Sorry, I beg your pardon."

"The person you are calling is in the hospital," the voice repeated. "Do you know Carle?"

"Yes, I know Carle, the hospital," I said.

"She is here in room 211. Are you her friend?" Before I could say anything, she continued, "She needs someone to be with her."

"Oh, OK." I said instinctively. Then she asked if I could come at once and hung up.

I got to the hospital half an hour later. A security guard helped me find the room. A small crowd of Chinese was already surrounding Alice's ward bed. When I came in, a young male nurse was explaining something to the group. Among them, a young woman with a confused look pulled up the strap of her leather purse, frowned at Alice disappointedly, and took her leave. A young couple was there holding hands with tense emotion. An undergraduate, obviously brought here by someone else, was hanging back, with a silly smirk on his mouth and a hairdo resembling something on fire. They all wore an expression of reluctance.

Alice, instead of lying down, sat cross-legged on the ward bed with her socks on, propped up against a cotton-white pillow. Her face was battered and covered with bruises and thin cuts. Her cheeks had swelled up, pushing up one of her eyes which blinked incessantly. But she seemed in high spirits; she insisted on having all her clothes on and refused to lie down.

"You have to lie down," the woman holding her partner's hand tightly said to her.

"I'm OK. I shouldn't be here!" said Alice, throwing a tantrum.

"Then where should you be? Look at you!" the woman said sternly.

"I'm OK, where is Vic?"

"Vic has been taken away!"

"It's a mistake. I am fine. Tell them it's not like what they thought," said Alice as if she was about to leap out of the bed.

The nurse put a clipboard down on a steel trolley and turned to Alice.

"You can go home to sleep for tonight. But there is the possibility of a concussion and skull fracture, so I need you come back tomorrow to do an exam," the nurse said.

The women gasped at the words – 'concussion' and 'fracture'.

Alice retorted, as if she was bargaining with a vendor. "What if I don't want to?"

"Don't want to? You have to," the woman cut in accusingly, still clenching her partner's hand.

"Well, I will let you go," said the nurse, now turning back to the woman. "She was drunk when she was brought here. Someone has to stay with her for tonight."

We all nodded.

The nurse turned back to Alice, "I need you to sign a few things, then you are good to go," he said, sliding closed a curtain hanging over the ward bed that screened the rest of us off.

"Are you a friend of Alice's?" The woman, having let go of her boyfriend's supportive grip, fixed her eyes on me.

"Well, we don't know each other very well. What can I do?" I stammered.

"Could you stay with her for tonight?" she said to me. There was pleading in her voice.

"Me?!" I was surprised that she'd ask me to do this. If they thought I was tough enough to defend Alice from any other man, they were absolutely wrong!

"Yes, can you?"

"I…can if nobody else is going to." I looked around at the others in the room. Their faces were as stern as stones.

"Oh, that's great. It's great." The woman was relieved. Then she handed me a sheet of paper.

"Give this to her when she's sober."

I took a glance at the hospital bill. This dramatic show, so far, had cost Alice seven thousand dollars.

## 18

Outside the hospital the high heat of the day had dropped off. It was cool and windy. Alice and I had sneaked into a bus. The bus was warm and empty, and the driver jaded, hiding behind a big wheel, swaddled in his uniform, staring forward unseeingly. We rode the bus for a few blocks and got off at a quiet residential area. We walked across a street, and then trod on a green lawn fronting an apartment building. It was already the next day.

To my surprise, her apartment had scanty furnishings. When we came in, her cell-phone was ringing. She apologized, quickly made for the bedroom, and pulled the door closed.

In the living room, a long couch in damask scattered with magazines was set behind a quaint tea table where an unexpected candle holder was towering over a pudgy tree-root-like tea pot accompanied by a few thumb-sized ceramic bowls. On the border of the living room and kitchenette, a dining table stood recklessly awry. I turned around; there was a wall of assorted shoes. They were stacked on wall-mount shelves, shinning, colorful and stylish in every possible way, but together made for an incongruent and noisy melange. They all looked as if they'd had their day, but now were abandoned, moored there accumulating dust.

"Nice shoes," I said as she was coming out of the bedroom.

"Oh, most of them are from Taiwan. Those girlish ones," she said with a flourish of her hand. "My mom shoved them into my suitcase."

"I used to believe in shoes," I said. "I mean you can tell a lot just from the shoes a person wears."

"You can?" she asked, as if I had said something silly. The alcohol in her blood must have worn off, but the black bruise on her cheekbones was all the more conspicuous.

"My mom used to force me to wear leather shoes with pointed tips." I meant to make fun of myself to lighten up the atmosphere.

"So you did it?" She smiled. It was an effort.

"Oh, they cost her 100 or some Chinese dollars in 1996. I couldn't throw them away, could I? If that was the look she really wanted for me, I would let her have it."

"Can you do me a favor?" Suddenly she changed the subject.

"OK, I'd like to," I said.

"Could you give me a hug?" she pleaded.

I paused. So gratuitously complicated the plot. "Yes, of course," I said. "Why don't you just hug me? I am bad at hugging or embracing or touching. Once I did it, and the girl accused me of groping."

"Really?" She let out a laugh, another effort.

"Well, when I was eighteen, I was such a hugger."

"How did you know I was in the hospital?" She let the subject of hugging blow over.

I told her.

Then she said gravely, "I am sorry I got you into this."

I consoled her, saying that I was an idler who'd been idling, and had nothing better to do but for the accident. Then I asked hesitantly, "What happened?"

"Oh, I just had a little fight with Vic. Do you know Vic?" she said, "He is my boyfriend."

This was what I anticipated, but I didn't know how to respond. "He... hurt you?"

We sat down on the couch facing each other. She crooked her arm and leaned her head back on a desiccated cushion. Then she slid some inches down, so I could almost touch her bare knees curled up in front of me.

"No, he can't hurt me," she said assertively. "I fell over and bumped into something, the table maybe. I really don't want to use the word 'jerk', but sometimes he really is."

"Where is he?" I asked.

"I really don't know." She was embarrassed, "I am sorry I was drunk." She grimaced in a sort of naughty way and said, "Thank you so much for everything. I have to go to bed before I fall in love with you."

"Oh, OK, I, ah, I…" I stuttered, standing up.

"No, no, no. You don't have to leave; please don't leave. I just need to take a nap, sleep it off and everything," she said and leaned forward towards me, giving me a brief hug. Then she went back into her bedroom.

It was three in the morning. After she left, an overwhelming sleepiness came over me. I curled up on the couch and dozed off.

I slept fitfully, having nightmarish dreams, and when the sky outside the window turned bluish grey, I heard the clogging footsteps of wooden slippers coming out of the bedroom. I kept my eyes closed, trying to squeeze in one more round of sleep before the sunrise. Then I heard, "Come in, it's cold out there."

19

"I am really fine out here," I said to her, feeling my clothes to make sure that they were still on me.

"Come on in. I want to tell you something," she prompted.

I took a look at my watch; it was not on my wrist anymore. If I had ever really dreamed of being invited into her bedroom, this puffy-eyed situation would be the worst I could imagine.

"Come on," she prompted still.

"Nothing will happen," I said to myself. So I got up and let her voice lead me to her bedroom.

The room was dimly lit, tidy and had the vague pervading perfume that was not what one put on necks and wrists, but rather like the scent of dried flowers and herbs. There was no place to sit except a twin-size bed, so I seated myself on the ledge of a windowsill. The sun was about to rise and birds were chirping outside. She was in her silky nightgown that hung loosely from her shoulders and cascaded down over her hips. While I was sitting down, she scrambled back under the bedspread, which must still have been warm. Then she wormed her head out from underneath a blanket.

"You said you had something to tell me?"I was trying not to look at her.

"Well, yes, I have a story to tell you," she was improvising, "you know a Chinese fable? A witless burglar wanted to break into a house and accidentally triggered a bell hanging on the door? The bell was ringing and ringing. But instead of running away, he covered his own ears to silence the bell?"

"He was arrested by a group of neighbors. Yes, why?"

"Well, it's supposed to teach kids not to have their own way because the majority are always in the right and will eventually catch you out."

"A pithy summary," I laughed.

"But the truth is that it's always the neighbors who want to break into *your* house and pretend there aren't any bells on the door whatsoever. You know what I mean?"

"No, I thought you were improvising," I said, "but this sounds like something profound."

"Don't underestimate me," she said languidly, her voice sweet with refreshed energy in it.

I was still sleepy. "Do you still want to write for the newspaper?" I recalled the mission Rachel assigned to me. I caught sight of her breasts underneath her dress, so I turned my head away again.

"Yes," she said weakly.

"Not interested anymore?"

"Yes, yes, I am interested," she confirmed, "I was thinking of something else."

"You know? Rachel wants someone dedicated." I was searching for a safe zone in the room to set my eyes upon while fighting off the voyeuristic temptations.

"Yes, yes, I am a drama queen. I want everything, but the moment I get it, I can't help impulsively throwing it away; clothes, boyfriends, reputation and everything."

"Is that so?"

"If I were you, I would stay away from a person like me. You are not in love with me, are you?" she finished, giving me a quizzical look.

"No, how could I be? That's impossible!" I let out a dry laugh.

"Impossible? Why?" she said, "I'm not hideous looking, am I?"

"It has nothing to do with your looks." I broke off. Then I said, "I have a girlfriend."

"You have a girlfriend? Then how dare you stay overnight at my apartment!" she said, teasingly.

"Yes, I am a bad person. I am morally corrupt." Since she was playful, I should just play along. "I heard that you are rich. How rich are you?"

To my surprise, she responded with a surge of enthusiasm. She propped herself up with a pillow and grabbed another one, put it under against her chin.

"My father is a tycoon. He owns a manufacturing company with one hundred plus branches all over the world, mainly in Europe."

"Then why are you here?" I asked.

"Where should I be?" she exclaimed, "Lying down on some beach letting dolphins surf around me every day?"

"You don't care for beaches?"

"Yes, I like them, but my father is very strict about money," she said. "Well, this is boring. Let's change the subject. Do you like America?"

"I haven't really explored much yet, so my opinion shouldn't amount to...much," I said.

"I have the exactly opposite problem," she said. "I feel I have explored everything in this country. What's the saying? I have turned over every stone." She finished the sentence dreamily.

"Found anything interesting?"

"I did."

"Then?"

"Well, nothing lasts."

"What are you interested in now?" I asked.

"I don't know, Alex!" She slid down on her back, holding the pillow up high over her face, and then thumped it down on her chest.

"I mean what would you really want to do if..." I was about to say if you had enough money, then it occurred to me that she might have already had it. So the subjunctive mood was for the first time inaccurate.

"If what?" she asked.

"If, you know, you didn't have all those mundane concerns: job, parents, school and everything," I said.

"Then I would sing!" she blurted out.

"What?!"

"I want to be a singer!" she said, gawking at the ceiling as if she was standing in a stadium before an audience.

"Oh, then be a singer. Sing, the hell with it," I raised my voice a little.

"I know. But I have wasted all these years on this nonsense. It's too late to turn back."

"Who say it's too late. I..."

My phone was ringing, vibrating on the coffee table in the living room.

"Excuse me," I apologized to her and walked out of the bedroom. I picked up the phone; it was Rachel and it was six thirty in the morning.

"What the hell?!" I muttered into the phone, "It's six thirty."

"You promised," she said severely at the other end.

"What?!"

"The picnic."

"My God. I didn't promise. I..." It dawned on me that this was the day when our microscopic photographer was supposed to take Rachel out on a date. "Listen. I really can't..."

"Alex, I swear to God!" she yelled.

"OK, OK, I'm coming. I'm coming."

## 20

It's a free country. This is admitted by both American intellectuals and ordinary Americans, and it is repeated by Chinese intellectuals and ordinary Chinese. But it's a lie, a profound one though. The truth is, rarely is a thing in the United States free. For example, you are not free to choose whether to get a college degree or not, if you understand the consequences of not having one. In addition, you are not free to choose what to think, since philosophies, if they exist here at all, are often ridiculed, and false activities — all forms of just-do-it logic — are fanatically prompted and favored over deliberation. It seems like you are free to choose one product out of a hundred, but if you have money, it's unlikely that you will choose anything made in China. So how is America such an exceptionally free country? If you throw this question at a newly employed immigrant, driving a newly purchased SUV, he will take you for a ride on a newly tarmacked highway and let you drive for ten minutes. If you still can't feel the freedom, the chances of you two being friends in the future are slim.

We were in a green sedan heading for a lake twenty miles away from the campus. When Andy Lu picked me up at the street corner outside Alice's apartment, he threw me a nasty look and started his car before I even buckled up. Rachel was sitting beside me in the back seat. It was hot on a highway, and I doubted there was any cool air coming out of the air-conditioner vent. So I rolled down a window. A draft of heat wave wheezed in, and it drowned out the driver's voice. I hastily pressed on the button to roll up the window.

"Excuse me," I said.

"I said I go to Chicago once every two weeks." Andy said. "I always take on two riders with me, to share gas."

*So we are supposed to pay?* I thought.

"My ex-girlfriend and I used to go to the lake very often," our driver continued, "I arrived in my department in 2007; she got in the year after. We are under the same adviser, James Hebert. Do you know Professor James Hebert? He's very famous."

"No. I don't," Rachel said.

"Oh, he's famous in our field," he said.

"It must be great since you are both in the same field," Rachel said.

"Who?"

"I mean your girlfriend and you," Rachel added.

"Oh, her!" he exclaimed as if a horse just stomped on him. "Yes, she is smart. My adviser said she is smarter than I am. The problem is that she doesn't care." He laughed.

"What's your research topic?" Rachel asked.

"Topic? Oh, I changed my topic this year." He hastened the word 'topic' and then the conversation seized up.

I was sitting behind the nape of his neck; it had multiple layers undulating as he was talking. He must have been in his early thirties, but he looked much older. From this privileged angle, I saw many streaks of grey in his thin hair, and when he laughed, in the rear-view mirror, crimps around his eyes and mouth turning into claws.

"How's the funding in your department, Alex?" he asked me.

I felt somehow flattered, so I answered seriously, "In general, it is meagre, and it requires teaching twenty hours a week or other kinds of jobs like editing journal articles."

"I don't understand these foreigners," Andy cut in impatiently, "I mean these white people. They want to talk about their work even after punching out. Can't you just talk about something else? Music, movies, arts. Do you guys play poker?" he said with both his hands hovering over the driving wheel, throwing some invisible cards in the air.

"Not really," I said.

"I can't do anything other than play poker during summer vacation," he said. "Are you guys going back to China, I mean eventually?"

"I haven't thought about it," I said.

"Me neither," Rachel said.

"I will go back to China. I mean eventually."

We arrived at a riverbank. A clear, frolicking creek flowed into it a short way from us. Above the marshes a stretch of green meadow was basking in the sunlight. We got out of the car. The photographer went back to the trunk to unload his barbecue gear. It turned out that he took this event more seriously than we expected. Not only did he have a classic kettle-style grill, as he explained, which had a 22-inch diameter cooking area with two hinged side openings that allowed one to easily add charcoal, but also a specialized camp table to facilitate the whole event. He laid out on the table two tongs, two brushes — one black and one red — a spatula, an instant-read thermometer to test the internal temperature of the meat. Instead of lighting charcoal directly on the grill, he had installed a chimney starter, a metal cylinder allowing one to light and heat charcoal before adding it to the grill. I was assigned to start the fire. As he was operating this metal gear with trained agility, Rachel could not but be entranced.

"Having fun?" I asked her.

"This is amazing!" she answered.

Andy came back from the car again, holding a fireplace lighter in one hand, a long canvas glove covered the other.

"Is he balding?" she whispered to me as if she was a matchmaker.

"Keep it down. He'll hear you," I said.

"China is screwed up if you ask me," he said out of the blue as he approached.

"You mean the country or our lunch?" I laughed.

"The country," he answered gravely.

"Isn't it rising?" Rachel asked sarcastically.

"If it's rising, why does everybody want out." He crouched down at the chimney starter beside me, mumbling words to it. "Everything is screwed up. Institutions, the culture, the government. How can you have a businessman who is also the judge and the general of an army. There is a book about this that everyone should read."

"What book?" Rachel asked, impaling chicken wings on skewers.

"I forgot the name," he said, "it's about Chinese socialism being a sham. It's a superficial rule above a hidden rule. Now kids are taught to be hypocrites. Being an open dissident is dangerous; believing propaganda is foolish. The Chinese no longer care about transcendental values; they only care about money. These kinds of people are easy to whip up. They're easily manipulated to do anything. This is the truth behind the so-called rise of China."

While talking, he occasionally took out a small camera from his multi-purpose jacket pocket and aimed it at something in some distance. He would snap a few shots and go on with his fireside chat.

"And higher education is corrupt too."

"You mean in U.S. or China?" Rachel asked.

"Especially in the United States. Students are in debt these days. Professors are teaching according to their whims if they care to teach at all. They don't know how to run universities."

"Do you?" Rachel asked good-humouredly.

The man blushed. "It's a business. If it's a business they should put businessmen in charge. They know how to maximize revenues."

Rachel grunted.

"I mean students are not receiving quality services from universities. They are not prepared for a career after spending four years in college. They have been forced to take useless courses just because there happen to be professors in that field."

"I can't agree with you on this," Rachel murmured to a skewer of mushrooms.

"For example literature, history, philosophy. Does our society need so many philosophers? They are basically forcing customers to buy things they don't need."

"So in your opinion, humanities are absolutely dispensable," Rachel snapped.

"No, I don't mean that."

"Then what do you mean by..."

I had a feeling that the photographer was not so much trying to argue with Rachel as actually trying to impress her with his pseudo-omniscience. So I left them to their banter, and took a walk in the sunlit meadow dotted with pansies and dandelions.

Andy might have thought his charlatanism combined with stubbornness was the very essence of Chinese masculinity. As a self-proclaimed scientist with all his material gear, he considered himself efficient, and actually believed in the future of the free-market economy with religious faith. Besieged and overwhelmed by academic requirements and resources, he fell short of one thing only: happiness. On top of microscopic photography and grilling, he was still not satisfied and felt the urgent need to cultivate another new hobby: discursive power – the power of language, the means of the chattering class. This time he wanted to express his anxiety directly, with words. He tried, but since his simple mind had been hijacked by academic imposters and pseudo-intellectuals, he could not help but mimic their way of talking, which has neither content nor the intention to communicate.

## 21

After the picnic, I sent Alice a text message, asking after her, and about the result of the examination or whether she had had it at all. She called me back and said she was blessed that there was no fissure or sign of a concussion. And what made the incident a blessing in disguise was that the doctor told her there was a tissue in her uterus, fluid-filled, small, but fortunately benign. For a moment I didn't know how to respond to such personal *good* news. But I was glad that she must have considered me a friend. So when she asked me to do her a favor, I said I was more than happy to assist her with any manual labor before she could fully recover. Then, she said she indeed needed some help because she was moving out of her apartment.

"I don't feel safe here. It has nothing to do with Vic," she added. "The room makes me feel anxious."

"Do you have a place to move to?"

"I just found a place this morning," she said.

"This morning?" I was surprised she could find an apartment in such a short time and had the freedom to move out of her apartment for no good reason except that she was just tired of living there.

"Yes, it's a little expensive but the advantage is that I can move in right away." She gave me the address.

"You need me to help you move out?" I was confused.

"No, of course not." She laughed, "I called a moving company. They are very efficient. But the old apartment still has eight months' rent to pay so I am wondering if you know anyone who would be interested in subleasing. You know, I don't have many friends in this town." Her voice flattened out.

I did have quite a few friends in this town, but none of them was homeless or in desperate need of a spare apartment. "I'll ask around," which I did, unenthusiastically passing it on.

The new apartment Alice moved into was in a high-rise building, a brand new residential tower built on top of a supermarket and surrounded by bungalows with worn-down stairs and roofs falling on boarded-up windows. The vicinity was still under construction. These new buildings were intended to cater particularly to rich, international students. Her apartment was on the seventeenth floor. The elevator roared treacherously, lifting me up, and I was having misgivings about how quiet and empty the place was. When the elevator split open, the interminable humming of a central air conditioner bloomed. The walls were painted bright green.

I stood at her door, unfastened my shirtsleeves, which had been rolled up and buttoned and let them drape down over my arms. I knocked on her door once tentatively, standing straight as if I was a hotel concierge.

"I am terribly sorry for the mess." She opened the door. "Everything is still out of place."

"It's a nice apartment." I stepped in, resisting the temptation to look around.

"Is it?" she asked. "I thought it was, too...I don't know. I liked it when they first showed it to me. I made the decision in a rush. I should have seen more places."

A black kitten with expensive-looking, fluffy fur, sneaked into the living room, cocked her head, and stared at me with amber eyes.

"I didn't know you had a cat," I said.

"Oh, I just adopted her from PetSmart. Do you know PetSmart?"

"Not really," I said.

"Oh, It's a wonderful place." She got excited, "You can adopt dogs, cats, fish, birds, even lizards; they call them dragons though. You can have a pet dragon. Isn't that wonderful?"

"Yes, it's wonderful, but it's a big responsibility. What else have you done?" I asked, teasingly.

"You can even have a hamster," she said without answering me, "really, it's so tiny and so cute."

She grabbed the kitten up, combing the poor animal's stomach, putting on a cartoonish voice, trying to communicate with the feline. "I'll take good care of you, don't you worry, Sooty? Her name is Sooty." Suddenly the cat let out a squeal, thrashed out of Alice's grasp. "Shit!" Alice cried, a long scratch appeared on her arm.

My heart lurched. "Oh, my God! Are you alright?"

"I'm OK. I'm OK." She twisted her arm, trying to see the scratch, and walked back into her bedroom. She returned with a vial of ointment. She handed the vial to me, and took off her sweater, discarded it on a couch.

"Is it bad?" she said, "I can't see it." she held her elbow up before my eyes.

"You want me…?" I asked, holding the ointment.

"Oh, yes, please, please."

We sat down on the couch. I unscrewed the lid, poured the thick oil out on my palm, and rubbed it on her elbow and arm. And one minute later, we started kissing.

I didn't know who actually started it. As soon as she closed her eyes, my arms encircled her waist. She pulled off my shirt and I eased her onto the couch. She had no bra on; I kissed her behind her ears and all the way down to her pubic bone, inhaling, exhaling, madly taking in her perfumed fragrance.

"Are you sure you want to do this?" I pulled myself back.

She didn't answer.

Then I asked, "Do you have a condom?"

"No, I don't," she said. "They have some downstairs."

"I'll be back," I said, breathing heavily.

The myth is that intelligent people usually have bad sex, and those who are less intelligent tend to have passionate sex yet bad relationships. In order to have good sex you have to be honest to your body, and the key to success hinges on your private fantasy. Since political correctness and viable sexual fantasies are usually contradictory these days, enlightened people are usually trapped in the vicious alternation between illegitimate orgasm and ungratifying, educational, salutary sex.

Too much reflective thought leads to a destructive result, just as talking about sex takes away from the enjoyment of just doing it. Sheer enjoyment evokes a sense of guilt: yes, you are honest to your body, but you are perhaps on the dark side of morality where honesty is actually evil.

I went down to the supermarket searching for condoms, with reality coming back to me in that excessively cooled warehouse. Members of the building staff were unloading goods half-heartedly as if they all knew my secret. My brain started to function again, "Does Alice still have a boyfriend? Is Alice even sane? What kind of trouble I am getting into? Do I still have a girlfriend?!"

The supermarket was a sad place. Everything there was decorated flamboyantly and cried out for attention, but all together made for an ugly place. I bought a 12-piece pack of condoms. Bright-colored tropical fruits on the cover were wrapped up in shinning waterproof cellophane, which would give me a hard time peeling it off. Some condom package designer thought fruit and a hard-to-reach-condom foreplay might somehow help sexual performance and in return facilitate the sale.

I took the elevator up back to Alice's apartment.

"Doesn't Vic know?" My hand was fumbling over the angles of the pack in my pocket.

"Oh, shit! Vic." She slapped down the book she was reading, jumped to her feet, searching for her cell phone.

I was flustered, "Is he coming? Should I leave?"

"No, no, stay." She retrieved her phone, leaned on an empty bookcase, trying to get someone on the phone. Around her feet were cardboard boxes; she poked them with her toes anxiously.

"Hello, Vic. I am leaving for Chicago. Call me if you need anything from Chicago. I didn't get your last call; I was unpacking. What's up? I will be back in one or two days, so give me a call if you need anything, bye." She hung up.

She sank back into the couch, sucking on her knuckles, trying to calm herself down.

I took out the condoms, "Seventeen bucks and ninety-nine cents. Share?" I asked.

She burst out laughing, and then she lowered her eyes as if she'd rather be left alone.

Part Three

22

On the second page of the latest issue of Corn-respondence, a banner headline read, "congratulations on your graduation." Under the festive, greenish words, two rectangular pictures acted together to convey the convivial theme. One was taken at a college graduation ceremony. In the picture, the incumbent chancellor of C_university was shaking hands with the commencement speaker of the year behind a podium before a row of seated professors in academic robes. This was the first time in more than fifty years that the graduation ceremony had been held outside due to widespread building renovations. The speaker was an alumnus NASA astronaut who'd graduated in 1993. A passage of his speech was quoted in a brief report, "Success for me is not what it looks like from outside. It took me 13 years and four tries to become an astronaut. I was turned down in 1995, 1997, 2000 and again in 2004." And it ended with, "Success is found in our own hearts." Astronauts are astronauts. The speech served the purpose as much as the picture did. If one would care to criticize, the frame and the angle of the picture were not exactly right, an injustice, considering that the photographer was a professional painter and art history expert.

I was trapped, at that time, in the matrix of an audience during an ovation. Having heard out the speech, a phalanx of students and their guerrilla parents and friends broke into pandemonium. The handshake between the chancellor and the astronaut only lasted for a few seconds, so there was no time for me to contemplate the angle or the frame or the depth of field about which I thought only a pompous person like Rachel would care. Anyway, camera technologies had come a long way. Narcissism, commodity fetishism, and consumer credulity were infinite if only you dared to exploit them. Many wanted to take pictures with the speaker, or the chancellor, or the speaker and the chancellor. While they were waiting, they chatted, shooting with their cameras randomly at each other, adjusting tripods, zooming in and out with telephoto lenses making wheezy automatic noises. Some of them were tourists from other countries. Most of them were Chinese. Suffering from jet lag, with small, puffy bags under their eyes, they were suddenly bequeathed college graduates who would unprecedentedly relish the idea of moving back in with them.

The other picture on the paper was essentially of verdant scenery except for a set of bronze statues covered with verdigris and two slim figures of young women lingering nearby. This was the Alma Mater Statue. It was a set of sculptures featuring an ancient Greek woman seated in long robes flanked by two male attendants holding hands behind her throne. It was a feminist sculpture, the symbol of C_University, and the most photographed spot on campus during graduation seasons. But over the years, the statue had acquired a hard green patina, because of which the three brass giants looked as if tears were streaming down on their grim faces. Rachel liked this picture more than the other one because it also captured the two young graduates unwittingly, giving the statue an offhand look.

On my way back from the ceremony, passing by the statue, I'd come across Jenny and Mary. Jenny and Mary were both Chinese. They were in the same grade and had both graduated.

"Hi, Alex. Come take a picture with us!" Jenny called to me.

I walked up to them, "Still taking pictures?"

Mary snapped a picture of me and Jenny, and then Jenny switched and took a picture of me and Mary. Then Mary intercepted a passerby, asked him to take a picture of the three of us.

"What's your plan?" I asked Jenny.

"I don't have a plan yet," she said, "plan for the worst though."

"At least you have *a* job," Mary said to Jenny, giggling.

"You have a rich daddy!" Jenny retorted.

Jenny and Mary had been party girls and went in for shopping, music concerts and luxurious restaurants. They didn't read much, so they were just as simple-minded as on the first day they'd stepped into this university. Jenny had three cats and was a waitress in a bar near the campus. That was her excuse for everything: *I have a job; I'm on my own; I'm entitled to be spoiled because I hold down a job; I don't have time to read because I have a job; I have three cats to look after; I can't abandon my cats, they're my family.*

I threw Jenny another question. "Going back to China?"

"I haven't made up my mind yet," she said languidly.

I smiled and knew that I would never see her again. She would be as free as a bird and when the time came, as hysterical as a raging bull.

"What about you?" I turned to Mary. Mary had started as a double-major in psychology and finance. But she stopped psy when she discovered that her procrastination might have been rooted in her traumatic childhood when both her parents had to go to work during the day and fought with each other every evening. She was also alleged to have asthma and a good many other minor ailments.

"Me?! I don't know either. I may take a gap year; I feel very tired," Mary said.

"You might as well take a gap life," teased Jenny.

"A gap year is a good idea," I said, "I wish you both all the best. And again, congratulations."

In the picture, these two young graduates looked happy, beautiful, optimistic and bound to succeed.


This very issue featured another graduation story. Two graduates died the night after the ceremony. One was in a motorcycle accident and another fell off the balcony of his apartment while he and his friends were having a crazy party on the 16th floor. Later, his friends said in an interview, "He was a very good man with a big personality." And his Facebook page was bombarded with 'best', 'greatest', 'most', 'super', exclamation marks, and confused remarks. Was this guy really that great? Or did humanity need a carrier; What better carrier for all those superlatives than a dead man? Perhaps it's easier to accept our own bestial acts when we assume someone else is carrying the torch of humanity on our behalf.

## 23

Once in a while, Rachel would clean up and rearrange the furniture in the office. I never liked it very much. It was not that I enjoyed a crowded, crummy working environment. There was only so much you could do to revamp a decrepit room without a budget. First of all, if the AC was turned on, the occupants not only could not hear each other, but if anyone accidentally turned on another electrical device, the entire floor would black out. This happened once. Having been showered by fluent streams of expletives in idiomatic English, even Rachel dared not try this again.

The walls, over time, were plastered with newspaper clips, academic posters, and portraits of Rachel's heroines. She would not allow me to take them down. The one she had to see first whenever she looked up was Virginia Woolf, one of Rachel's favorites. The only thing Rachel could not agree with her about was that women should have rooms of their own. "A woman not only should have a room of one's own; she should have an office of her own," Rachel was wont to say.

It was one of the days when I came in later. I expected she had started the cleanup routine. But when I got in, she was sitting in the office, with dishevelled hair and the clothes she'd worn the day before.

"Had sex?" I asked her. "When was the last time you had sex anyway?"

"I woke up in the middle of the night and could not sleep again." She looked really tired.

There was an unfolded blanket on the couch.

"You haven't answered my question."

"Stop it. I don't need sex," she returned.

"You don't need it, or your ego has been too big to believe that you still need something from someone else?"

She said, "What's wrong with you today?"

What was wrong was that I wouldn't hold up much longer, and with the workload she had been forcing on herself, she probably wouldn't either. I finally found the courage to put it to her because Alice had told me that a doctor had told her, ironically as a piece of consolation, that he had been seeing quite a lot of anguished doctoral students with tumors developing in their bodies.

Rachel was an addict. People get addicted to drugs and alcohol because their lives are so empty and also so demanding. However, with a stretch of imagination, you can get addicted to anything. Anything can symbolize anything else. I saw a doctoral student get addicted to knitting. Knitting could symbolize a grandmother's retirement lifestyle, it could also symbolize suburban leftist revolutionaries. Many Chinese students were addicted to cooking: collecting recipes, buying culinary tools, steel, plastic and ceramic, telling me that there was a world of difference between them. Then one day, they'd lose interest in cooking completely and start to give away or undersell gear and utensils at one tenth of their original price. These are harmless addictions.

Rachel was addicted to the office. It was her object of desire par excellence. She would go to the office at 6:30 in the morning. She would stare out through a small window at an empty lawn while she was having her breakfast. Her breakfast was invariably made of a bowl of soy milk, an apple, a boiled egg, and a bread bun. She used to drink milk. Having watched a documentary about the dairy industry, she cut it out and made up the loss of calcium with calcium pills. One day she just moved her fridge into the office and said she didn't need it in her apartment because she had been having all three meals in the office. She got to work at 7:00. The first three hours would be distributed to her own research set on one of the desks, and then two hours to the newspaper. This was before noon. Then she would do the routine over again in the afternoon unless something came up. And she insisted that she still considered the newspaper a hobby. She would go to the gym around 6:00 pm. With her spirit refreshed afterward, she would go back to the office and read under a floor lamp for another three hours before she went back to her apartment at about 10:30 in the evening. She had been doing this routine for years with occasional interruptions. She had been decorating the office to suit her needs: hanging up a curtain and changing it, sticking up a poster and then replacing it as more and more activities came and went, and the more time she spent there.

Her routine had started to hurt her back and neck, and she had become grumpier and more and more fastidious. She gradually and unreasonably believed that she could not trust anyone with her work and the arrangement of the office. Once I put a dustbin in the wrong corner, and got yelled at. This was the real reason she had been turning down interns and volunteers. "I can't control what others think of me. I can only control myself," she said when people cast strange looks at her, and she would tighten her grip on her routine all the more.

"You need a vacation. You haven't gotten away from the office since I met you."

"I'm fine. I work out every day," she said. "Is Alice still coming?"

"She said she would, but I don't want to press her."

"She's rich, isn't she?" she asked abruptly.

I wondered where this was leading.

"Allegedly," I said. "So?"

"Nothing. The international student affairs center hired a new director. Lisa has been replaced."

"So?"

"They had someone check our office yesterday. They're going to put another organization in here."

"What?!" I was surprised. Did she know this the whole time?

Before I could say anything, a bout of footsteps boomed outside in the corridor. Since last month, students in the military tuition assistance program had been using the building for combat training.

"We have to move some stuff out," she said.

Some clumsy trainee in the corridor bumped the doorknob.

"Fuck! I'm going to teach them a lesson today." She was about to storm out of the office and probably confront a U.S. Marine.

I seized her, "Don't lose it. What organization is that?"

"I don't know. Either the ROTC or a group affiliated with the counselling center," she said, staring at me as if this was the last day of her life.

In the afternoon, a woman came to the office. She introduced herself as Molly Wang, pulled up a chair, and struck a plump, statuesque pose. She was the chief editor of a newsletter for the Student Counselling Center. The center provided services to help students with emotional, interpersonal and academic problems. It offered individual, couples, and group counselling. All of these services were short-term and paid for through a health services fee. She handed a pamphlet to us, detailing all the information above.

Molly Wang started to chat with Rachel. She was an Asian American. Her mother had emigrated from China when Molly was a high school student. She warmed to Rachel immediately as some women did. She was a writer too. From the pamphlet she gave us, I could see that her writing was of the style of Chicken Soup for the Soul. But the real reason why Rachel would not make friends with her, I thought, despite Molly's sheer stature, was that she seemed to be very happy, gratified, healthy, and not particularly an addict.

"I am thinking of installing a fish tank beside the window. I like living things. What do you think?" she asked Rachel.

"That's an idea," Rachel said.

"Then, what about…"

"It's your office, too. You can do whatever you want," Rachel interrupted.

Then, Molly left, and two hours later she came back hugging a big moving box. She started to arrange and decorate her desk and the walls around it. A few minutes later, I could see what she was aiming for. She was turning half of the office into a Chinese antique shop. She had stuck up an ink painting of Chinese Peonies Blossoming, flanked by two Chinese calligraphy scrolls about prosperity and blessing. She laid on the shelves a few terracotta warriors standing or kneeling with one leg, as well as framed photos of her and her monstrously built boyfriend on her desk where a visitor could immediately see.

After that, she boiled water in a glass kettle with a long neck on a flaming crucible. And then she poured the hot water into a gold trimmed porcelain teapot and started to distribute tea into porcelain teacups resting on gold trimmed porcelain tea saucers.

There was something 'too Chinese' about her. It was like a remote memory rooted out of its origin, broken off, and romanticized, like a piece of an ancient Chinese song played in a western concert to add exoticism and perhaps commercial profit. Or this was the only identity after having failed to seek out a new one, because society itself was having its own identity crisis.

Exoticism in America became the only form of assimilation for many immigrants.

"This is my dad," she said, pointing to a photo with herself and a smiling white man in it. "And this is my sister, Elizabeth. She's different because she is a mixed, Eurasian baby. One of my friends in the biology department tells me Eurasian babies are supposed to be smarter." She added quickly, "She is a professor. I don't think being smarter than others is being better off, though. I want her to be as happy and stupid as I am. Ha, ha, ha." She finished up her tea.

Suddenly the door opened. A pack of gibbering, garish young women poured in. Molly stood up, and they plunged into each other, kissing, squawking and squalling, calling each other's names and that of Jesus and God. They were deciding on which restaurant they were about to head to and who was going to drive whose car, and then all left.

Recovering from the horseplay, Rachel said to me, "It seems we have no choice this time."

24

When Rachel liked an article she would cut it out from a paper, or print it out from a website, or even take the trouble to transcribe it from a book, and then stuck it up on the walls. She was serious and meticulous about these tasks. When she liked one very much, she would take pains to highlight the title with a thick fluorescent marker and underscored a lot of words in it with various colors and symbols.

She was not in the office when I came in. That Rachel was late for work was strange and ominous. Since Molly's arrival, I had been admiring the transfiguration this small room had undergone. Molly had brought in more of her stuff, and Rachel had removed the posters and newspaper clips which were on the walls of Molly's corner, despite Molly's earnest insistence on having them there as they had been. They had been taken down, and a mound of these eye-catching pieces lay on Rachel's desk.

When she finally crept in, I was reading a book review in a scrap of the newspaper.

"Is Molly here?" she asked quickly.

"Jesus, you scared me."

"Is she here?"

"I don't think so. Where were you?" I said with indignation as I was startled.

Then she said she had something very important to tell me, but she refused to do it in the office. "Let's find some place across the street."

"Across the street?" I asked incredulously.

Across the street was the main building of the business school. Business students were coming and going in suits and carrying Louis Vuitton handbags. Rachel disliked this place despite its very convenient coffee shop. She had been shunning it for years for either grabbing a bite or having a nap in its spacious, genuine-leather-upholstered chaise lounges. *So*, I thought, *it must be urgent.*

We found a table in a concourse-like lobby. It was big, sleek and sturdy compared to the old, rickety junk in our office.

"I like this desk," I said like a country idiot.

"We will have even better ones if we win this." She handed me a leaflet as if she was a devious mafia boss trying to seduce a simpleton to take the fall for a heist.

"What is this?" I asked.

"The university is offering two office places in the new student union for two preeminent student organizations." She pointed to the leaflet. "If we get it, we would not only have an exclusive office but two new Mac computers. Look at the pictures."

The picture showed an office chicly decorated and two state-of-the-art computers facing two upmarket swivel chairs.

"What are our chances?" I asked tentatively.

"We need to write an obscenely good proposal and get two powerful figures to write us recommendation letters." She gave me a radiant smile, and had a sparkle of genuine affection in her black eyes as if she was deeply in love. And then she added, "I've already written the proposal."

25

There was a legendary Chinese woman at C_University. She was a tenured professor and was alleged to be the most prominent scholar in Chinese media and communication research. Her last publication was a long diatribe against big media corporations in China and in the United States. Rachel was a secret admirer of her work, secret because she hated to be seen as a teacher's pet. The idea that Chinese women should look after Chinese women repulsed her. But now she was in need. Rachel thought that the scholar, as a vocal opponent of media conglomerates, would definitely support a local newspaper like ours.

And just as Rachel expected, the legendary woman agreed to an appointment and invited us to her lake-view house. My first impression was that the professor was more like a Wall Street CEO than a suburban intellectual. She was in a business suit, led us into a living room stylishly decorated to the height of modernity, which suited her sleek, chin-length, bob haircut. When she spoke, her very wide eyes behind a pair of Gucci glasses became wider and larger. A Hermes floral, silk scarf set a pearl necklace vibrating around her neck as it shifted up and down. She was fluent in English, talking with tremendous vitality. She had successfully gotten rid of everything of the girl from the Chinese countryside, except when she laughed: a snorting, charming, energetic laugh. It made me feel relaxed. I never judge a person by her title. To me, the professor was still a daughter of ordinary Chinese farmers.

Yet, I had never seen Rachel so intimidated in front of another person.

"It's an independent, collectively-run, community-oriented publication," Rachel almost stuttered. "Our goal is to provide a forum for topics underreported and voices underrepresented…"

"Ahh." The lady continually nodded as we sat solitarily in her enormous living room.

Rachel continued, "All contributors to the paper are volunteers. The budget goes for printing costs. Everyone is welcome and encouraged to submit articles or story ideas to the editorial collective. We prefer, but do not necessarily insist, that articles be on issues of local impact written by local authors."

"Hmm." The lady stroked her knee, lowered her eyes, seemly contemplating something.

Then Rachel had no idea what to say next.

"You two wait here for a moment," the lady said, leaving for the kitchen. A few minutes later, she returned, bringing tea back.

"Did you see the Olympic opening ceremony?" she asked.

"No, I didn't," said Rachel and turned to me.

"I didn't, either," I said.

The lady seemed surprised and so were her mini-chopstick-like earrings.

"You didn't?! But it was in China. You are Chinese, aren't you?" She laughed.

"I don't have a TV," Rachel said, "I had a class to teach that day."

"Oh, it was a wonderful ceremony and I was full of tears when the national flag was ushered in by fifty-five kids. Do you know what the number fifty-five means?"

"Fifty-five ethnic groups," I answered.

"Yes, but do you know who was not there?" She grinned.

"Who?"

"Farmers and Workers!" she said. "How could a self-proclaimed socialist country host the Olympic Games without farmers and workers ushering in the national flag?"

I pictured a Soviet Union style marching band of sickles and hammers proceeding in a grand stadium.

"China has become a neo-liberal regime," she said, "do you know what neo-liberalism is?"

Rachel nodded like an apprentice, and I said, "I have heard of it."

"Good, good, then you are all set. Ha, ha, ha." She laughed again, muscles on her neck flexing.

Rachel was agitated, "So you think socialism is still possible for China? Is it still worth fighting for?"

"Of course it is possible! Let me show you something." She took out a smart phone, tapped it on, pinching, spreading her fingers dexterously, called up a picture and held the screen to us.

"See this; I took it in a street in Shanghai."

An elderly beggar sitting on a dirty street curb was reading a newspaper.

"Who says that the lower class doesn't care about the world? Who says they're of low quality? If the culture is not dominated by the market elites, we still have a chance for sure."

Rachel was about to ask another question and the scholar continued.

"OK, I am sorry. I have to get back to my work. I can write a recommendation letter for you."

"Thank you," Rachel said promptly.

"No, thank you two for providing the service for the community. I wish I could do more, but as you see, I am very, very busy," the legendary lady said, leading us out of her house.

Two days later, the professor sent us an email, asking for further information about Corn-respondence. Rachel never replied to the email. She said to me with a change of attitude, "Either she is really stupid, or she is a profound intellectual prostitute." I didn't reply because I couldn't tell her that, to most sensible daughters and sons of Chinese peasants, what Rachel was doing seemed really, just stupid.

## 26

Our microscopic photographer sent us an email saying he was leaving the newspaper. He had given quite a few irrefutable reasons, and said he would like to assist until a replacement could be found. Of course, Rachel saw his grand gesture only as an insult. She immediately wrote him a thank-you letter, ordered a book of *Journalism Photography for Dummies*, dredged up from the bottom of the ocean a dust-worn compact digital camera, and then shoved them all at me. Her cruel, Stalinist style had no limits. Andy Lu didn't just quit for no particular reason. It was neither wise nor respectful to be invited to a picnic and criticize the host, saying, for example, that escaping into nature wouldn't cure our social ills, and that the host's opinion on Chinese immigrants was platitudinous. Rachel refused to censor herself to a fault, even if it meant instantly losing an active staff member.

Compared to Rachel, I was a poltroon, and my cowardice was infinite. I would never confront anyone with anything, let alone cross one on purpose. Fighting was not my thing. I was an incurable pacifist. I would rather die alone, isolated on a deserted island than be entangled in conflicts. For I could not stand being disliked; it would drive me crazy. This quality obviously had many benefits, but the lack of vibrancy in my life had made me fall victim to quite a few hysterical girls and their crazy sisters.

For a few days, I felt someone was following me. Then, I realized a young woman often wearing big aviator sunglasses was everywhere I happened to be. Each time she saw me, she stopped, standing a few feet away, taking off her glasses, and bearing down on me with a strained mouth. She had long, black hair, big gold hoop earrings setting off a gold peace-sign necklace dangling ostensibly outside her sleeveless blouse. Her gaze would last a few standstill seconds, and then she would move on, leaving my confused head pondering, *How did I attract a Bohemian?!*

In the age of the Internet, if we are shy about confronting a person in reality we can confront her on Facebook. I ran through my friends' profiles, and then my friends' friends', and then my friends' friends' friends' avatars to find a face match. Before long I had found two pictures that bore a striking resemblance to the bohemian without the necklace and earrings. Fortunately, neither of them had set their pages in private mode so I went into their posts and picture albums.

A coward is usually a resourceful schemer. *God, this is exciting.* I soon excluded the one whose name was Poppy who was modest, and didn't post narcissistic selfies or make personal comments.

But the other one was a real whiner.

She wrote on a Monday, "I want to get married." And on the same day, she wrote, "I want to marry my sister." And then she wrote some nonsense, which I could not decipher. Then she vandalized her page, writing:

"I need more sessions at the counselling center."

"Who can give me a ride to Chicago?"

"Who can lend me a bicycle?"

"I want to go to Japan!"

"I only cook for the ones I love!"

"I can't be myself without being with you."

"Guys around me make me want to date girls, seriously."

"Dying because of the dry air in Illinois… I need to live somewhere near the sea in the foreseeable future…"

"I used to tell my ex that I have a lot of dreams like what is shown in this painting." And a surrealist painting was posted under the comment featuring a mutilated lady floating on a waterless riverbed.

And last, "Check this out!" A hyperlink to a song. I clicked, and the singer's voice must have been hers!

Her name was Lily. She seemed to be an average, self-centered young woman typical of these days, a Facebook friend of one of my friends. *Why does she hate me?* I thought, *She must have the wrong guy, or maybe something I did unwittingly in the past had a butterfly effect and is finally backfiring on me.* Then my train of thought branched off to campus shooting, mafia conglomerates, and my visa status.

*I have to clear this up before something bad happens,* I thought. I could send her a message. I typed in the dialogue box a felicitous letter, and eventually I deleted it. Once again, my cravenness prevailed.

"I can't believe you two run this newspaper all by yourselves!" a Singaporean woman exclaimed. The director of the center for East Asian studies was the second most powerful figure Rachel resorted to for a recommendation letter. The director had agreed to a meeting with Rachel, and then rescheduled it twice.

"Why don't you have interns work for you?" she asked in her office. "You know we have a journalism school, don't you?"

"Yes," said Rachel. "But I am very bad at management, let alone managing undergraduates."

"What's to manage?" she said. "You just tell them what to do and give them the credit. They would be very happy to get some experience. It would be good for them."

"Yes, yes, and I am also very bad at democracy. You know, I tend to be very bossy." Rachel cast a fake smile at me.

"Democracy?!" The lady seemed to be offended.

"Letting the kids decide what they want to do? It doesn't work, at least not in my experience. Give them democracy, and they prefer to stay home playing video games."

"Well, maybe," said Rachel, "I am very fastidious about words and everything. He calls me Nazi woman." Rachel laughed, pointing her finger blindly at me.

The Singaporean let out a dry snort. "I can't believe you did this all by yourself. That must be a lot of work. Seriously, do you need interns? You can assign them some errands for a start, making phone calls, making coffee, cleaning up your office, so you can focus on your work."

Rachel seemed not sure if this was a suggestion or a prerequisite. So she gave it another try. "Well, I'm not so sure about giving drudge work to volunteers. I can't trust them with editorials either. It's not that bad. But we're looking for an ideal candidate. And we almost found one, right?" She turned to me again. She looked exasperated.

"Yes, we are searching." I said to the lady, nodding.

The lady walked around her desk, drawing up a chair to sit close to us.

"Actually, I want to ask you a favor," she said, lowering her voice, and then closed the door.

This unnerved me, and Rachel said, "Yes, what?"

"I assume you know Confucius College."

"You mean Confucius Institute?"

"Yes, it goes by several names. The university will sign an agreement establishing a Confucius College on the campus. There is going to be a ceremony.

Representatives from the Chinese General-Consulate in Chicago, a few university presidents and department directors will be there. It's all high class, but you know they don't want it to be too sumptuous. I think it would be good if your paper could cover the event. And there would be a lot of networking opportunities."

Rachel paused, and then she leaned back in her chair, "We really don't want to have anything to do with the Confucius Institute."

"Oh, why?" the lady was taken by surprise.

"The paper just doesn't want to associate with government propaganda," she said sternly.

"Oh, no, no, no, you misunderstood me," she said, "I am not asking you to stretch the truth or anything. I am just asking if you can write a report, I mean, objectively. I know it is an independent newspaper. You must be aiming for objectivity."

"Objectivity is not our priority," Rachel said slowly and assumed a newly required air of nobility. "We established the paper aiming for cultural criticism. It is a pro-liberal newspaper in the Chinese context, and we don't shun politics."

This abrupt and provocative reply proved indigestible for the bureaucrat's cold stomach. The sudden dispensing with the social mask and the short circuit of ironic distance and sincerity shocked the powerful lady to a pause.

In Rachel's world, everyone deserved celebration when she first met them. She seemed generous enough to give anyone the benefit of doubt. But she also had draconian measures to tease out friends from enemies.

Rachel wanted to save the office and the newspaper. But what she wanted to save was not just the room and the mere existence of a Chinese weekly in an American college. Then, the Singaporean burst out laughing. The laughter was loud, dry and ominous.

"Then forget about it," she said, and it was a final. "I wish we could talk about this in some detail. But as you can see I am very busy. I have never been as busy as these days," she said, walking back behind her handsome mahogany desk, giving us the sign to leave.

"We're pro-liberal?" I asked Rachel as we left the office and stumbled onto the pavement.

"Why not?" she said with rancor in her voice, "we are pro-liberal from now on."

## 27

I was ready to stand up to the Bohemian. Perhaps people who seemed to be so menacing were not that menacing after all. After seeing Rachel blow the recommendations from the powerful ladies, I discovered a piece of courage within myself, a sense of my own power to confront enemies.

But once I decided to square up to the menacing girl spy whose name might or might not be Lily, she disappeared. She was nowhere to be found, not in the dining hall where I first saw her, nor at the ice cream kiosk around which she had had a strong presence, nor the undergraduate library where I ran into her once. "Is she planning an ultimate attack?" I was deflated. I stood in the twilight descending the campus; the dogged, insecure, and confused feeling was flooding back to me with a vengeance. It's easy to imitate an action, but it is hard to acquire the style.

I wanted to be amongst amiable people to feel safe; a party would be welcome at the moment. I, like many people, needed distractions in order to stay sane. So when a young friend casually invited me over, I took him up on it.

However, I didn't ask what kind of party it was. An ideal piece of decadence was hard to come by. For one, my turning up gave the friend a start. It turned out that the invitation was just a gesture. He fudged his welcome and minced his footwork at the door. There was no rule to restrict an Asian doctoral student from going to a college party. But you had to have a real knack to pull it off or you would soon be pegged as 'that creepy guy'. And what a bummer that would be, as I found out soon after, in the garage where the party was blooming the girl spy reincarnated in a black dress, barefoot, a pair of high heels in one hand and a beer in the other.

"Excuse me, are you Lily?" I walked up and accosted her.

"What? No. Why?" She seemed to be stung.

I didn't expect she would deny it.

"I'm Alex, I see you everywhere."

She regained her balance, and suddenly grabbed my arm. She took me out of the garage, dragged me along until we were under a whitewashed wall where there was a garbage can that had gobbled a trash extravaganza: pizza boxes were semi-folded and squeezed into it; so were the remains of donuts and pretzels, seeds and rinds of watermelon, chicken bones, chilies and baked corn; to spice it up, a greasy, roasted squid was sleeping on top of it all, oil droplets dripping down on the ground, forming rivulets. The worst was that someone had accidentally stepped in it and smeared the entire driveway.

We stood against the wall beside the trash can, and my first remark was full of jitters, "Do I know you?"

"I know you," she said assertively. Her hair was tied behind her slender neck in a loose bun. Now she was staring at me with earnest eyes, her high nose pointing at me haughtily.

"I am sorry, but what's up?" I asked.

"You know Alice?" she asked coolly.

"Yes, I know Alice."

"Are you fooling around with her?"

"What?" My heart thudded. "Who are you?"

"She is very innocent; don't play on her innocence," she said without a blink of her eyes.

Then, I realized that the girl was very naive.

"Well, I am not fooling around with her," I said. "We're just friends, maybe not even friends. We're just casual acquaintances. Is her boyfriend Vic? Excuse me, but who are you?"

"You slept with her, didn't you?" she said contemptuously.

"No, we didn't," I denied.

"OK, you're not honest," she said, "I don't want to talk to you anymore."

I was agitated, "I don't have to explain this to you, but we didn't do anything outside the norm."

"Then why are you talking to me?" she asked.

"Because you're following me!"

She narrowed her charcoal-circled, attractive eyes.

"What is this?" I let out a nervous laugh.

"You're a hypocrite."

"Really? Why?"

"Maybe I'm wrong. But I just want to protect her from fooling around with jerks."

"Good for you!" I said. "Are you warning me to stay away from her? Seriously, who are you?"

She paused, and then she eased up a little as if she had soaked up my words, and then she sighed theatrically, "You don't know her."

"I am trying." I was wondering whether I should have ended the conversation.

"If I were you, I would stay away from her. You're biting off more than you can chew. She and Vic are planning something dangerous."

As she had lightened up, I pressed home my advantage. "What is it?"

"Stay away from her. She's a trouble maker." She meant to leave, waving her hand as if she was dispelling a cloudy curse.

"Are you sure you're not Lily? There is a whiner who looks exactly like you on Facebook."

"Don't lose touch with reality, Mister." She left.

I stood there, besieged by the smell of fast food residue, profoundly mortified. I had never expected that a man, at least in my inexperience, who wanted nothing from anyone, after offering a bit of help, would be treated in such an insolent manner!

## 28

She warned me not to contact Alice. It is often a suchlike warning that tempts an innocent into becoming a convict. With my college of corn education, I understood my human weakness, so I discreetly avoided letting it affect my feelings and judgment. Spur-of-the-moment action was not my style either. I snobbishly spent more time reading Victorian literature than exercising in the field. I had my own, unique way of vindicating myself. I immersed myself in books and grappled to find clues to distill the proof that I was better than my nemeses. It worked. Dostoyevsky was a big help:

> ...these young men unhappily fail to understand that the sacrifice of life is, in many cases, the easiest of all sacrifices, and that to sacrifice, for instance, five or six years of their seething youth to hard and tedious study, if only to multiply tenfold their powers of serving the truth and the cause they have set before them as their goal such a sacrifice is utterly beyond the strength of many of them.

What an exquisite expression of my vindication. And Proust, the profound coward, was also an excellent source. What one could accomplish in one's bed was after all wondrous. And Henry James and Edith Wharton and many others. It was interesting that all these great minds, with a little self-serving twist, could stand by me and speak in my favor. But when Alice asked to see me, I answered automatically, "Sure, why not." I was sure Dostoyevsky wouldn't feel betrayed. He was a deceased literary giant. What did he care?

Alice and I met in a dining hall. The welt on her face had completely gone down and all the bruises had disappeared. She had no appetite, but ordered a small bowl of fruit salad and only gave it a few indigestible pecks. I fixed myself up with a big slice of pizza and a cup of coffee with cream and sugar from a rickety, dribbling coffee machine. Before we could strike up a conversation, a plump middle-aged Iranian woman came up to our table. Something about her doubtful eyes revealed that she was an insecure immigrant. But she spoke fluent and idiomatic English. She seemed to be astonished to see Alice here, letting out a cry, bending down to encircle her in a suffocating embrace.

"Oh, my poor girl!" she said plaintively as if somebody had just died. "Are you OK? Are you...? Is Vic in jail? Did they put him away? I would have come, but..." She made an excuse.

"I'm fine. He's out. We're fine. It was an accident," said Alice.

"Can I sit down?" the woman said and took a look at me, nodding.

"Sure, sure." I scooted over and let her sit down.

The woman continued, "Promise me you will take care of yourself, or I'll call your mom. You hear me?" She grasped Alice's hand.

Alice welled up with tears. "Thank you."

The woman turned to me, "I'm sorry, I'm Nazanin."

"Oh, never mind, I go by Alex," I said.

Then they seemed to have nothing else to say to each other but still held hands.

Alice said as if something just came over her, "What is neo-liberalism?"

"What?" The woman didn't follow her.

"Neo-liberalism," said Alice, "they were talking about it in the seminar. Is it something important? Is it something I'm supposed to know?" Alice was pleading.

"Sweetie, don't stress yourself out," the woman said. "Take it easy. I didn't know half as much as you do when I was your age. And if you know what I don't know by now, you must think I am an idiot!"

"But they all seem to know!"

"Let me tell you something. When I got in; they invited me to their parties; and I was so frustrated when they talked about those singers and music groups I had never heard of. I even thought of having an American boyfriend to catch on. Now I think I was just being stupid."

"Really?"

"If you don't know what they think neo-liberalism is, you can just ask a professor."

"Can I?"

"Yes, you are entitled."

"But I have a lot of things to catch up on: what structuralism really is; what post-modernism is; what the hell Judith Butler is talking about."

The woman burst out laughing, "It's OK, it's OK. Lesbians talk about being lesbians. Trust me, you'll be fine. Now I have to run."

She hugged Alice again and patted her on her shoulder, and then left, her spindly fingers waving goodbye.

"Who is she?" I asked.

"A friend. We used to hang out," Alice said.

"I thought you were close; she said she would call your mom."

"Oh, that's her way of talking. She's a very nice person, though." She lowered her voice, wiping tears on her cheeks. Then she sat straight, braced herself, even smiled a little. The smile was disdainful and seemed to mean: "I will figure out what neo-liberalism is. I will figure them all out and, one day, I will beat you all down with all I know." But the silver lining only lasted for an infinitesimal moment. Soon she became as melancholy as ever.

"How is Vic?" I asked.

"I don't really know." There was a soul-outside-of-the-body note in her voice.

"Where is he?" I asked.

"I don't know."

"Do you still want to join the newspaper?"

She paused, "Yes, I want to," she said weakly.

"Are you sure?" I should have warned her about how Rachel would mercilessly handle a loafer.

"Yes, yes, sure, sure." Her voice was impatient, and at last tailed off.

"OK, so you want to meet. Is there anything I can do for you?"

"So, I am not allowed to see you just because I want to?" she said, as if she was irritated.

I said, "Sure you can. I mean what do you want to talk about?"

"It seems you don't want to talk with me." She was flaming.

I was quite experienced with this kind of womanly hysteria, having seen it often in spoiled girls, and knew what would make her even crazier. So I said, "Yes, as a matter of fact, I wanted to ask you..."

"Academia is full of bullshit and bullshitting people," she cut in. "Do you know ninety-five percent of scholars are rubbish? People get stuck, and new bullshit keeps pouring in. Most people got in not for the sake of their studies at all. Do you know why they are here?" she asked as if she had discovered a cure for an epidemic.

"Why?"

"They are here for their private little pathetic dreams. They are enjoying their secret enjoyment while wishing that this big bullshitting edifice would never fall down."

"Well, that's really nothing new to me," I said.

"Oh, you are so sophisticated," she said sarcastically.

I sighed and said, "You know, all the people in this world..."

"I am sorry," she said before I finished.

"Never mind."

"Can you stay at my place tonight, please?" she said suddenly, beseeching.

"What?" I exclaimed, "Did something happen?"

"Nothing happened. I just don't want to be alone."

I thought she must have had a fight with Vic again, or someone else, and had exhausted the available friendship. Maybe she had to resort to the last person she could mess up with.

"I can't stay overnight at your apartment," I said.

"Why?"

"I just can't. If you're afraid of being alone, you should make friends."

"Aren't you my friend?"

"Yes, I am. But..." It occurred to me that I really could not talk any sense into her at the moment. She was a patient. So I said, "How about this; if you are really afraid of being alone, I can ask a friend if she can put you up for tonight."

## 29

"I am sorry for the mess," Priscilla said, fixing up chairs for Alice and me to sit down.

When I'd asked Priscilla whether she could accommodate a young woman who just had suffered domestic violence, she immediately agreed and asked me to take the poor woman to her apartment at once. She hung up the phone before I even had the time to explain the deal further.

"I found the guitar; it's under my bed; I am free tomorrow; come if you want to play." She directed her words at me intending to break up the uneasiness that descended, due to our stranger being present.

"She's my guitar tutor," I told Alice. "It sounds ridiculous, but she just found her guitar."

Alice laughed, "What do you do in your guitar classes aside from playing?"

"Laugh if you must. She is very disorganized. Last time we spent a whole class trying to figure out where it was."

The first few minutes went as smoothly as possible. This was what I expected. Pricilla was a woman with all the required eccentricities, and not the easiest person to get along with. Normally, she would not relish the idea of tidying up her apartment to the extent of liveability, to accommodate a battered young woman for an unfixed term. But Priscilla had been through a lot lately. It was not so much sympathy as the feeling of taking control and being useful that allowed her to become Alice's benefactor. And the spontaneous air of Pricilla's living room chimed with Alice's notion of a free spirit. This temporary union was bound to unravel, as any friend circle could only afford one free spirit. But for the same reason, the acquaintance was rapidly maturing into a friendship. A camaraderie, which had taken Pricilla and Rachel years to achieve, began to develop.

The dark cloud that had been hanging over Alice's face cleared up in this messy-but-homey room. It was hard to believe that just a few minutes ago she was still on the verge of a mental breakdown. She was again a beauty and a mystery, and seemed ready, as an interlocutor, for any subject of conversation.

"I'm really sorry about the mess," Priscilla said with mock chagrin.

"I like your shoes." Alice pointed to a shoe shelf.

"Oh, they are old shoes; I don't wear most of them anymore," Priscilla said.

"That happened to me, too," Alice said, "I bought a lot of shoes when I was young and stupid."

"I thought your mother bought them for you," I said casually.

Alice glared at me in surprise. Then I knew she was not completely at one with herself and was still trying to be amenable.

"Are you a doctoral student?" asked Priscilla, "I think I might have seen you somewhere before."

"Yes, gender woman studies," Alice said. "What about you?"

"Music; musicology as a matter of fact."

"Interesting!" Alice exclaimed.

"It used to be interesting," Priscilla said. "Now I just want to graduate and get out of here. Do you mind my smoking?"

"Is it gonna set off the fire alarm?" I reminded her.

"It's OK. I disconnected it." She waved her hand.

"You are a heroine," I said mockingly.

"Can I have a cigarette too?" said Alice.

Priscilla fetched a pack of cigarettes from the top of a worn-out mantelpiece. She drew out two cigarettes, and handed one to Alice. Priscilla conjured up a plastic lighter and they huddled together and lit them up. Then they went back to their respective seats, crossed legs, cigarettes clamped between fingers, hands relaxed on the arms of chairs, and smiled to each other.

"I don't like my program either," said Alice, "but I've changed my major, so I can't change it again, otherwise I would stay here forever."

"Same here. I used to be in the anthropology department," Priscilla said. "What are you planning after this?"

"I want to teach. Because as long as I stay at school, my mom will leave me alone. But I don't like it here; I prefer cities."

"Hmm, same here. I am wondering whether I hate my major because I hate this school." Priscilla sighed. "And you?" she turned to me. "Why are *you* here?" It was a rhetorical question meant to break the serious air and spare my feelings from being left out.

"Why? I'm a social pariah; I have no place to go," I said.

"Don't believe what he says. He thinks he's too

wonderful to have a real job," Priscilla said.

"I am wondering if I'm not just afraid of having a real job too," said Alice. "Last summer, when I was in Prague reading the *Unbearable Lightness of Being*, I was suddenly filled with energy and wanted to be a war correspondent."

"And then?" asked Priscilla.

"Oh, it was just an impulse. Of course, it didn't work out. It's unrealistic. It's silly, isn't it?"

Priscilla didn't address her question directly, she said, "I used to want to be a singer, and I can't even sing."

"What a coincidence. Do you want to be a singer, too?" I asked Alice.

"No, I don't," she answered quickly, and her face went all red.

So I dried up. And Priscilla dried up.

Alice reactivated the conversation, bringing up a gay pride parade she went to in Chicago. Priscilla happened to be there on the same day. Every woman around me, all of a sudden, had become savvy in gender, sexuality, and various other feminist agendas. I was ignorant, so I nodded while being accused of homophobia, class-blindness, xenophobia, Sinocentricsim, Eurocentricsim and, at one point, racism.

Priscilla and Alice kept going from topic to topic, carefully avoiding why we were here in the first place. They seemed to have so much in common, so many shared interests, and remarked how it was a shame that they had not known each other long before. They both loved cats; they both had a brother who was a snooty asshole with bad taste in everything and proud of having a stupid job; and they both had had an absent father when they were little. The only difference was that Priscilla thought her father was a sheer scumbag, while Alice only made him out as an abusive chauvinist.

## 30

Despite their seemingly infinite resources, Americans like competitions just as much as the Chinese, with such finite resources, like bluffing. Competition was supposed to cultivate elites and eradicate lazy free riders. But sometimes it went awry. It spawned one-dimensional egoists who were good at nothing except for uncannily qualifying for either a job or an award. These competitions turned out to be competitions between specialized, humanoid machines and flawed human beings. Over time, more and more flawed human beings had been turned into specialized machines. As long as it was allegedly a country of dreamers, a mechanical life was more acceptable. Immigrants had left their rotten homes to come to the United States to seek the American dream. But from the first day they landed on the continent, they realized that they had to compete to survive.

We didn't get the new office. There were, of course, many reasons: we underestimated the importance of the proposal writing workshop; we were not a group best representing multicultural assimilation; we didn't make a strong argument about why we needed a multi-media working environment, etc. The mortifying subtext was that even we had not thrown away the recommendation letters we still would have had no chance to win.

And Rachel didn't tell me what the stakes were. On filling out a form and signing up to join the competition, Rachel had automatically given up our current office as a prerequisite.

She told me the result over the phone. "We are moving out." Her voice was affected, yet clam with controlled emotion. And she was not calling me just to inform me of the failure. She said she had already registered a desk in the student organization center where over one hundred RSOs were squeezed into the entire second floor of a three-storey, old office building. I had been there on errands many times. Students hustled in a dim, narrow corridor and bustled about the grey, worn, cement floor full of cracks.

My immediate reaction was to get to the office to see if she was committing suicide or making a more sensational scene. On the contrary, she comported herself with great grace and dignity. She was packing, separating out our purchases from what belonged to the office.

"We can have it back next semester, can't we?" I asked.

"Sure, we can win it back," she said. "Take down those books, and put them into these boxes, please."

The second floor of the student union was a spacious, open room with fluorescent ceiling lights. It had been divided into a maze of cubicles by shoulder-high partitions. The incessant hubbub enveloping the floor might die down momentarily but would never be eliminated. Against the noisy background, two Muslim students kneeled down just a few feet away from us and started praying. This would come around several times a day. In a corner, a group of Korean students were dancing to the beat of drums.

Priscilla had heard of the shakeup.

"They knew each other?" Rachel said at a distance, seeing Priscilla and Alice walking toward us.

They offered help and showed their support. We were arranging our cubicle to accommodate all the essentials we thought we could not do without. I was expecting high spirit from Priscilla and Alice; however, they acted out their moral support cheerlessly.

"It's a small office," said Rachel laughing. "Let's change it around a little so we can make more space. What do you think, Alice? Are you still decided?"

"It's alright," Alice said aimlessly, then raised her voice a little, "I mean the space."

"It's an unimpressive working environment, isn't it? But the good news is, I don't have to break you into the office. You can see everything at a glance now."

"Well, we can discuss this later," said Alice. She leaned on the desk, lowered her head, and looked at her finger-nails.

"Any reason why this is happening?" Priscilla frowned at me as if this was my fault.

I handed her the rejection letter with the feedback on it. This proved to be a mistake as Rachel made a quick and impulsive move with her hand as if she wanted to snatch it away. Her face was frozen in embarrassment as though I'd insensately let our house guests in on our delinquent son's report card.

"Oh, my God. You guys are so hardworking. This is... strenuous," Priscilla said after searching for an adjective and putting down the report.

Then Alice picked it up, and Rachel glared at me accusingly.

"Do you have a website? I mean a digital version of the newspaper?" Alice said, reading the report. "It says you didn't prove why you need a multi-media working environment."

Priscilla sat down on a chair and looked up at Alice and then turned to Rachel. Rachel, with a hand covering her stern chin, threw an exasperated frown at Alice.

"We don't have a technician to set up a website," I said.

"Why? It's very easy." Alice got a little excited, "Actually, I was thinking maybe we should get rid of the print version all together; I mean print media is dying anyway. Let's move it online. We can build a newspaper website; it's much more efficient, and it will cut the cost almost down to zero."

"How do you know that?" Rachel seated herself on the other of the two chairs, crossed her arms in front of her chest, a crooked index finger sinking into one side of her arm.

"Isn't it obvious?" said Alice, looking at me and then Priscilla for support.

"I don't know," I said, "I am not familiar with websites." I cleared myself from the battlefield.

"Well, if we don't do it, I think somebody else will; just think about how many Chinese students are coming each year; they will take the market. I mean, somebody will do it anyway."

Then Priscilla said, "I was also wondering why you guys haven't made it available online. Everything is online now."

"Seriously, you were wondering?!" Rachel blurted out.

Priscilla was dumbfounded.

Rachel stood on her feet and turned away from us, "I have to go to a meeting." she pulled on her backpack and stormed into the bustling crowd.

"Don't you think it's a good idea?" Alice stared at me as if she had been bullied.

"It's not your idea; it's your attitude," I said.

"What's wrong with my attitude?"

"Yes, what's wrong with her attitude?" Priscilla said.

"If you don't get it, that's fine," I said. "Actually, we have been talking about moving it online..."

"Then what's wrong with my saying it?" Alice was agitated.

"Calm down," I said. "Don't you think you should earn her trust before proposing shake-up ideas?"

"I don't think so."

"Then you are spoiled," I burst out.

Alice was astounded and then was breathing with fury. Priscilla looked confused.

"I am sorry. I don't mean to…" I apologized.

Alice interrupted, "No, you don't have to apologize. That's your opinion. But I'll show you how narrow-minded you are. I'll show you." She said, with the vigor of a fantasy running wild. She meant to make her words resonate. But her imagination, which was built upon nothing, would only occupy her hysterical mind for a little while, though that could be long enough to hurt someone else. Then it would be forgotten in a few aimless days.

"What's happening?" Priscilla turned to me, mouth agape. "Did I just piss Rachel off?"

### 31

Alice never came back to the office again. Instead, she thanked Priscilla for her hospitality as if she had finally found her course in life, and went back to her own apartment and started a war against the newspaper, which I knew she had no intention of winning. She posted an ugly poster on her Facebook page, looking for partners to co-found a Chinese news website. She whipped up a string of pretentious phrases ending in exclamation marks. She must have copied the job description and employee requirements from somewhere else. In a dialogue box, she replied to a friend's comment, saying she was willing to pay for articles.

I told Rachel about it. A tight smirk struck the corner of her mouth, and she knitted her calculating brows. "I don't want to see it; it's stupid," she said and she un-friended Alice on her Facebook page. Alice considered this as throwing down the gauntlet. In another poster, she offered to pay everyone a five-hundred-dollar-a-month salary. In return, a few students whose dates of birth went back to the nineteen nineties sprang up. And a few days later, a loud, gaudy website popped up with chicly-designed slogans and empty columns.

Having had enough of her shenanigans, and being deprived of an office to work and study in, I hid in the basement of the agriculture library. This was the library with the least traffic on campus. It was damply cool and ethereally quiet, known as a place for self-discipline, self-rehabilitation and repentance. I had not opened a book or done any research for God only knew how long. So, a cup of hot coffee in hand, I went there, fixed myself up with an armchair and found myself restless, wondering whether I could still write or read at all. An open book lay in front of me; page five; and I was thinking millions of things that might or might not concern me. My impulse was to do some online shopping, but the idea immediately went away. I wanted to have a new notebook, I meant one with paper, but maybe a new computer was also a good idea. I wanted to watch a movie. I needed to check my email. I wanted a person, preferably a girl, to sit by my side. I wanted to take out one of those fat books written by Tolstoy or Dostoevsky to heal my attention span problems, and the chair was not comfortable at all.

I had not made much progress besides covering twenty-five pages of reading, and felt wistful when a librarian announced the library was closing. I went back to the new office, now only a desk, and Rachel was there.

"Guess what," she said coldly.

"You are pregnant."

"I am not kidding," she said. "Your Alice took out all the books that have to do with my research topic from the library, fifty five of them in total."

"What? What does that mean? How do you know?" I was perplexed and also annoyed that she said, 'your Alice'.

"What else could it mean?" she said. "It means she wants to take a revenge on me."

"For what?!" I called out.

"You'd better ask her," she said, "and you'd better be quick; I need a book by this weekend."

"Why should I talk to her?" I was irritated.

"Oh, isn't she your new girlfriend?! You introduced her to Priscilla, didn't you?" Rachel said sarcastically.

"Now you're taking this out on me?!" I muttered.

And I thought, *After all these years of free labor and moral support I gave, you gave me this nasty attitude?* I stared at her.

"You look like you want to beat me." She stood up slowly, leaning back against the glass partition, hands in her pockets.

"Can I go?" I said.

"It's a free country." She mimed finger quotes for the cliché, and stepped aside theatrically implying that no one was in my way.

I shrugged my shoulders and closed my lips in a pout. Inside, I was as mad as a crazy dog.

## 32

A year earlier, a young Chinese graduate student, a watercolor artist, was brutally murdered by her ex-boyfriend. The murderer was also a graduate student and was said to be a quiet man, a cool, level-headed mathematician. He confessed afterward that he loved her, wanted to give everything he had to impress her, pamper her, and look after her for the rest of her life. But in the end, the woman was not so impressed, didn't want to be looked after by him, and wanted out. His supposedly rational mind failed him. He felt humiliated. Humiliation led to violence. He had threatened to kill her, and was given a restraining order, and then broke into the woman's apartment, tied her up, stabbed her in the throat five times with a dagger.

The university immediately claimed that this was an isolated case and the campus was still safe. The Chinese community was absolutely silent, except when the Women's Resources Center held a candlelit vigil. People called, complaining in Chinglish about the event not being in daylight, as is the Chinese custom. "To talk about the case in public will further damage the girl's reputation and dishonor her family," an anonymous woman said passionately supposedly upholding Chinese tradition on behalf of the victim's family. Rachel was disgusted and cut off quite a few friends who thought the victim might have cheated on the murderer, giving the murderer an excuse to kill her. It seemed that a Chinese woman's death was of little consequence to the Chinese community. The community was charged with rage and confusion only because white people took over and meddled with our deliberately ignored dirty laundry. That was the time Rachel coined the epithet: Chinese fanatics, which meant behaving with uncritical zeal or obsessive enthusiasm for one's own interests. And she had categorized Alice as one such zealot.

I thought otherwise. I thought that calling each other fanatics was hopeless. Though I admitted that Alice went way overboard with her tantrum. My instinct was to catch her and give her a timeout lecture. But I understood that I didn't have the authority to do so. She was a grown-up, and what made the situation more complex was that she was rich.

So I restrained myself from calling Alice. "I am a liberal man; I haven't done anything wrong; it's none of my business, so keep it that way," I said to myself. I expected Rachel to call me to apologize, but she didn't either. So I stopped turning up at the new office. I held my silent protest for a week until the editing deadline of the newspaper came around. Then I went back and saw a handsome young man, an American-born Chinese, in a stylishly tattered university hoody, sitting at the desk.

"Hi," I greeted him.

"Hi, can I help you?" he asked.

"Oh, I am fine. Is Rachel here?"

"She said she would be back soon."

I broke off, and for a few seconds, I was speechless, "OK, Then I'll come back later."

"Do you want to leave message?" he asked earnestly.

I said I didn't. I went downstairs. Stepping outside the building, I was caught by a shower. Summer was getting old; the rain became cooler. Real Americans could strike out in the rain without the shelter of an umbrella. I never was that scrappy. My phone rang, and I went back inside; it wasn't Rachel; it was Alice.

I picked it up. "What's up?"

"Am I interrupting anything?" she asked nervously.

"No, you're not interrupting anything."

"Can you come to my place?"

"No, I can't. But we can meet outside; I want to talk to you, too."

A long pause ensued, then she said, "Me too. Can we meet at the Student Union?"

I gave her my consent and didn't tell her that I was already in the building.


Sitting near the front gate, waiting, I bought a coffee and a donut. She didn't show up until long after I had finished them. I had nothing to do but listen to a student pianist playing a half-baked melody on an old upright piano on a small semi-spherical stage. Students were coming and going. Occasionally he sang to it.

And when he was singing, passers-by would linger wistfully for a few judgmental minutes.

Then Alice stumbled into through the door. I saw her first and instantly admitted that it was a mistake to insist on meeting her outside. There were bruises on her arms and thin cuts fresh with congealed blood on her cheeks. Her clothes were mismatched and had dirty stains on them. She must not have washed her hair for days, for it was straggled in tendrils and with split ends springing up here and there. I waved to her.

"What have you been doing?" I said as she came up to me. "You took out her books to get back at her? For what?"

"I'm sorry; I made a mistake; I blew it. I've returned them."

"Don't apologize to me!" I muttered.

Her eyes were brimming with tears.

"Don't cry; please don't cry; if you start to cry…" I shook my head and averted my eyes.

"I'm sorry! I'm sorry. Don't go." She was crying, but also fighting back her tears.

I felt I was getting caught up in something really messy. I did bite off more than I could chew, and my instinct was to pull out at once.

"What can I do for you?" I said.

"I don't know; I just want to have someone to talk with. I hate being alone."

"Why me?"

"Don' t you want to talk to me?" she beseeched.

"I have to go," I said.

"Please don't," she said, "I want your help."

"What is it?" I said impatiently.

She broke off, then she said suddenly, "Can you go with me to Boston?"

I turned back to her, "To Boston? The city?"

"Yes, Boston, the city. There's a conference; I want to go to the conference." She hurried her words.

"No, I can't go. I..." I was about to say I had an editorial deadline to make, but it occurred to me that I might have been fired. So I said, "I just can't, I am sorry."

"I'm leaving tonight. Aren't you worried?"

"Are you threatening me?" I said angrily.

"No, but I'll go anyway." Her voice was stubborn.

Suddenly I wished I had never met her, "Well, it's really your choice, but I sincerely suggest that you stay." Then I left, without turning back to look at her for once.


I went back to my apartment, turning over in my restless mind what had just happened. I was thinking of the young woman whose name must have been Lily, and of what she said about Alice's being a troublemaker. *But why did Lily warn me? To protect Alice? To protect me? To monopolize her? To con her out of some money? Where did those bruises and cuts come from? Is there some sort of secret society or cult club for these rich kids, in which they beat each other up? Is Vic really a monster?* As I was fantasizing, I landed on a disturbing theory I had been denying: Alice was a captive. Someone was playing on her innocence, and she might have been caught up in a devious setup! I mean, she was obviously into sufferance; there was no doubt about that. Once I reached this conclusion everything fell into place. My wild imagination was satiated, and that also explained why Alice was alienated from her friends; somebody was trying to separate her from them.

8:30 pm. When my conscience and composure finally found me, I decided to call Alice to apologize for my abruptness, and to check whether she still needed any help. She picked up the phone to a hubbub of background noise and broadcasting speakers.

"Hello?" she said.

"Hi, I'm calling to apologize," I said.

"Sorry, I can't hear you!" she yelled into her phone.

"I am sorry!" I yelled back.

"Oh, it's OK."

"Where are you?" I asked.

"I am leaving for Boston." She must have found a quieter place. "Are you coming?"

"So you're really going to Boston?" I said. "Is there anybody with you?"

"No, I'm alone. Can you come?"

"I am afraid I can't make it. Have a safe trip," I said.

There was a silence. I was waiting for her to hang up, and she was waiting for me.

"OK, I am coming," I said. "Where are you?"

## Part Four

### 33

I met Alice at a train station. She was dressed in a garish Indian kaftan dress, wearing light blue eye shadow and glossy orange lipstick. She stood beside a brown piece of luggage, looked heartbreakingly vulnerable.

On seeing me she quickened her step in her leather pumps and hugged me theatrically.

"I knew you would come," she said.

I was dreading that someone might see me; I dragged her to a corner and eased her into a seat. I looked at her; her hands grasped the ticket tightly. I wanted to persuade her to stay, but she looked so determined, I gave it up.

"How long are we going away for?" I sighed.

"Just a week or two," she said.

I grunted with laughter, "I can't be away for two weeks."

"Then one week."

"I can't," I said. "Can I just see you through settling in and come back, I mean, if there is a conference at all?"

"You don't trust me?!" she muttered.

"Yes, I trust you," I said. I had bought a ticket, after all.

The windy Midwest took to flexing its muscle. We sat near an automatic door, waiting for a night train. I sneezed while the door was being set on and off by travelers, deprived beggars, vagabonds lugging around their luggage, prostitutes in gaudy clothes, and sanitation workers with tired eyes. This run-down station was just one mile away from the prestigious C_University. But this was the flip side, where funds and disbursement were permanently cut off.

"Did you see that prostitute?" I asked.

"Who? Where?" Alice turned around.

"Don't turn. Just look at her; she's on your ten o'clock," I whispered.

She took a fleeting glimpse, "How do you know she's a prostitute?"

"I saw her write down her number on a card and hand it to a man," I said.

"That doesn't mean she's a prostitute. How do you know it's her phone number?"

"I can't prove it, but I think so."

"Maybe they just know each other, and they haven't been in touch."

I didn't know whether she actually believed what she said or whether she was really that ingenuous; I dropped the subject.

I strolled around the station as the surge of my adventurous impulse dissolved into shivering. It was a fairly small station. I was nosing around for something to distract my attention so as to calm my disturbed nerves, until a security guard started to squint in my direction. Trying to look innocent, I sidled up in front of a coffee stall, and ordered a medium hot coffee. The best way to blend into an environment and appear benign and ordinary was being a consumer. To have the power to consume in this country meant you were a responsible citizen, had something to lose, and cared about yourself and your society. The coffee cup changed hands, from the Chicano young lady's to mine. I clutched the rim; the coffee smelt artificial and tasted bland. It was two dollars and fifty cents and getting colder and colder every second in the air of this effectively air-conditioned lounge.

I was wondering what Rachel would say about this. She would say it was a bad decision. And she would say if you made the right decision the outcome would be alright; if you made a bad decision the eventuality would be bad, and you would end up feeling shitty. All you had to do was make the right decision at the right time, starting with staying off cheap coffee and away from screwed-up people and doomed escapades. Rachel thought life should be like a ledger filled with as many positive digits as possible, and when negative digits came up, greater positives should be put in to balance them out. That's why she was so infallible, and I, as a humanist, failed all the time.

I tossed the coffee in a garbage can; still feeling thirsty, I walked up to a vending machine, standing in front of it, bemused. In addition to the same old stuff, it featured a few new brands of soda I had never seen before. All of a sudden they made me nauseous. Then I felt cold, sad and lonely.

A train arrived at 10:30, unceremoniously. We boarded, found our seats, and it started up and went on with its trip. A dispatcher walked alongside the train on the platform for a minute and was left behind.

A woman in uniform popped her head out from behind a canvas curtain. "Do you need anything? Light snacks and drinks?"

"I'd like to have a coffee please," I said.

"This is the second one," Alice said.

"Oh, yes, I'm addicted." I sunk into a recliner. "It takes more than two to hurt my stomach and screw up my nerves. I can't stop it. Maybe because nobody ever died from drinking coffee, or it's a sort of auto-sadism. I don't really understand it myself."

"Then stop it," she said.

"I should. Well, who cares?"

"I care." She slapped my hand reaching out for the cup.

I looked at her; an adorable face with a serious look. I took up the cup, "I will quit, I will, I promise." I sipped. "By the way, is it politically correct to say that your shoes are beautiful?"

She took a look at her shoes.

"Who is the girl, Lily or Poppy?" I asked.

"Poppy?! How do you know her?" She was surprised, staring at me, and poured out, "She is a strange, strange little woman; we went out for a while, actually, we lived together for a while. She is so, so unconventional. Then I found out that she and her friends were taking drugs, getting Nazi tattoos, reading books written by religious nuts and that sort of thing. So I decided to cut her off. How do you know her?!"

"I don't know her," I said archly, "She ferreted me out and told me to keep my hands off you."

"Really?! When?" she exclaimed.

"It doesn't matter. But I don't have to worry about it, do I?" I asked gravely.

"She was really protective of me," she said.

I was annoyed by her only being able to think of herself in this situation. So I closed my eyes and leaned back in my seat. The coffee was kicking in. I was lying on the chair like a fully charged battery.

"When was the last time you had sex?" Alice asked.

I swiveled my head toward her. "You mean real sex?"

"You masturbate?!" She got excited.

"Yes, I do. Excuse me if I've disgusted you."

"Interesting!" she muttered, "then when was the time you had real sex, I mean with a woman?"

"One year ago," I lied. It was actually seven months ago in a hotel room with my ex-girlfriend who had not had broken up with her ex-boyfriend back in China, so it was an affair.

"Why don't you find a girlfriend? You don't have any trouble finding girlfriends, do you?"

"In order to have sex?" I asked, "I used to have a morbid interest in sex, yes, but now I've lost it."

"Maybe you're gay!"

"I don't know. I believe everyone has a quota for good sex. I used mine up before I was twenty-five. So I don't really care now."

"Interesting! But…"

"Have you figured out what post-modernism is?" I interrupted, as any further discussion related to my sex life would make me permanently impotent.

"Oh, yes, but I don't want to talk about it. I've read a thousand pages on it. Bringing it up again would turn me into a cold-blooded killer," she said in mock anger, drawing her head and shoulder back from mine, leaning on the window. It was pitch dark outside.

"Is that so?" I laughed. "Can I ask you a question?"

"Don't ask me anything about my research."

"What about the conference?"

"What did I say?!"

"OK, then what's the deal with Vic?" I thought I'd caught her off-guard.

She paused, "What's the deal with him? He is the opposite of my ex-boyfriend. My ex-boyfriend is a very nice guy, and too good to be my boyfriend."

"I hope you haven't said that to your ex-boyfriend. It's humiliating."

"Excuse me; I am not just saying it. He is really very nice and romantic. He writes poems; he is a poet. One day he said he had written me a poem..." She turned back to me. Her raised voice made passengers around us uneasy; a plump lady and her skinny daughter were squinting at us from across the aisle.

"He's a poet? He writes poems for a living?" I lowered my voice.

"No, he is an accountant. Anyway, he wrote me poems. Once he wrote me a one-word poem."

"I have heard of that, but I don't know if it really exists," I said.

"He gave me a card; I opened it; there was the one-word poem; guess what it said?"

"Alice," I whispered.

"Oh, my God," she muttered, grasping my arm. Then she sighed, "Then I broke up with him."

"And you hurt his macho pride?"

"He had a hard time getting over it," she said dreamily. She dozed off at last on the train, and didn't wake up until the train glided into Boston.

## 34

There indeed was an academic conference coming up at a Hilton hotel in Boston. But we arrived two days early. A pale and weary concierge gave us a wan smile from behind a mahogany counter.

"Checking in?" she asked.

Alice stepped up to the counter. "Yes."

I was hanging back in the lobby. It was 7:00 in the morning. The lobby was large and empty at that time. A young couple was standing beside a marble pillar with eyes riveted on their smartphones. An elderly woman was sitting in a wheelchair with her hands gripping both sides, gazing blindly into space.

Alice came back to me in ebullient spirits. "Seventh floor; room seven four seven; it sounds like a plane."

An elevator took us up to a floor of labyrinthine corridors. Like two rats in a maze, we searched around and came across a sturdy Mexican charlady pushing a trolley cart loaded with tablecloths and cutlery.

"Excuse me, can you tell us where the room 747 is?" Alice asked.

The lady stopped her cart, took a look at us, smiled inwardly and then moved on without saying a word.

"Maybe she doesn't speak English," I said.

"That was so rude!" Alice glared at me.

We found Room 747 at last. Alice liked the room very much. It had a partial view of a back street where a fruit vendor was putting up a stand, selling grapes, tangerines, and watermelons, big and mini.

"Do you want to take a walk?" she asked with excitement.

"No, I don't feel up to it," I said, "I didn't sleep a wink last night. I just can't sleep on a vehicle. I'm sorry." I slumped into one of the two mattresses in the dimly-lit, yellowish room, and breathed the sterilized air in and out.

"I don't like the smell of hotels," I said to the ceiling.

"Why? I like it. It's where you feel at home in a foreign country," she said.

"I simply can't agree with that," I snorted.

"No, you don't understand." She shook her head emphatically, "I've been in a lot of countries, Paris, Berlin, Milan, Tokyo, Istanbul, you name it. Hotels are your home when you travel from country to country." She sounded like a tourist commercial, so I said, "It's the smell of capitalism. It's a sterilized smell."

I fell asleep, starting a cycle in which she was asleep whenever I was awake and vice versa.

I didn't know how long I had been sleeping until I heard someone groaning in my dream. Someone was moaning, slurping, and growling on and off continuously. I swivelled to the other side, but the voice was still present.

"Oh, my God, it's not a dream." I came around and realized, "Someone is moaning in the room! Someone is having sex!"

I turned around. Alice was sitting cross-legged on her bed with a remote control in hand, entranced in a porn movie on TV.

"What are you doing?!" I called to her.

"I've never watched one of these before," she said.

A man's penis was shuttling frantically in and out of a lady's vagina. The camera panned out to a wider view, revealing another penis doing the same routine in the lady's mouth and yet another one in the lady's fist.

"How did you find this?" I was flushed.

"I knew they had these adult channels," she said, "I just never got around to watching them."

"Now that you've watched it, how do you like it?" I said reprovingly, "Could you turn it off or at least turn it down, please. It gets on my nerves."

"They are really doing it!" she exclaimed, "I thought they were just faking it."

"Depends on how you define faking. Please turn it off. I am getting a headache."

She turned it off and said, "we can have this for 48 hours; I paid; feel free to watch TV when I am not around." She laughed.

"I really appreciate your hospitality."

Then, I was about to say I was getting ready to depart since my mission had been completed.

"I bought you something," she interrupted and conjured up a plastic pack from behind her back. It was a bag of men's underwear. "I bought you some shorts." She was sizing me up. "You wear a medium, don't you?" I took the bag of the underwear; it was labelled Calvin Klein.

"I buy my shorts from Old Navy," I said. "These would make me feel…"

"Please stay," she begged suddenly. She looked like an abandoned child pleading for parents.

"Alice. I'm not your father," I said.

"Just one more day," she said, fighting back tears.

I was irritated. "Well, OK, I will, I will stay until your conference starts." I thought I was doing her one last favor.

She didn't get it. She leapt out of bed, full of excitement, holding her arms out, inviting me for a hug.

"I am sorry, I stink," I said.

She stepped toward me; her arms encircled my neck, pulling my face down against her chest.

"I don't like this," I said weakly. Then I put my arms gingerly around her waist, tightened a little and pushed her away. I liked her so much that I could not accept anything less than love.

The rest of the day, Alice treated me as her real lover. She asked me which dress she should wear for the conference, which color of lipstick went with it, and how she looked in her ballet flats.

"Are you giving a presentation?" I asked.

"No, my paper was not accepted," she said briefly.

"Oh, then get your revenge; make them regret it."

"I don't care what they think of me. How do *you* like this?" she was standing in front of a mirror, twirling and stooping.

"I think you're beautiful." I smiled.

"You know, it's unfair because women have to please men," she said. "We're constantly asking the questions like: what do you want from me? Am I likeable?"

"You don't care," I teased.

"Well, that's what doctor Freud said!" She paused, "Or someone else said it; I can't remember who said it, but it's true; women don't know what they want. You see, I used to have a perfect boyfriend, but I couldn't resist having an affair."

"You're not talking about me, are you? If you are, I want out," I said.

"Relax, Alex. Vic was my affair, and I was also his," she said. "But I did have an affair when I was with Vic, too. Do you think I'm a nymphomaniac?"

"What is that?"

"It's a psycho disease," she said gravely. "It's a person who likes to have sex all the time, and with lots of different people."

"It's a disease, or a hobby?"

"God, I am not kidding. Check it out on Wikipedia if you don't believe me. It's officially called hyper-sexuality or nymphomania." She repeated the strong word again.

"Tell me about your affair when you were with Vic," I said while helping her put her dresses, pants, jewelry, sunglasses, and belts with beads and feathers back into the closet. She had narrowed the choices down to three outfits.

"Oh, that." She hesitated. Then she sat down, taking a deep breath.

"His name was Howard. I met him at a party. Vic and I were both invited. Vic was drunk and flirting with a girl, Lana, from Ukraine. I was embarrassed and angry with him, so I went walking in the backyard. I found a very quaint hammock installed there. It looked like a cradle, but it was a hammock. There was nobody around at that time, so I climbed upon it, lay down, one leg draping over the canvas and swayed back and forth. I remembered the clouds cleared up; the moon was so big and shinning that I had the impulse to touch it and held it up as if it was a giant bubble of water. Then, I heard someone walking into the garden. I closed my eyes as if I was asleep.

'Do you mind if I smoke?' a man's voice said.

I said immediately, 'No, it's fine. Thank you for asking me though.' I could not see his face in the darkness. He lit up a cigarette and smoked quietly. 'What do you smoke?' I asked him. He said it was just a cigarette, and then asked me if I thought he was smoking weed. Then he walked up to me, holding a cigarette butt before my nose. He said, 'I am sorry, but this is the last one.' I stared at him, pretending that I was offended. But, I swear to God, he was so handsome; maybe that accounted for his boldness. I thought I would scare him away, but guess what?"

"What? Vic walked in?"

"No, my God, he didn't back off. He was holding the butt and looking into my eyes. That was so intense. I must have blushed like a monkey's ass. My heart was racing, and I finally understood why those ladies fainted so easily in novels."

"Then what happened?"

"I sipped at it and he took it back, having his turn and passed it on to me again. I accepted it, and we took turns smoking until we finished it. It was just one or two minutes, but it felt so long, and my mind was totally blank. Then he leaned down, holding his breath, and I pushed up his shoulders. I said, 'my boyfriend is in there'; he said, 'I know.' Then he kissed me, and I kissed him back. I stuck my tongue into his mouth and he scooped me out of the hammock. His arms were as strong as tree trunks."

"You were lucky that nobody interrupted you," I said.

"We sneaked into a guest room, and we made love. I was…"

"That's enough. I got the idea," I said. "So it was just a one-night stand or did you see him again?"

She paused, "He's dead," she said with melancholy.

"What?!" I was surprised.

"He died from a car accident a month after we had the affair," she said dreamily. "And he turned out to be an orphan."

"That's…that's incredible," I said.

Finishing her story she claimed that she was tired and sad and wanted to have a nap.

I left the room and went down to an Internet service center to check my email. Then on sudden impulse, I did some research on students at C_Universtiy who had died in car accidents in the last five years. There were three cases, two men and a woman, but none of the victims was named Howard, and none of them seemed to be an orphan.

## 35

The third day.

Alice and I explored the city. I was quite cheerful and more enthusiastic about sightseeing than I'd been the other days. I gathered that a short trip in New England was not a bad idea for my sedentary, screwed-up spine and Midwest-bleached soul.

"Do you want to go to Harvard?" I said, "You are an alumna."

"Oh, I am fine. I don't really care for it," she said.

"Then would you be my guide? I haven't ever been there."

"OK, if you really want to go. But I can tell you there's nothing much to see. It's a small campus full of self-important snobs," she said, like a young mother complaining about her spoiled son.

I let the idea blow over. So we strolled the street aimlessly. We passed by a live band performing on the pavement. A woman was singing:

*Won't you please let me back in your heart?*
*Oh, darling, I was blind to let you go.*
*Now that I have seen you in his arms,*
*I am trying to live without your love as a long sleepless night.*

I stopped to listen while Alice went on walking. When she was out of sight, I felt obliged to catch up with her. Turning a corner, stepping down a flight of stone stairs, we stumbled onto a plaza. Street dancers and skateboarders were dancing and jumping from banisters onto short ramparts, and then landing on the ground. More of them were standing around, stretching legs and arms, chatting with each other. Music suddenly boomed out from a big speaker. The music was familiar, but the name eluded me. And suddenly the whole plaza came to life. Dancers were twirling, holding up their legs high at breathtaking angles and then smashing and stretching onto the ground. A young woman leaped upon a young man's shoulders, flipping her legs and turning herself over in the air elegantly; then the man launched her out and she landed back on the ground as if gravity had ceased to exist for her for a second.

"These people make me feel so old," Alice sighed.

"I know. It's a different life's path," I agreed.

For the rest of the day, she was humming and whispering now and again a song she had picked up in the street: *"Why is it so hard to make it in America; I tried so hard to make it in America."* A sweating African American man had plaintively sung it in the plaza. Alice rendered it as if a school girl was complaining about too much homework. She was singing it absentmindedly above the sink in the bathroom, taking out her contact lenses.

"Are you feeling alright today?" I said, "You look zoned out."

She walked out of the bathroom, wearing glasses. "Oh, I'm sorry." She paused. "I deleted a lot of emails yesterday; some of them might be from my advisor. Now I'm worrying that I might have missed something important."

"You deleted them by mistake? You know you can retrieve them from the trash can."

"No, I deleted them on purpose, and I emptied the trash can."

"Why?" I asked.

"It's unfair to reply to so many emails every day. I hate emails. Do you hate replying to emails?"

It occurred to me that she had been abusing these words: unfair, hate, and I don't.

"What is so unfair about that? I don't understand."

"Can't they just leave me alone?" She finished her words with a growl under her breath and squashed something invisible in her fists.

When I was about to talk her out of this childishness, my phone rang.

"Hello?" I picked it up.

"Hi." A woman's voice. Then the phone on the other end changed hands.

"Is Alice there?" a man said with a grumpy, impatient voice.

"Yes," I faltered. "Just a second." I handed my phone to Alice.

She was calm as if she was expecting the call all along, holding the phone up to the level of her ear without touching it. Then she said slowly, "Hello."

Hearing her voice, the man started lashing out on the speaker, and in return, Alice yelled back at him. It was too much for me so I sneaked out of the room.

I consulted the concierge about train tickets back to Illinois and had my first coffee of the day. After an hour of meditation on a chaise lounge in the lobby and a few pieces of intensely self-conscious inner monologue, I was ready to go up to say goodbye to Alice.

Stepping into the hotel room, I was absolutely stunned. The room was completely trashed. White towels and bed sheets were strewn on the floor; the TV and a lamp were knocked over with electrical cords still plugged into sockets, stretched taut and tangling each other ominously; a glass tumbler was shattered, shreds scattered in a corner where lay a toothbrush and a plastic tube oozing sticky transparent gel, smeared all over the carpet.

"What the hell are you doing?!" I shouted.

She was sitting on the top of the toilet cover, sobbing, and mumbling something hateful.

"Bastard, bastard." She kicked her feet and swung her arms frantically like a caged animal.

"Another boyfriend?" I said.

"My brother," she said. "It's none of his goddamned business; I was talking to my mom!"

She had bruised her arms and shins and was trying to bump and hurt herself on the head.

"Stop it!" I said, "Are you fucking out of your mind?"

I seized her hands, dragged her out of the bathroom, trying to sit her down.

"You have a brother?" I didn't know what else to say or do. I wanted out, but it was too cruel to abandon her at the moment. I regretted the whole affair.

"I'm OK," she said, "I'm sorry for messing up your bed; but you are leaving anyway, aren't you?"

"Yes, I am leaving," I said.

"Oh, OK," she said with a dazed expression, "I'm sorry I lost my temper." She broke off. "Then good luck with your trip." She started sobbing again.

"Do you want me to pick up the room for you?" I said.

"No, please leave it! I will do it later. I will, I promise. It's unfair to you."

"Can you take care of yourself?"

"I'll have a nap. Then I'm gonna be alright. Don't worry about me; you have your things to do."

I sighed and looked around at the expensive mess she had just created. She must have gotten used to the idea that someone would pick up after her and rescue her, giving her what she wanted at last, without judging her, still loved her for just what she was. Then she could drop her messy bomb again on whomever else. I refused to go down that path. I gathered my belongings, said a few parting words, then I left.

There were rumors about devious city taxi drivers targeting Asian students. I sent for a taxi at the front gate. Ten minutes later a minivan arrived with a middle-aged man in the driver's seat. I acted like a veteran traveler to keep him from ripping me off. The trip from the Hilton hotel to Boston South Station only took ten minutes, and it cost me twenty dollars.

I was standing in the middle of a bustling concourse, but found myself with no intention to buy a ticket to leave. The uneasy feeling of leaving Alice alone at the hotel was turning into a dilemma. *Should I at least take her home?* I thought, *I did escort her here. Maybe I should finish what I started. Should I? And why was I so cold to her anyway? Is it because she's rich? What if she were just a poor girl, a young woman without any means in a foreign country? Then I would definitely help her out. Why am I not helping her out now? Oh, I'm such a snob, thinking that money has the power to elevate a person to a more respectable position, and that rich people should have more dignity and self-discipline.*

I sat on a bench set between two colossal marble pillars. Over my head was an enormous star-spangled flag, the remains of the 4th of July. I watched people scuttling around and I conjured up a good excuse. I had not settled the rent with her, which I'd promised I would pay half of. Once I made the decision, I started dreading what she might be doing now. Hurrying out of the train station, I hoped that the taxi was still around.

"Left something in the hotel?" The driver gave me a quizzical smile.

"Yes, I left something behind."

Rushing back into the hotel, I took the elevator up to the seventh floor. This time, I had no trouble finding the room. I knocked on the door. No one answered it. I tried the doorknob and it was unlocked.

"Alice!" I called out, stepped into the room.

Her luggage was still there, but she had gone off. The room had been picked up by hotel maids, I supposed, for instant coffee packs and tea packs were refilled in two new tumblers wrapped with new paper slips.

Feeling thirsty, I fixed myself a cup of coffee. I picked up a travel magazine to fan my sweating face, pondering what Alice might have been up to.

Then there was a creak at the door. Alice stumbled into the room. She was as drunk as a monkey, stumbled about, took a few struts and a twirl, and plunged into the bed. She flipped her body around, facing the ceiling.

"Kiss me," she said drunkenly.

"Where were you?" I asked.

"Kiss Alice. Don't you want to kiss Alice?" she said as if there was an unacknowledged person in the room or she was speaking through a dummy's body.

"No, I don't. Where were you?"

"I won' tell you unless you kiss Alice." She sat herself up straight, breathing heavily. "Kiss me!" she yelled. Then she sprang up and grabbed my collar. "You are not a man!"

"Get yourself together, Alice, get yourself together. I am not a man for sure. So don't play little girl for me," I said.

She let go of my collar and fell back on the bed, started her lachrymose routine.

"What's that for?" I asked coldly.

She didn't answer my question and was crying and crying.

"Do you want to go home?" I said.

"I don't have a home!" she cried out, "This is my home!"

"Then let's go back to Illinois; go back to Vic," I said.

"No, I am not going back," she said waywardly, "I won't give up; that's what they want."

"Who wants what?"

"My brother. He wants me to quit. Then he can be the model son. I won't let him have his way until I am dead." She sunk her teeth into her lower lip with hatred. "Wait until I become a Harvard professor. Then they'll know who's a piece of shit. I will beat him down. I have to beat him down."

## 36

The next day, in the lobby of the hotel, a gentleman with a British accent asked me where he could find a copy machine. I told him that there was one next to a vending machine on the second floor. Then he asked me if by any remote chance and against all the odds I happened to be attending a conference he was attending. I said yes and no, and he asked whether he had the privilege to inquire the reason. We ended up talking on convivial terms for about fifteen minutes, and parted without exchanging names.

Then two big buses dawdled in under the awning of the hotel. The check-in counter was soon thronged with people wearing formal suits and business casuals. Some of them had name badges hanging from their necks. They all looked serious, anxious and compulsorily sociable.

Alice had gone to bed early the night before because of her mental and physical exhaustion that day. But she got up at 7:00 am; went jogging in the hotel gym; then put on a sleek pantsuit with shoulder pads and two ivory white buttons in front. She asked for my opinion, and I said it was exquisite and lovely. I was jealous of her being able to recover so thoroughly, but had misgivings about her erratic behavior.

Having no interest in hearing out long-winded, verbose pedants bashing movies in which women had too much flesh and no dialogue, I opted for going out shopping. I'd promised to stay in Boston, so I bought a towel, a toothbrush, three pairs of socks, and two books: a paperback novel and a copy of *People's History of the United States* at a discount, and a canvas duffel bag for 30 dollars. I put everything in the bag and went to a movie to spend the afternoon. The duffel bag attracted a great deal of attention. At the entrance, I had to open it up for inspection to prove that it was not a potential threat to public safety. The computer-generated imagery put me into a trance, then a fitful sleep. I woke up when the villain thought he had killed the hero, and another time when the hero thought he had killed the villain.

When I got back to the hotel, the conference had taken over the whole vicinity. Conferees were standing around, leaning on walls and sitting on the floor. Young scholars huddled around academic veterans in corridors, chattering, listening to a star holding forth on his postulate, nodding their assent. Laughter was heard occasionally and often encouraged. For even younger scholars, it was more of a festival to celebrate their newly acquired lexicon, newfangled theories, in which academic jargon, profound phrases, convoluted sentences, and redefined common words were finding first release as if deformed, grotesque babies were floundering toward premature birth.

I saw Alice in the lobby. She was chatting with a young woman, and they seemed to know each other very well. The young woman clutched a thick hardcover in her hand, stood erect and alert. She was thin, and, instead of pretty, she was handsome. She had a high, aquiline nose rare for an Asian woman and an assertive manner enhanced by her finely chiselled chin and self-possessed eyes. Her hair was short, and she wore a white, long- sleeve shirt fastened by a wide leather belt and tucked into beige slim-fit khaki pants. But what really made her look distinguished was her black equestrian style boots, standing apart firmly on the floor like a young officer and giving the impression that she'd just gotten off a pedigree horse.

Alice waved at me; it was too late to escape. So I walked up, introduced myself modestly, skimped on anything concrete to avert the distaste for wordiness. I didn't want to take too much of their time and attention.

"Where have you been?" said Alice. "We were just talking about Lacan. You are interested in Lacan too, aren't you?"

I smiled and colluded, "I read a few of his books."

It was a lie. The truth was that I had never read anything first-hand the prestigious clinician ever had written. I read a book titled: *Lacan: a beginner's guide*, and that was all. I had no interest in being an imposter, making myself look erudite or well-educated or even slightly more intelligent than I really was; however, I felt obliged to lie about having read or known of some writers or essays only because in the academic world, it is impolite, off-putting, and even haughty to admit blatantly that you don't know an author or a theory. I had got used to playing along with their assumptions, and in return, unwittingly invited them to talk at me, let off their steam and have their therapy. The truth was that I was one of the few in my circle, who was not a pedantic egoist in that small world. I was disinterested.

I said, "I especially like his theory of unconsciousness; it makes more sense to me."

"Interesting, my paper is about the political unconsciousness of the late Qing novelists," said the equestrian.

"Interesting, interesting, I'd like to read it. How can I read it?" I asked.

"I'd like to read it too!" Alice chimed in, "and what's unconsciousness for Lacan and who does it make more sense than?" Alice stared at me and then directed her question to her friend.

"Oh, he argued that the unconscious is made of language instead of libidos—" the woman made an air quote, tucked the book under her arm, and continued, "—signifiers, instead of commonly trusted instinct."

"Then where are the instincts?" Alice asked.

"I doubt that he had a theory about instinct at all, or he simply refuses to use this word. He talks about drive and desire, though."

Alice refused to give up. "What are they then?"

"It's complicated." She stepped back a little so that she could make both of us out better in her view. "Drive is obviously different from desire, right?" the woman looked at me for consent.

I nodded, lowering my head, stroking my chin as if I was contemplating.

"Desire is not what you absolutely need, like air and water, but something extra, and something you cannot simply demand by using language. It's what gets lost in language. So what you ask for is actually not what you really want. As a result, desire can never be fully satisfied." While she was talking, her right hand slowly rose in front of her chest, clawing its way up as though holding an imaginary crystal ball for her witchcraft.

"Hmm, very interesting," Alice said; she turned to me. "What's the name of the book you read?"

"Of course, I'll give it to you later," I said.

People started to pile into conference rooms. Another session was about to start. Alice's friend thus said it was a great pleasure to meet me and definitely would like to talk with me later about Lacan especially through the perspective of Hegel and Kant. I contrived a smile and shook her hand nervously. After she and

Alice walked away, I was left in the lobby shuddering at the flagrant lies I had just told, and trying to digest and stash it away into my or possibly Lacan's unconsciousness. Why couldn't I just be myself? I don't know!

I didn't figure that Alice would ask me to have the dinner with her. So I had bought a lot of junk food, processed food made from almost nothing but sugar whose American name is fructose corn syrup. I would get diabetes if I kept eating like this, but the perennial shortage of time, space and money was winning out over the Chinese diet my parents brought me up on. It is said that it takes seven years to change every cell in one's body, but my tongue had not changed. The food still tasted like junk. My phone had two missed calls from Rachel. But I deliberately ignored them, for I didn't feel up to explaining why I came to Boston with Alice. She would never understand it because I didn't fully understand it myself.

When dusk fell, Alice called me saying she would take me out for a decent dinner. I told her that I was perfectly fine eating frozen dinner boxes in the hotel room by myself. She would not hear of it. She said if I turned her down, a suicide note would be sent to both me and a local newspaper. "Then fine," I said. "But nothing fancy because I have nothing decent to wear." We decided on a Chinese restaurant.

"How is your conference so far?" I asked.

"It's fine," she said while flipping through a menu. She'd brought a book she bought at the conference. It was laid aside, and the title on the spine read: *The Ideology of the Aesthetic.*

"Your friend is interesting," I said.

"You think so?" she asked me, scowling.

"Why? Who is she?"

"Oh, we were close when we were at Harvard," she said. "At that time we both thought private schools were full of right-wingers and pretentious pseudo-scholars. She went to Boston University afterward. We went our separate ways."

"She seems to know a lot of things," I said.

"Does she?" Her scowl intensified. "She seems more knowledgeable than I am? But she used to..."

"I don't know," I said quickly. "I can't tell."

"Be honest with me." She folded the menu.

The boss of the restaurant, a Chinese northerner, who had been murmuring something to her calculator behind a counter, was sizing us up in the periphery view of her puffy eyes encircled by black charcoal. Waiters lingered around listlessly but eager for tips. We had been seated near a set of Chinese screens featuring round-faced fairy-ladies floating on colorful cotton candies, giving us the luxury of a little privacy.

"I really can't tell because you are both more intelligent than I am. That's my honest impression."

"Oh, God," she burst out, "I am wasting my time at a public school! Most of my classmates ruled out public schools, and now I know why."

"Why?" I asked.

"Oh, I am sorry. I don't mean to offend you or anything. You must think I'm a snob."

"No, seriously, I want to know the reason."

"They said there's no real education in public schools. It's just vocational training and preparing white collar proletarians for mediocre corporations."

"To some extent, I agree," I said.

A waiter brought us noodle soup and a plate of shrimp dumplings drizzled with soy sauce.

"I'm so hungry." I dug in.

"Oh, really? Feel free to have mine. I may just want one dumpling."

Then it occurred to me that she'd never had a real meal since the day we arrived. She always just poked and pecked at whatever was in front of her like a dyspeptic cat.

"Why? What's the word? Anorexia?"

"No," she said, "I wish though. I am gaining weight like a crazy cow."

To get her to eat and in revenge for what she'd said about public schools and proletarians, I was deliberately munching, slurping and gobbling my food with table manners that would easily make a right-wing lady faint.

"I like the way you eat." She smiled.

"Oh, I will take it as a compliment," I said with my mouth full.

"I like staying with you." She lowered her voice. Then, out of the sheer blue, "Alex, is your family rich?"

I swallowed a dumpling, and washed it down with a mouthful of mineral water.

"Why? You want to borrow some money?" I said gaily.

"No, of course not," she said, "I want to ask you a favor, but it has nothing to do with money. Well, actually it's about money, but… never mind… I'll tell you later."

"You'd better tell me now, or you'll spoil my appetite."

She apologized and then turned her head around as if making sure nobody was eavesdropping.

I was in a rather talkative mood, "My parents are both retired. They live on their pensions, which are fair enough according to their provincial standards. I mean, they're by no means rich but willing to subsidize now and again if I ask."

"Are you the only child?" she asked.

"I am," I said, "I'm the only child in the family. We're not on speaking terms lately, but…What favor do you want from me? You don't have a sixteen-year-old daughter to marry off, do you?" I laughed.

"Guess what," she said, "I do have a woman I want to betroth to you though she is not sixteen."

## 37

A worn-out waiter brought fortune cookies and a yellow tab to the table. "Tips are not included," the waiter said unceremoniously. The dumplings left on the plate had become clammy and stiff. I glanced at my watch; it was 9:30 p.m. But it was actually 10:30 p.m. because of the time difference. I was unwilling to adjust my watch, knowing I might leave the city at any moment.

"And you are not kidding?" I asked. "You're not in love with me, are you?"

"No, no, it's not what you think," she said. "OK, it's my brother. My father has put him in charge of the family company, and my brother keeps my mom from giving me money. I don't know how he did it, but he talked them into believing that I am wasting the family money on luxuries."

"Are you?" I asked, siding with her brother momentarily.

"No!" she groaned dramatically. "Do I look like I'm living a life of luxury? I was thinking of applying for a job at the GAP!"

"I know a lot of students who work at the GAP. What's wrong with the GAP?"

"I will!"

"Well, I am sure you can. But what does this have to do with getting married?"

"My brother got married last year, so he was given a house and the big sum of money my parents promised to each of us when we got married."

"So you want to get married and cash in?" I was amused. "It sounds crazy."

"Yes, and you know why?" She stared at me.

"Why? Not because you are greedy and devious?" I assumed an air of seriousness and continued, "It sounds like a melodrama and really over the top."

"No, it's because my brother is in charge of the company, and he is a moron, and my parents are totally blind to his stupidity; because he is a boy! If I don't claim the money, my money, now, the company will go under in his hands, and nobody in my family will have anything."

Now I knew that she was not kidding and was deadly serious. "Are you sure?" I said.

"Who can be sure?" she said, "My grandparents were just poor orchard farmers. My parents used to be poor too. They don't know anything about capitalism. They think they have made it to high-class society because they are capable. They don't know what financial crises are. They don't know who the hell they are! They just believe in money and their retard son."

"But…" I wanted to say something, but lost my train of thought.

"Oh, you don't have to decide now." As she had vented her feelings, she leaned back. "If you think it is too crazy, it's fine. I am telling you this because I think I can trust you."

"What about Vic?"

"Vic?" She paused. "Vic is not trustworthy. You are an artist; you don't care much about money, do you?"

"I should be more careful about money," I said, leaning far back on my chair. There was a newly established free-fire zone over the table between us; I felt like if I leaned in, I could be shelled to pieces.

"Will you help me?"

"Probably not, it's too romantic for me," I said.

"I understand, I understand," said she wistfully.

I finished up the dumplings; she settled the check, tipped the waiter; we left the restaurant. Outside, it was dark. The street was empty but treacherously so. Just as we landed on the pavement, a band of motorcyclists parking their bikes on the street corner, hailed us, revving their engines with heavily tattooed arms, yelling gibberish which when it occurred to me was actually garbled words of Chinese. Alice grasped my hand; we hurried away, and turned onto a main street.

"I don't feel very safe at night in this country," I said, relieved.

"Oh, really? I feel OK. Just keep away from some places at night," she said while tightening her grip on me.

The ten minutes of sauntering back to the hotel was amorous and short. She extracted her hand from mine as soon as we saw the lighted windows in the driveway.

"Care for a drink?" she said, "I feel a little hungry now."

"I am sorry I ate your dumplings," I said.

"Don't be silly, it's not your fault." I felt she was pulling my shirt.

"I am very tired; I'd like to lie down," I said and realized that this was the time that her day usually began. Her face lit up with a glimmer of hope and her chest seemed to be filled with a fanciful prospect. She was transformed into a person who was very capable of any excessive entertainment and diabolic activity. I pictured parties sluiced with expensive alcohol, drugs, condoms, and syringes, all the debauched dreams that oriental peasants had imagined for the last thirty years.

"Take care." I waved to her, as she entered the hotel bar.

## 38

I woke up in the middle of the night. It was pitch dark; the curtain hanging over the window was too thick to let in any light. A clock on the side table displayed greenish, incandescent numbers. It was two o'clock in the morning and Alice was still at large. A surge of anxiety, which would attack me once in a while and particularly on waking up at odd hours of the night, enveloped me. I groped my way to the window, peeked out from behind the curtain. Window walls reflected neon signs, which were reflected in myriad other window walls. I found the window behind which I was standing in the reflection, and soon lost it. I felt dizzy and sick, as if I was in a whirling boat. *Where is Alice?* I thought.

At dawn, I was puttering about in the bathroom, brushing my teeth while taking a shower. I managed to skip masturbation, and it made me feel positive and confident. This was the last day of the conference, and the adventure was officially coming to an end. I was brooding about never having to see Alice again. I had practiced several versions of my farewell speech and conjured up a few scenarios for each, all of which I firmly concluded with, "see you in the next life." For example, if she didn't turn up by noon, I would leave her a message saying: "I can't stand your whims and histrionic nonsense, so please don't contact me again." Or, if she turned up before noon and was willing to make amends and began to cry and beg for mercy, then I would be kind enough to take her back to the university immediately. If she refused to do what she was told, I would simply defer to the first solution. There might be other possibilities, but they wouldn't be at variance with my will to cut her off.

At 9:00 am, she breezed in. Seeing me, she deliberately cringed like a little girl having misbehaved, caught out by her stickler father. What a prima donna!

"Good morning," I said pointedly.

"Good morning," she murmured.

"Have you had your breakfast?" I kept my eyes off her, pretending to mind my own business.

"No, but I'm not hungry."

"Oh, really? Then I have something to tell you," I said.

"I have something to tell you, too," she said.

A rage came over me and a scream went up on the top of my lungs. *What the fuck is it?!* I imagined yelling at her.

But I said, "What you said to me last night is strictly your business. I won't tell anyone anything about it. You have my word."

"No, it's not about that. I figured it was ridiculous and childish. I didn't know what I was thinking."

"Then what is it?" I demanded.

She sat down, looked at me with her wan and tired face.

"I met a guy last night, an assistant professor," she said. "He's a film director, I mean, he is a real film director. We watched a movie he made; it's beautiful;

he's not a fraud. And he said he's going to shoot another movie, and he wants me to play a role in it!"

I was sure this was just one of her crazy ideas. So I said, "Then do it. By the way I am leaving for Illinois today. Will you come with me?"

"But we are going to Buffalo, and I want your company," she said.

"Now?" I felt curiously helpless.

"Yes, we are leaving after lunch."

"Then, I'll pass." I turned away from her, jerked open the curtain in the vain hope that the sunlight would have a sobering effect on her.

"I know you're angry at me, but I really want to go."

"Then go." I slumped down on the edge of my bed, the mattress buoying my stiff body.

"But I don't know anyone in Buffalo. Won't you worry about me?" she said.

"Why's everything always about you, Alice?"

"But I really want to give it a try. I like acting," she burst into tears.

"It seems you only care about what you like."

She started to cry, and a long pause ensued.

Suddenly I had an evil plan. "OK, let's go to Buffalo." I thought maybe I should have let her fell on her face; as Americans would say: get a taste of her own medicine. "But you have to promise that this is the last time."

She nodded, sobbing.

"How do we go?"

"We can go by plane and meet him at his place."

"Are you sure he's not a serial killer?" I asked. "Who is this director? Asian? White? Black?"

She didn't answer my question because she couldn't. Once she had my assent, her crying became even louder and harder. It seemed as if she was deliberately trying to cry her heart out and her eyes blind for a momentary catharsis.

I couldn't bear it. I left the room.

We arrived in Buffalo when the sun had sunk down and a breeze from the north dissipated the heat of the day. I carried on mindlessly as she was getting more and more excited.

The city was depopulated. It was one of those places suffering from post-industrial unemployment and sporadic recession. It was a city of vacant and deserted buildings and bungalows. A bus carried us through the downtown, an eerily empty, clean, and quiet cityscape. Alongside a boulevard were stores and theatres, shut down with doors and windows clasped in rusty chains. I could hear music broadcasting from somewhere and reverberating through the street. The scene gave me the impression of a nuclear apocalypse.

"This place is so spooky," I said to Alice sitting beside me.

"Yes, it's like a movie!" she exclaimed.

We got off at a bus terminal. I was coming down with the flu. It started with a headache when I left the hotel. It turned into a cold when I boarded the plane, and an air vent, which could not be turned off over my head on the bus swishing my head mercilessly, exacerbated it.

While we were getting further disoriented, a Toyota sedan stopped across the street. A tall Asian woman in a white blouse came out, negotiated the traffic with her long legs, and walked up to us. She stepped close and asked, "Are you Alice?" She was taller than either of us; Alice looked up, and I tilted my head.

"Yes, I am," Alice said.

"Steven told me to pick you up." She directed the first half of the sentence to Alice but finished it on me. "How are you?"

"I'm fine." I sneezed. "I'm OK."

"Something came up at the set. It's a mess. They are shooting tomorrow, so he is dealing with it. Do you have a place to stay?" she asked.

Alice said, "He said we could stay at his place."

"Oh, really? His place?" she said as if she was surprised.

"Yes, that's what he said," Alice insisted.

"We can find a hotel if it is inconvenient," I said, sensing that there was some misunderstanding that must have been Alice's fault.

The woman looked at me with a faint relief on her brows, "Oh, that would make my life much easier," she said calmly.

Seeing the lady convinced me that there was, after all, a movie project going on. She must have been a model or an actress or both because of her statuesqueness and her oval-shaped face with perfectly arranged features. However, other than that, she was nothing like a sensitive thespian type; her efficient and business-like air was more of a professional agent, a movie agent maybe.

The lady started the introduction to cover the silence as Alice and I sat in the back seat while the car was speeding through the city. "Buffalo is an abandoned city. But it has one thing that attracts tourists from all over the world. It is on the eastern end of Lake Erie, opposite Fort Erie..." She drove fast, or at least the darkness enhanced the impression. "...and at the beginning of the Niagara River, which flows northward over Niagara Falls — I assume you know Niagara Falls — summer is the peak season, so it's hard to make a hotel reservation." She paused, making her words resonate with foreboding.

We tried two hotels; they were indeed all booked up until the next month. Walking down a flight of stone steps on the terrace, Alice asked the lady glumly, "Can I call Steven?"

"Oh, sure, you can. I bet he is busy now, though," she said. "Just an idea, if you guys don't mind, I can put you up at my apartment for tonight."

Alice was about to say something, and I cut in as I was very sick and tired, "Thank you, I think that's a good idea."

It was an on-campus apartment at Buffalo University. When the hostess turned off the engine in the parking lot, she turned back to us, gauged the situation, and said her roommate had gone and there was a couch in the living room. The living room, though having its own light fixture, had light bulbs plucked out of their outlets in the ceiling, leaving black sockets presiding over the sparse furniture. It was lit only by a floor lamp, like an enormous spindle, wrapped from bottom to top with rice paper, giving off a soft, glowing, oriental air. And there was the couch beside the lamp. I was to sleep on the couch and nobody seemed to have any problem with it.

"Feel free to use everything," our hostess said.

I thanked her, and apologized for putting her to so much trouble; she said never mind but didn't look very pleased either. Alice took a shower; I took a shower. I felt hungry, but I decided to sleep it off and wait until the morning.

The hostess led Alice, wrapped in her selfish pyjamas, into one of the bedrooms. I lay down on the couch with my clothes on, curled up, trying to go to sleep.

"Do you need a blanket?" Having changed into a dressing-gown, standing beside me, the hostess asked.

"Oh, please. Thank you." I sat up in a fluster.

"Are you hungry?"

I sneezed, "To be honest, I am hungry," I said, grimacing and trying to shrug off my embarrassment.

She laid down a blanket and went into the kitchen. After a while, she brought back a cup of warm milk, two pieces of toasted bread with garlic melted on them, and a bowl of strawberries mixed with apple dices. She had transformed from a super model into a keen nurse, and this overwhelmed me. I gibbered with gratefulness, apology, praise, and superlative adjectives. She sat down in an armchair, tilted her head, her temple resting on her knuckles, nodding smiles to me. Her smile was bewitching in the dimmed light.

"Where are you from?" she asked.

"I'm from China," I said.

"I can tell." She laughed. "Where do you go to school? Are you a student?"

"Oh, I am from Illinois," I said.

"How is your school's funding?"

It was not an amorous conversation at all; I coughed and said, "There were severe cutbacks last year, but everyone seemed to have survived one way or another."

"They make you earn everything you need," she said.

"Yes. You have to make an effort to beat someone else down to survive in the system."

"True. We spend most of our time writing grant proposals rather than making films. No money, no film."

"We're running a local newspaper, and it's the same," I bluffed.

"You're a journalist?" she asked.

"No, I am a graphic designer," I exaggerated, and I was afraid she would push, so I asked, "And you?"

"I used to study psychology," she said. "It didn't turn out the way I expected."

"Why? If you don't mind…"

"It's OK. Maybe I didn't expect psychologists would work in labs. I supposed they were more like the ones we see in films. I was very naïve at the time." She put her arms down on the sides of the chair. "Well," she sighed, "I'll leave you to your sleep. Good night." She stood up.

"Good night," I said, wondering if I had said anything inappropriate.

I pulled the blanket up on me. It fitted snugly from my feet to my nose, warm and fluffy.

I was thinking about the woman. *She must be the director's girlfriend or mistress who takes care of the lofty artist's mundane life.* Then I started to imagine her naked, her long legs, and her body beneath the dressing gown. I was thoroughly civilized in terms of manners and appearances and irrevocably perverted underneath the thin veneer. I put a stop on my prurient thoughts and fell asleep.

I was woken up by the sound of someone tinkling about in the kitchen. I looked at my watch; it was 8:30, so it was 9:30. I'd overslept, abusing the courtesy of being invited to stay in an apartment as a guest. But I had an excuse.

I got up, caught by a pang of splitting headache, as I shuffled my way into the kitchen. The hostess was cooking breakfast if it wasn't lunch.

"I'm sorry, I overslept," I said, "I caught a cold last night."

"Oh, don't worry," she said. "You can sleep in the bedroom now if you want to; she's gone to the set."

I thought, *If Alice had been kidnapped or raped, I would become the biggest idiot and standing joke for the next ten years.*

"Where is the set?" I asked.

"They're shooting on a train today," she said.

"A train?!"

"Yes, a real train. They have it just for a day, so they had to start early," she broke off. Something seemed to occur to her, and I guessed that it must have been something about my presence. And she continued, "and they don't want anyone except the crew on board."

"She didn't tell me about this." I stopped pressing.

"What do you want for lunch?" she asked, "I'm going to a food court."

"Please let me help. I feel very sorry for putting you to so much trouble."

Then she arranged on the kitchen table a bowl of milk-soaked oatmeal, a boiled egg, strawberries, halved kiwi fruit, and again apple dices served on a china platter flanked by a silver fork and a spoon.

"Coffee?" she was cradling a coffee cup in both of her hands, smiling as I started to wolf down the eggs and the oatmeal.

"I do like coffee. I am sorry. But please," I mumbled.

## 39

The shoppers in organic food stores seemed more-educated, greener, and taking shopping more seriously. And the shop assistants are not serious shop assistants, more like liberal young painters or budding writers making a little money on the side. My hostess and I were at the organic food store when a young shop assistant said hello to her without looking at me once. The young man went back to making an inventory while she soon got lost in the aisles of cheeses, beers, wines, fruits and vegetables, and nuts and nut butters and flours and various grains.

"Smell this." She held a bulk of cheese to my nose.

"What? I can't smell anything. My nose's stuffed up," I said. "What is it supposed to smell like?"

"Never mind. It's goat cheese. It's my favorite," she said, putting it back into a fridge where hundreds of these milky bricks were stacked.

She started to tell me that there were seven kinds of goat cheeses I had to know. I never could recall any of the exotic names, let alone pronounce them. All I could think of afterward was the absence of Alice, overdue phone calls back to Rachel, and occasionally the hostess' long legs sashaying down an aisle, mincing in front of a rack.

She was a little disappointed with me, having no interest in learning more about organic food. So she went on browsing solitarily, paying close attention to every item she happened to hold in her hand. I felt she was deliberately frittering time, reading details on labels, comparing one thing to another, and even doing miniature research now and again with her smart phone. I much regretted my not having been more amenable, and decided to be absolutely sycophantic when the next opportunity came up. None came. The shopping lasted for an hour, and at length it didn't end voluntarily. It was rather interrupted by an urgent phone call. Then she put everything in two brown paper bags and said, "We have to run; I have to babysit this afternoon at a professor's."

On the way to the professor's she stopped off twice; the first time, in a boutique, where she changed a jar of preserves, which she said she had bought the week before: it wasn't sealed properly. And the second time, she picked up a skein of wool in a Jo-Ann fabrics and craft. There were magazines and pamphlets I didn't notice the night before bulging in the bags in the back seat. She was not only a savant of food but must have been a keen reader on knitting, homeopathy, Chinese herbal medicine, and cupping therapy. She suggested that I go back to the apartment, but the prospect of waiting alone in an apartment where I was only a guest was not attractive. So I had asked if I could come along. She laughed and said that if I was bored I should not at least show that in front of the kid.

"I've never tried cupping before," I said in the car.

"It can suck humidity out of your body," she said.

"Is it expensive in this country?"

"Oh, I can do it," she said with cheerfulness. "You want to try?"

I pictured myself laying down half naked while she was manoeuvring firing cups over my body. "It would make me too comfortable," I said, "I mean, thank you so much but… I mean I really appreciate it, but…"

The baby's mother was a big woman standing impatiently on the porch while her two-year-old daughter was crawling on a yoga mat, pounding a rattle on a glockenspiel and then reaching for a tambourine. The mother was anxious for our arrival. When she saw us, her face lit up.

"Hello, Ming, my lifesaver," the professor called to us. So my hostess's name was Ming.

"Hi," then she said to me, "I am Helena."

"I am Alex." Ming had called her, saying she was bringing me along.

Helena could not wait but apologized and said the baby had a temperature, yet it was fine to leave her awake. She paid Ming and left. Seeing the chance to reciprocate for Ming's hospitality, I took the liberty of starting to hobnob with the little princess.

"How are you?" I said.

She didn't answer, absorbed in a foolish, fruitless affair, legs worming around, kicking away rag dolls and wooden building blocks.

"What's your name?" I asked the kid pointlessly.

"You have kids?" Ming asked.

"No, of course... I mean— No."

"You can talk to her in Chinese; her mom wants her to learn Chinese."

"That's popular now," I said.

I gave up and decided to leave the baby to her business. I found her babysitter in the kitchen making apple cider.

"Interesting kid," I said.

"Do you like kids?" she asked, then whispered, "She's a little devil; her mom is a linguist professor; her father believes China is the future." She was twisting and straining pureed apple through a cloth, extracting the juice which was dribbling into a jar.

"I like children," she resumed in a natural voice, "so much that I'm pessimistic about humanity."

"Well, I can't speak for humanity, but we are doomed if we keep doing things the way we are doing them now." I couldn't believe what I just said. I sounded like a member of Greenpeace.

She had decanted the cider into two cups, closed a cabinet. "Are you sure you don't want to try fire cupping? They have a set here."

"I'm fine," I said, "unless you want to experiment on me."

"Oh, you don't have to feel obliged." She said gravely, possibly offended by the word 'experiment'. I wanted to explain that it was meant to be a joke. But I thought it would only make it worse. So I backed down, did a brief, aimless survey of the kitchen while she was giving the cider some final touches. The kitchen was a full-fledged arsenal of cooking utensils and gears: bowls, platters, a timer, cutting boards, mittens and knives stacked up according to size. A pile of coupons and receipts were clipped together with bills. A digital calculator lay authoritatively on top, displaying a prophetic zero. I strolled back into the living room. Suddenly, I wanted all this to be mine. My wife would soon bring apple cider from our kitchen. And our baby would sit on her lap, and she would swing her long legs, mumbling some endearment that would make a stranger embarrassed because this all belonged to me. The idea seized me only for a fleeting moment, but it was poignant and devastating. For I thought I had been searching for the absolute opposite with my ludicrously pretentious and seemingly unconventional life until then.

I had not seen Alice for 48 hours. After the babysitting, Ming had to head to a Japanese dance theatre show. She had had the Kabuki arranged days before and would have requested an extra ticket if she had known I was coming. "Never mind. Don't give it another thought," I said. So I went back to her apartment by myself.

I was lonely at the apartment with absolutely nothing to do. No new book to read; no laptop to idle with. I boiled a pot of spaghetti and got carried away with the miscellaneous ingredients I found in a kitchen cabinet. After supper, I ferreted out a copy of Madame Bovary in Ming's bedroom, and dozed off on the couch when Emma was about to have her first love affair. Then I was woken up by Alice calling me on the phone. It was ten in the evening (I had adjusted my watch accordingly). She said ecstatically that she'd had an exciting day, and the crew was nice to her, and she had managed to invite me to the shoot the next day. I was exasperated by her incessant and detailed narration, and said congratulations on her new experience, but I was tired. I realized that I didn't really care about Alice as much as I was eager to find out where Ming was, and whom she was with. Neither of them came back to the apartment that night, and their whereabouts remained a mystery to me to the last.

In the morning, having shook off my cold, I felt fresh and high-spirited. I decided to take Alice up on the offer she'd made the night before, hoping that it still held.

I followed the map that I had found in the kitchen and went to a subway station to catch a northbound train. I was one of only a dozen passengers. After five stops, the ghost train coughed me out onto a platform overlooking a row of dilapidated buildings. I walked a block and went into a building that Alice had designated. I climbed a flight of rickety stairs, and then found myself standing on a carpeted landing opening onto a long, dark corridor. The carpet was slimy and worn-out with holes in it. I faintly heard the muffled bustle of people laughing and stomping behind the doors. Then, a head popped out from behind a door in the corridor. The silhouette waved at me and pulled its head back right away. Trying to quell my apprehension, I walked down the corridor; the floor was creaking under my feet, and the air smelt of mildew. I knocked on the door that was left ajar, pushed it open.

The room was a movie set. The crew in shirts and jeans were sitting on fold-up chairs, cross-legged on the floor, or were leaning against walls and windowsills. They were half-heartedly watching a football game on a tiny monitor. All the partition walls had been torn down except a pillar holding up the ceiling in the middle of the room. There were geometrical gaps in the carpet. A mock-up of a bathroom had been built and decorated. An intricate and expensive-looking camera was mounted on a big tripod and was overlooked by stand lights with big heads and bar-doors, training their light bulbs at a shinning, porcelain bathtub. Seeing me coming in, Alice scampered up. "I'm so tired," she said as if she was a shrivelled flower.

"It seems a long time since…" I broke off. "Are you shooting the movie?"

"Yes, we are. We're waiting for twilight. We need diffused light. Now the light is too hard to work with," she explained as if she had become a lighting technician.

Then I saw Ming. She was sitting in a corner singularly, staring unseeingly at the screen. On noticing me, she nodded with a balmy smile.

"Who is Steven?" I asked under my breath, afraid of being intrusive.

"Oh, you haven't met him?" She grabbed my arm and led me to a young man in a baseball cap. He was a thirty-something Caucasian. Doubts and anxieties were hanging around his otherwise funny face where all the features were bunched up in the middle.

He stood up, "Nice to meet you." He shook my hand. He was slightly shorter than me and had a big head. But whatever he lacked in physical attractiveness he compensated for with his close, assertive eyes and manly voice.

"We're waiting for the light," he said.

"Yes, I have learnt from Alice. Sorry for interrupting your work," I apologized.

"We're not working; we're watching a football game; you like football?" he asked.

"Yes, a little," I lied.

"Great, great." Then he sat down and went back into not so much the game as whatever he had been contemplating. A lotus was tattooed in faint relief on the nape of his thick neck. I had been expecting something like an introduction to the crew, but it seemed that it was not a reasonable expectation.

The sun had ducked its ridiculous head behind a grey, derelict building opposite. The sky went from deep-blue-gold to crimson, and streaks and bands of white and dark cloud adorned it. Those who had been sprawling their limbs all over the room and those in chairs with their yearning mouths agape, arms draping down, were now picking themselves up reluctantly.

"We only have an hour," The director announced.

I stepped back and retreated to a corner. Lights on; the temperature immediately rose and put everything except the bathroom setting in darkness. A cameraman pressed his eye on a viewfinder, exchanging words with the director; a hunky soundman was stretching out a long rod attached to a microphone wrapped in a windshield that hung down like a dead cat. A cosmetician was preparing Alice's face so that she would look barely like herself.

"Camera?" the director raised his voice.

"Camera ready."

"Sound?"

"Rolling."

A young woman sneaked onto the set holding a slate. "Scene 49, shot 2, take 1." The slate fell down.

"Action!"

Then Alice walked into the frame, turned her back to the camera, stopped at a washbasin, looking into a mirror hanging above it. She stooped forward, clutched a strand of hair, pulled it back behind her ear and began to take off her clothes.

"Cut!" the director yelled.

Alice pulled back on her blouse and looked at the director in confusion.

"Pick up the pace. It's too slow," he said. Then, without further ado, "Camera?"

"Camera ready."

"Sound?"

"Rolling."

"Scene 49, shot 2, take 2."

"Action!"

Alice walked into the frame, stopped before the mirror, clutched a strand of hair, flung it backward, and started to undress herself.

"Cut!" The director yelled again. He sighed.

Sixteen times.

It took sixteen takes in total for the crew to see Alice, nude, getting into the tub and sliding a curtain closed. As the twilight outside the window was getting dimmer so was the face of the director. Alice became more and more nervous and self-conscious. The young director did everything he could: demanding spontaneity, asking her to concentrate, helping her invent a back story and encouraging her to explore on any slight improvement. But Alice had no talent for acting or, to put it pragmatically, lacked the life experience which she could draw upon. Her compassion for other people's trouble or feelings just could not go beyond basic, infantile emotions.

I could not stand it; it was torture for both Alice and the bystanders. So I asked Ming during a break whether I could go back to the apartment, and she handed me the key.

## 40

I felt relieved as I left the building. Mission completed. Nobody would find any fault with me or cause Alice any trouble. She was after all an adult, and from now on, I thought, I was going to treat her like one. There was only one thing that needed to be done before I fled the city.

I took it into my head to buy Ming a gift. I would have bought her a book if she had expressed any interest in literature and if I had not had a hard time finding a bookstore: a Barnes & Noble drawn on the map had been closed down and a mattress seller was renovating the shop. A book would be uncommonly nerdy, but I was not afraid of being reduced to a cultural stereotype. I don't have a knack for picking presents. But it didn't matter. Who would despise a music CD with a card, preferably recyclable, to go with it? I had heard her humming a song in the food store, and I happened to know that it was U2.

I had my gift prepared, wrote tautologically on a thank-you card: "To: Ming. Thank you for your warm hospitality. Good Luck with your film and studies. — Alex." I bought a plane ticket without even telling Alice about it. The plane would take off around the middle of the night, and I would arrive in Illinois the next morning, no matter what shenanigans Alice would come up with this time, I decided.

I waited at the apartment until nine o'clock. Nobody showed up or called. "Fine, then I'll call." Alice didn't answer, so I left her a message. Then I called our hostess.

"Hello," I said. All I heard was music booming and people carousing in the background.

"I can't hear you. Wait." She took the phone for a ride and found a quieter place. "Hello."

"I am sorry to interrupt, but I'm going to leave. I am wondering how I can give the key back to you."

"Oh, you're leaving?" she sounded confused.

"Yes, could you tell me where you are? I'd like to give you the key back."

She paused, and then she gave me an address and suggested a bus route.

"Never mind, I have to take a taxi anyway," I said. Now the gift CD seemed gratuitous.

It didn't take me long to find the pub. I told the taxi to wait, and I went into the busy place. After searching around, I found Ming sitting beside a pool table, a tumbler half filled with gin in her hand.

"Can I talk to you for a minute?" I walked up to her.

She looked surprised but followed me outside.

"You said you're leaving?" She asked in the halo of a street light, leaning on a railing.

"Yes, I am leaving. But I have something for you. Thank you for putting us up." I handed her the CD.

"Oh, you don't have to do this." She was not only surprised but unnerved.

"It's just a CD. I heard you singing one of the songs, so I figured you might like it."

"Really? Oh, then thank you. How much is it? I mean— thank you so much. You really don't have to do this," she said.

"You're welcome," I said. "Now I have a plane to catch."

"Does Alice know you're leaving?" she said.

"I left her a message." I added, "We're just friends. And I figured she could take care of herself."

She was about to say something, but I cut in.

"OK, now I have to run."

"Wait," she said, "are you sure? Wait. What's your name again?"

"I go by Alex. I am sorry I haven't…"

"I'm Mingming."

"I know." I sensed she was trying to prolong the conversation so as to work out what the situation was.

Then she gave up. She leaned back on the railing, giving the CD to the more dexterous hand, waiting for my next move.

I felt like initiating a hug or at least a handshake as we stood on the sidewalk looking at each other. I chickened out. Shrugging my shoulders, I walked hesitantly back to the taxi. She turned and waved to me with the CD in her hand. I knew that this might have been the last time we would ever see each other, and I wished she had tried harder to get me to stay. Then it all made sense: the wolfing down her meal in the kitchen; wistfully keeping her company; tracking her down instead of Alice; the CD. This was love at the first sight. A younger, more romantic and passionate version of me, if we were in China, would surely have sent her a flirty message with an inquiry about whether she liked me, too. But I was neither an optimistic flirt nor romantically passionate anymore. And this was not China. I would assume she was also entangled with something or a handful someones, and did not have the time or inclination to explore an affair. And in this digital era, farewells had lost the powerful, dramatic effect that prompted lovers to confess, kiss, with men holding women tight, or women crashing into men's chests like in the old movies. We no longer believe in passionate love or a final farewell, maybe because we're all permanently connected by Internet. We, together with our love, had become insipid, and in this insipidity, we were all superficially united.

41

In the age of Romanticism, it is easy to give special credit to eccentrics or even to a sheer sociopath, for individuality has never been so vaunted. I have been writing as if the community of overseas students is made up of Alice, Rachel, Ming, Priscilla and their like. This could not be farther from the truth. The main constituents are of a different nature.

Illinois. Nothing seemed to have changed since I left, and nobody seemed to have noticed my leaving. Nobody but for a Chinese Ph.D. in the biology department. The man was one year younger than me. Both of his parents had been elementary school teachers in a small town of China and were retired. The last time I saw him, he invited me over for a baby shower. Several people were there taking care of the child and the frail, post-pregnancy mother. Old folks believed women should have babies before turning thirty. So he got married when he was twenty-eight, his wife twenty-six. I had not seen him for two years, so I assumed that he had had a two-year-old daughter and probably another child as this was the standard practice in the community.

He emailed me to ask if I had time for a little gathering. "Nothing in particular, just a little chat," he wrote. It was a little strange because we were not even friends, though we had known each other for years. We'd been assigned to the same group for a campus orientation. I remembered that he was very capable and eager to make friends, but soon he had figured out which lot he belonged to and had been sticking to it.

The email had been in my inbox for several days. I just had to apologize and explain why I was unable to make it. To my surprise, when I replied he insisted on the invitation. Perhaps seeing him and talking to him would help me to retrieve the bearings I had lost somewhere since mingling with Alice and her like, fantastic people, people out of my own league. So I decided to meet him.

He replied to my letter with a sense of renewed immediacy and said he wanted to invite me over for a dinner at his place as soon as I was available.

"Tonight?" I replied.

"I can give you a ride if you need," he wrote back earnestly.

Then, I realized it was for more than just a little chat.

I turned up at his door with a six-pack of beers clutched in my hand.

"Come in." He grabbed my shoulder. "You don't need to bring anything to my place; my fridge is full of beers and leftovers from a party last week. Is this the first time you're coming to my place?"

"No, I was here for the baby shower," I said.

"Oh, right. You should come more often. But you're busy, aren't you?" He led me into his living room.

We sat down on a couch set behind a coffee table cluttered with coasters, clammy mugs, various remote controls, and video game consoles. We faced a big plasma TV screen connected to a laptop computer, an X-box, and other boxes I could not identify, green and orange signal lights flickering incessantly.

"Where is your daughter? I've never seen her since..." A quaint mahogany baby cradle stood next to the gaming center with an ultra-modern trolley parked beside it.

"She and her younger brother, her mother and my wife's parents are on a trip in Las Vegas. Have you ever been to Las Vegas?"

"No, I haven't been anywhere near the West Coast," I said.

"Really?" he exclaimed, "how long have you been in America?"

"Seven years. Just like you."

"Did your parents ever come to visit you?"

"No."

"How many times have you gone back?"

"Once"

"Oh, my God!" he called out and looked at me as if I were a terrorist. Then he opened a bottle of beer for me and one for himself. He sipped and smacked his lips loudly, "You're the kind of person I look up to," he said, "and I want to ask you a favor."

I put down the beer bottle. "What can I do?"

"You know, I have a hobby on the side." He leaned forward, installed his elbows on his knees as if he was about to confide in me. "I write things."

"Oh, that's great." And I asked, "What do you write?"

"I write all sorts of stuff, short stories mainly. But I just finished a novel, and I want you to read it."

"A novel? Wow, that's something. What's it about?"

"Of course, you don't have to read it unless you are interested. That's why I want you to take a look at it and decide whether you want to take it home to read." He stood up, and then he sat down again.

"I'm glad to and thank you for giving me the honor," I said.

Then he stood up again as if he was mentally challenged. "Oh, you don't have to say things like that between us. I think you have good taste and fine breeding, unlike other ordinary Chinese. I mean, what's your opinion on overseas Chinese?"

"I know very few of them; too few to pass judgment."

"Overseas Chinese are the worst. That's my opinion," He said angrily, suddenly evoking a nation, a continent and the entire immigration history. And he strode into one of the bedrooms and came back with a mound of print paper.

"See if you are hooked by the first five pages. If not, you don't have to read it; it must not be good enough."

"OK, I'll be completely honest with you," I said, taking the novel, written in Chinese. I started to read.

The story started with a description of his hometown and childhood. His father was the breadwinner, but the boy despised the father and was brought up by his grandma. This caregiver died when he was sixteen, and there was a long paragraph about his memories of the older woman. She used to own a small grocery shop. When the communists took power in 1949 and no private owned business was allowed any longer, she lost her property. However, since she was by no means better off than anyone else and was utterly illiterate, she had not gotten into too much trouble except for a few perfunctory meetings in which there were fists raised and slogans chanted. Then she was believed to be completely transformed into a communist shopkeeper in her own shop. She and her grandson spent a lot of time together when he was a klutzy toddler and, later on, a model school boy. I laughed when he wrote that times out of count, he was pissed off by her illiteracy and her barbarian way of babysitting and, in return, he brooded over various possible measures to assassinate her.

Since high school, he stopped paying his respects to his working class father all together. The boy became a refractory snob. Believing that civilization and modernity dwelled far beyond his hometown, he hung his hopes on going to the most prestigious college in China. He made it and won various first-place awards and scholarships. Puppy love was not acceptable because it was a bona-fide distraction from becoming established. When he met his wife, he was still a 'man virgin'. I burst out laughing as I read the word.

"What?" he was very content with my joyful reaction.

"It's funny," I said.

"Where? What is it?" he asked gaily.

"Nothing, it reminds me of something else," I said.

"Oh, continue, continue," he prompted.

"Is it an autobiography?" I asked.

He paused and said thoughtfully, "No, it's a fiction."

And I thought it was, too, because if it wasn't, he would have been a dishonest autobiographer. Despite the early memories, the character bore little resemblance to the author. He wrote that in the boy's heart he was a rebel. He never liked those who were supposed to be in his own league. All his real friends were juvenile delinquents. Despite his perfect scores, he never studied hard, but was into playing billiards at some seedy joints run by alleged underground big brothers. He had his way of lighting cigarettes, passing them around, inhaling and then puffing out smoke rings while laughing and swearing pointlessly. He was also a frequent visitor of seedy video sheds where action movies from Hong Kong and porn from all over the world were screened day and night. Once in a while, there was some real excitement, a fight between two boys or a scrum between two gangs. Blood would be shed, usury debt would be redeemed, and, in some cases, the police would be called up. I thought he had experienced none of these things. There he'd mixed reality with Hong Kong action movies to give himself a little edge. But for most of the time, he concluded, the same pathetic uncle was watching over his business absentmindedly and scratching his newly purchased lottery card. The same dim light, the same hopelessness and boredom accompanied his teenage life until he went away to college in Beijing.

I could relate to parts of his story. Aspiring kids became sorts of actors and actresses. He wrote that nothing could erase an atrocious scene in his memory: a bunch of children clamoring for attention, love, in a bone-fide vanity fair, getting reassurance from the school authorities and their peers with no choice but to get up early, shout the rights answers in class, obstinately cheat on tests and appear more and more like little politicians. The most grotesque behavior got the best reward. And there always seemed to be some other kid understanding the tricks better and earlier, willing to bend a little further, more sycophantic, more shameless, and subtler.

I said, "I'm absolutely hooked."

"Really?" a complacent grin appeared at the corner of his mouth.

"It's great. Why don't you become a novelist?"

"Oh, you know," he said, "that would be a little unrealistic. You see, I have a family to support, and a Chinese writer living in America doesn't stand a chance."

"That's probably true. Although you could write in English."

"Write in English?" he exclaimed. "That would be one hell of a competition in and of itself, since I'm Chinese."

"You don't have to see it as a competition," I said.

"Oh, everything in this country is a competition. Even shopping is a competition in this country. Speaking of shopping, my wife is totally addicted. She said she couldn't read after giving birth to Molly, so she discovered this new hobby. First I thought it was just for the baby. Then it went out of control. Do you want to see what she's been hoarding?"

"I can imagine," I said and let the subject of being a novelist blow over. "But you can't blame her; there's the whole advertising industry."

"I thought it was her hormones, then..." He changed from psychoanalysis to medical diagnosis.

"I'd like to take your novel home," I said.

"Sure, take your time. Let's hang out sometime. You and I should hang out more often. One last thing, although this is all fictional, don't let anybody read it. That's why I'm giving this hard copy to you and nobody else," he said gravely.

## 42

In our era, even if you die, your life doesn't automatically stop. For example, you still receive emails, the funds in your bank account still earn or lose interest, and your various virtual accounts still act as a squad of miniature receptionists, collecting date, teasing out the paramount from the insignificant, sending alerts after the headquarter has been permanently shut down.

I finally found the courage to log into my Facebook page, thinking what if it's teeming with responsibilities, and what if my life really was so empty that nobody needed me except Alice. In the latter case, was it me who actually needed her? My Facebook was a shame. It was inundated with pictures of ferociously happy people, jumping around strangling each other, and comments meaning nothing except how awesome, how amazing, and how incredible this sightseeing trip had been, exceeding all previous ones in terms of enjoyment and happiness. In two weeks, I only had one friend request. It was disappointingly from the autobiographer. He also seemed to be a very happy person. There were hundreds of pictures of his babies, him and his wife tightly embracing each other as if they were in an invisible lifeboat. How could such a sunshiny person have so much anxiety and frustration that he eventually had to resort to writing a jeremiad novel to prove that he was still alive?

By the way, I hadn't turned another page since I brought his manuscript home. Perhaps no one likes to hear another's complaint. We are modern warriors who prefer to celebrate our victories together and die individually. Or everyone thinks their own story is more interesting and more worthwhile because they are not only the storytellers but also the protagonists.

Only in one's own head, as a character instead of as an author, can one experience the precious and delicious details of a story and the emotion and the meaning it evokes. Adult life has the power of boredom and embarrassment, but it is going to be forgotten and disappear forever very soon. The uneasy and ticklish feelings will invariably find their vent in writing that no one except the author cares to read. That's the reason why the survivors of a massacre, the victims of the Chinese tragedies, and bitter, old folks keep telling their stories until everyone begrudges lending an ear. Let's be brave, let's be happy. Joy and happiness has become a burden, an obligatory performance, and a default setting everyone is supposed to tune into. Once again, I deactivated my Facebook to finish what I had ill started.

Sorting through my emails, I found that Rachel, my boss, had sent me one two days before.

> *Dear Alex,*
>
> *I am sorry for my abrupt manner the other day. I was stressed out by all the hustle that's been going on lately with the newspaper. I hope you can understand and forgive me. We had an intern student when you were on vacation. He has been very dedicated and helpful but needs some training and advice from you. I hope you can come back soon. The newspaper needs you.*
>
> *Sincerely,*
> *Rachel*

I knew this probably was the humblest position Rachel could ever descend to. But it was not her condescension disguised as humbleness that made me forgive and reconcile with her. It was 'the newspaper needs you' that had all the persuasive power. Having passed the period of romantic, juvenile egotism one just wanted to be needed, wanted, asked for one's opinion. I didn't have a child. I remembered some famous writer once said that one of the best things he could imagine in this world was being a wanted criminal. I needed to be wanted.

So I met her at the new editorial desk. If there had been a setback, it was all over. She had revamped the cubicle; now it could accommodate three staff members. It had three desktop computers, a coffee machine, and all the files from the office. "Get to work. Chop-chop," she smiled, seating me in a chair.

I never stopped dreading that Alice would make a mess and have no one to call except me. Then, she called me up just like that. She was mumbling some drunken words on the telephone. I asked where she was, and hoped Ming was with her. Then, I figured out that she was not in Buffalo at all and had gone back to the hotel in Boston, and had been staying there for a week.

"What are you doing there?" I asked her on my phone.

"I'm OK. I am..." She switched between English and Chinese.

"Why don't you come back?" I asked.

The voice broke up, and then we were disconnected. For the first time, I wanted to call her parents and ask them to bring her back home. But I dispelled the idea immediately. "She's a grown-up; she's a thirty-year-old doctoral student; she has resources that ninety-nine percent of the world doesn't have!"

I knew she would not be coming back herself. Meanwhile, it was very dangerous for her to stay out there alone, and every minute I denied that fact, she could be getting killed or raped or kidnapped, and the police could soon track me down, and I would be looking at an interrogation...

After all my attempts, I managed to get through to her another two times, trying to persuade and then trick her into coming back. Having failed repeatedly, I bought a ticket in a rage, took the train to the airport, and boarded the first plane from Chicago to Boston. The flight was badly delayed due to a thunderstorm. When I arrived in Boston it was nine o'clock in the evening again. I stormed into the hotel. I must have attracted a lot of attention on the way and along the corridor, but I didn't care. I dashed up to the room, thumping and yelling at the door.

To my dismay, no one answered the door, and I got angrier as I called and listened to her cheerful voicemail message saying "Hi. This is Alice, I am not available now. Please leave a message."

I paced the corridor anxiously, tired and helpless. Suddenly the door to the room opened. Almost at the same time Alice popped out of an elevator and walked down the corridor in my direction. I didn't fly at her because of momentary confusion.

I simply said, "What are you doing, Alice?"

She opened to me like a flower and ran into my chest. "You came! I knew you would, I knew you wouldn't leave me alone."

I smelt alcohol and a strange odor in her hair, "Is that your room?" I pointed to the door left ajar.

"Yes. It's our room," she said.

"Who is in there?" I was alarmed.

"Oh, Jessie! I almost forgot. Jessie was sleeping in there," she said and, as uncoordinated as a toddler, stamped her foot.

"Who is Jessie?" I was confused.

"Jessie?" she looked at me as if I'd asked something stupid. "Jessie is unemployed and has no place to sleep."

"What do you mean he has no place to sleep?!"

"Yes, he lives in the streets. He's a tramp," she said. "He was sleeping on a street corner when I was walking back last night. I thought since the room has two beds, I could do him a favor. It was his lucky day."

It occurred to me that whoever was in the room must have been listening to our conversation.

"A tramp?" I muttered, "You let a tramp sleep in your room? Where is your stuff?"

"He must go because you've come," she exclaimed.

Suddenly the door swung open; a grubby young man emerged from behind the door drawing a soiled duffel bag on the floor.

"Hi, Jessie." Alice grabbed my arm, hiding half of herself behind me. "This is Alex," she said.

"Hi." the young tramp muttered and looked at me without expression.

"Hi…"

The young tramp went on walking toward the elevator. My first instinct was to seize him and hold him up until Alice was sure he had not taken anything that was not his, but of course I didn't and thought it was lucky enough that Alice was still in one piece. I turned to Alice, "What are you doing here?"

"Oh, it's a long story, it's a long story, and I don't want to talk about it."

"You'd better tell me," I said paternally, "I was this close to losing it." I gesticulated like a mad monkey, a fool. She had turned me into the very authoritarian figure I hated.

We entered the room together as she still refused to let go of my arm. The room was an absolute mess and smelt as if something was decaying.

## 43

We were back in the same hotel; Alice was drunk. This was the pattern of her life. She was trying to break away from it, but her wings were too weak and her will too fragile. I chastised her for bringing a stranger, not to mention a tramp, in. This time she didn't argue with me. Then I asked what had happened in Buffalo and about her acting career. She didn't answer me. And after a moment of silence, she started to bash her brother and her father and finally her mother for letting these two men always have their way in the family. "These capitalist scum and their slave women," she snorted.

I asked her what this had to do with the escapade, and she could not come up with a word in answer.

I asked, almost demanded, that she go back with me immediately. But she insisted she neither wanted to go back to the university nor stay in Boston any longer, and said wilfully, "I want to go elsewhere."

"Oh, you are definitely not going anywhere else," I said. "You and I are going back to Illinois right now."

She refused to give in, and said if I had to go back, I could just leave her there alone. I could not reason with her any longer. I thought I had no choice but to inveigle her into believing I was in love with her so that she could have something to hold on to and, just for once, do as she was told.

"Alice, you know what? I love you, but you keep breaking my heart," I said, and a dangerous and chilly feeling came over me. But I braced myself for whatever would come out of this Pandora's box.

"Really?" she stared at me in a state of stupefaction. "You love me?" she asked weakly.

I wanted to retract what I had just said; I should have confessed, *No, I don't love you. You are drunk, you are spoiled, you are selfish. Nobody will love you or care about you except for those who want to take advantage of you.*

"Yes, I do," I said.

Her lachrymose routine — I cold-heartedly saw it as a daily routine now — flared up. She lunged into me and kissed me and, as she was clumsy, bit me on the lips. I was hurt and disgusted, and got hold of her head on the temples. She still looked very pretty and innocent, and now believed what I had said. *It was a white lie*, I said to myself, *and it was good for her*, I thought, saying goodbye to all the feminist theories, the critical thinking classes, and whatever I promised myself, when I came to this country, about being a liberal, honest and suave gentleman.

"I was lost," she said, full of tears, "I was confused; I have been wasting time with those I don't care about."

"What happened in Buffalo?" I seized this opportunity.

"Steven lied to me. He's married," she said, "but it doesn't matter, it doesn't matter now."

"What about the film? You weren't there just for a married man, were you?"

"The film?" she sighed, "I don't know, and I don't care any more. Maybe I'm not cut out to be an actress. I was so tired out. And I was so pissed off. I was in his car, and he told me he had a wife. I asked him to stop the car. I said 'stop it!' He was so rude that he kept driving on. Then I opened the door."

"You what?!"

"I opened the car door."

I could not believe what I heard and doubted whether it was even possible.

"Where were you?"

"We were on a highway. He was so rude; he wanted to hold me against my will."

I stared at her, "Against your will? You wanted to jump out of a moving car?"

"I told him to stop the car!" she yelled.

"But it was on a highway, wasn't it?"

She could not answer. She said, "You think I was wrong?"

"I think holding you against your will is one thing. Keeping you from committing suicide is another, isn't it?" I asked her.

"Maybe you're right." She seemed to be contemplating something for an instant, and then regained her cheerfulness, "You will take care of me, won't you?"

"I will if you listen," I said, "Let's go home tomorrow."

She pulled herself up, looked at me waywardly, "No, I don't want to. There is nothing for me there. I have nothing to do... Please, anything but going back."

"Then where do you want to go? You can't stay in a hotel forever."

"Let's go to Prague!" she said.

"Where?"

"Prague! Let's go to the Czech Republic. I know there's a film festival coming up."

"We are not going to the Czech Republic. We're going home!"

"Why? Last time I was there, I felt so proud of myself, and I figured out what I wanted to study in grad school."

"But you lost it."

"Yes, that's why I need to go back. I may find what I want to do next. Let's go."

She was holding my hands with both of her hands, pleading.

"I will not let you go to the Czech Republic. I can't believe I'm even having this conversation. I am... I'm your mentor, and you have to defer to what I say from now on."

"What are you?" she laughed.

"I know it sounds ridiculous. But I am your mentor," I said gravely, "From now on, I'm responsible for knocking you back to reality when you are having a reverie."

"Oh," she sprang up, letting go of my hands, "I have a mentor! Nice to meet you, my mentor. But I have a question, mentor; according to Lacan, it's really hard to tell the difference between reality and reverie. One man's reverie is another one's reality."

"I don't want to listen to this bullshit."

"Wow, you sound like an authoritarian mentor."

"I thought you liked men with big shoulders." I did sound like a big idiot.

"I can't remember whether I told you, but I trust you." She smiled, jumped up on the bed, crawled and sat down cross-legged at the other end like a pearl resting in a clam.

We had dinner in the hotel café. It was her first meal in many days. When we went back up to the hotel room, she became very sick. She knelt down on the tiled floor in the bathroom, hugging the toilet bowl, retching. Then she came down with a fever. Several times, I felt I had to call an ambulance, but she stopped me and said she would recover soon, and she wanted to smoke and asked whether I could fetch her a bottle of wine. We had a quarrel about her request until she said she felt very cold. I pulled a thick down blanket out of the closet and covered her with it. Then, she said she still felt cold and was suffocating and asked me to hold her. I held her from behind her back. She was shivering and hot from head to toe and could not keep from sobbing. At last she was exhausted and fell asleep or just passed out. I didn't know.

She slept through the night and half of the following day, and I watched over her closely. This was America; going to the hospital was not an easy task to carry off; one could easily run into a big bill by using medical services without knowing the ropes.

Nine o'clock in the evening. Alice woke up again sweating.

"Sweating is good; it means you are getting better," I said to her, mainly for my own consolation. As I said it, her nose started bleeding. Blood was dripping down on the white carpet and got smudged everywhere as she was wiping her nose with her fingers. She ran into the bathroom; I followed her and had completely no idea what to do or say or think.

"Let's go to the hospital," I said.

She was coughing as she was splashing water on her face. More blood was coming out of her nostrils. But she was unexpectedly calm and handled it with practiced ease. She pinched her nose together between the thumb and the index finger, pressed it to her face, stooping with head tilting forward until the bleeding stopped. Then she sat down on the toilet cover quietly, keeping her head high and straight.

"Could you bring me some ice cubes from the fridge please?" she said with nose plugged-up.

I did it.

"Wrap them in a towel," she instructed.

I followed her instructions. She took the towel and pressed it on her nose and cheeks.

"Are you alright?" I asked.

"Not the best moment of my life," she said, wearing a survivor's smile.

Later in the evening, we got into another fight over whether I should inform her family of her whereabouts. Since Alice stubbornly refused to pick up their phone calls, I had been the messenger, informing her family about where she was and how she had been. She warned me not to do it anymore and insisted that her whereabouts was strictly private. She told me that she and her family were not on speaking terms, whereas I argued that this was due to her monstrous behavior toward them.

"Either you go back to Illinois, go to the hospital, or your mom will come and take you home," I said.

"They have no right to do that," she yelled.

"Then be responsible for yourself! You're a student; you should stay at your university, not a hotel."

"But I don't want to study what I am studying anymore."

"Change your major or get a job," I said.

"But doesn't Alice have to find her calling in life first?" She talked in the third person as if she was out of her body.

"You think you can find your calling in a five-star hotel?"

"Alice told you she wants to go to Prague. Alice has to live. She can't find her calling in life by avoiding life!" she said as if she was a mad woman. Her face was pale, and for every breath and word, she had to make an extra effort. She was a person on the verge of collapse.

"Let's talk about this later," I said. I let her lie down, and covered her with a new blanket.

## 44

Alice was right about one thing: one can't find one's calling by avoiding life. But what she failed to understand was that she was living in a world where most of us had not had the resources to explore our potential. In the real world, human labor was being hijacked to generate capital and buy commodities that we mostly didn't need, yet still desired, while succumbing to political power to keep the status quo. And if one asked what is the meaning of life for the new, rich Chinese whose grandpa died from the Great Famine, one would very likely hear: money, luxury, morally or immorally earned money and luxury.

And if one doesn't have freedom in the first place, one could be genuinely interested in chains and torture. One's calling, though having an individualistic appearance, is essentially social: we live in a world where most of us don't have a calling, and so fail to see the value of it, so what exactly can one use as a reference to confirm whether one has a calling, and how does one know that such a thing actually exists? We, Chinese people, are pragmatic atheists, but at the same time deeply mystical and superstitious. We don't believe for a minute in things that don't work in reality in the short term. But we are very willing to believe what we don't understand, and the more we don't understand it, the more we give it mystical credit. Therefore, one's calling is either practically inconvenient, or transcendentally worthless.

Alice claimed that her problem was a loss of interest. Gone were the days when she could earn freedom, an allowance, and praise from her parents by working hard at school and winning first place in a contest. Despite the degree she had been pursuing for six years, she now had almost nothing to be proud of, to prove that she was not wasting her precious youth cooped up in a small town where winter was brutally severe and summer was unbearably torrid. The library had millions of books. One could find any subject or author one was interested in, but none of these mattered to her anymore. Her brother had become a vice-president of a transnational corporation. Yes, it was her father's company, but his career was nonetheless impressive. He was a successful businessman, a responsible husband and the father of a cherubic daughter. Alice had even begun to miss those days when they could squabble over trivia all the time and hate each other's guts, when they were equals except that she was a dominant sister simply because she was one year older than he was. Gone were those days. The last time she went back, her brother asked her about her studies like a father asking about the daughter's homework, implying that she was squandering the wealth of the family. And when she was about to fly at him, he just walked away saying he had a meeting to catch. Meanwhile, she had to explain to her mother why she needed an extra four hundred dollars to make ends meet because her laptop was broken, because her landlord unreasonably delayed giving back her deposit, and because her scholarship was reduced to twenty-five percent without including a fee for using the gym. Plus, she had not seen her advisor, her supervisor, and none of her dissertation committee members for God knows how many months. The longer she procrastinated, the more frightful it was for her to think about it.

I made a mistake; I said I loved her. And then another one: I called up her family in the hotel. I thought they were the only ones who cared about her in this world. Her brother answered the phone and asked whether I could bring her back to Illinois. If not, they were able to send someone over. I said I would try, and told Alice what had been settled between me and her family. Hearing it, she stared at me with her mouth agape as if she was squalling without sound coming out of it. I had never seen a person so filled with anguish and despair. She had lost her pride, and now her hope and simple dignity. She lowered her eyes, sat beside a window for an hour like an old, dying folk woman waiting for the devil to take her away. Then, she stood up, fell to packing her luggage wilfully, and when I offered my help she accepted it without saying anything.

We didn't say a word to each other on the way back, not at the bus station, not at the airport, except for a few occasional remarks like, 'thank you', 'sorry', and 'never mind'. Back in Illinois, we had to wait for three hours for the next bus setting off from Chicago to the university. I bought us two cups of coffee, two hot dogs and a pack of gum. She took a bite of her hot dog and then set it aside, leaving her drink untouched.

"Americans are very interesting," she said after the long silence.

"What is it?" I prompted her.

"I bet that all the people in this station were told when they were young that they were excellent and bound to be successful."

"I'm sure."

"And then they're put down by reality, and every one of those people who told them those lies has disappeared."

"What should they do? Tell a kid she is a piece of crap in the first place?" I asked.

"Yes, they should. Tell her the truth."

Then she resumed her silence.

There wasn't any drama afterwards except for a bit that I later attributed to my paranoia. It was ten minutes before the bus was going to leave. Alice went to the bathroom and didn't come out. Passengers lined up, streaming into the bus, filling all the racks with their suitcases, adjusting seat belts, earphones, and closing their eyes.

"Are you coming on?" the woman driver asked me with one leg on the ground and the other scuffing the ramp.

"Oh, yes, my friend went to the bathroom. I'm waiting for her."

"OK, five minutes." She scrambled onto the driver's seat, chewing gum, ticking off something on a list on a clipboard.

I went asking a student in a sorority blouse coming out of the bathroom if she saw a young Asian woman wearing a purple T-shirt in there. She said she had not, and then went back in to check, and ten seconds later, walked out, pouting her lips, shrugging her shoulders, asking for further clues.

"Never mind, never mind, thank you so much," I said.

The driver craned her neck, looking over the platform at me quizzically. And just at the point where I would have had to abandon our travel plans and come up with a new one that would likely involve a police investigation, private detectives and other sorts of craziness, Alice turned up. She was walking across the concourse like a fazed little bird searching its way back to a nest. She came up to me, "Is the bus coming?"

I grabbed her elbow, "It's leaving. They are waiting for us. Come on." She almost tripped as I dragged her along.

I didn't ask where she had been and why it took so long; I didn't care. But as soon as we sat down I couldn't help glaring at her contemptuously.

"What's the matter?" she asked.

I turned my head away from her pale face. A dull stretch of corn field spread outside the window from the shoulder of the highway to the horizon.

Part Five

## 45

We got back to her dingy apartment; I was to call her parents once again and finish this dreary mission. But first, she asked whether I could do her one last favor and help her to sort out some of her books. "Books? Why?" I agreed, and she started taking paperbacks and hardcovers down from a bookshelf: *The Marx-Engels Reader, Culture and Society 1780 – 1950, The Poverty of Theory and Other Essays, Orientalism, Prison Notebook, Critical Dialogues in Cultural Studies, The Sublime Object of Ideology, Four Fundamental Concepts of Psychoanalysis, Amerika* by Franz Kafka. All went into plastic garbage bags, and then got dumped in a dumpster downstairs outside the gate.

"You can sell them," I said pointlessly, looking at the soiled book covers.

"Who's gonna buy these useless, useless books," she said emphatically.

I leaned on the two-arrow-clash button as the elevator door was closing, as if this would expedite my leaving. But as soon as the elevator started to lurch, I had another qualm. I wondered whether I had been acting the cold blooded prig that her brother was said to be. I was the only child in my family, so I'd had no devious siblings to compete with. And I was a man, though an Asian man, but still a man, so culture and society would grant me partial immunity, sparing me the plethora of self-weakening ideas, self-contradictory values, and self-demeaning aesthetics that shape women into a powerless, inferior-feeling species obliged to be nothing beyond having beautiful appearance. As Rachel once said, "Living in a Chinese woman's body is like living with a disease."

Deep down, I had no rancor against Alice, just sympathy and frustration. I, like most people, simply became more cynical. We felt lucky for ourselves each time we saw an innocent fellow getting drowned in treacherous adulthood. And in this foreign country in particular, as an international student or immigrant, the moment you wanted to do something for others, you would infallibly find that you had already had enough trouble yourself.

I went back to my apartment, took a shower, cooked a skimpy supper, and drew a chair up in front of my laptop. I had one hundred and forty mid-term essays to grade for an undergraduate class. I was one of the two graders who had fallen behind schedule. And I knew I would quickly work up a migraine by reading bad essays. There were also emails from the writer asking me whether I was ready to discuss his novel, a journal article I was supposed to review for the department, and a grant application deadline, which would leave me penniless for the following semester if I failed to meet it. We academics were entangled, over the years, in the menial tasks of polishing the nuts and bolts of the academic machinery, so the paper-generating monster could run all the more efficiently to snare more of my kind, consume our labor and pay less for it. No one liked it. The only difference between me and Alice was that I saw it as a duty enshrouded in work ethics, and she saw the naked truth. But seeing the truth and reacting to it directly is hysteria par excellence.

Finally, I decided to put off everything until the next day, except an email from Priscilla. It was strange; she rarely emailed me.

> Hi, Alex
> What's up? I heard you have been in Boston. By the way, I am getting married. Can you make it to my wedding? This is not the official invitation, though. Ha, ha.
> Sincerely,
> Priscilla

The 'ha, ha' seemed affected, full of suspension as if uttered by a person who had been frightened rather than cheered. "She's getting married? Who is she marrying?" Something told me that the person was not Pim. And it felt like a quick solution to some prolonged problem as instant love is often convenient when things get seemingly incorrigibly bad.

I tried to brush it aside; it was none of my business. But my thoughts kept going back and forth from Alice to Priscilla! What were they doing?

Later in the evening, I made an excuse for myself. I thought the last type of person I wanted to be was a self-appointed agent who would pacify women whom the society thought of as rebellions. They were besieged by these pacifiers, so when they tried to break out, and acted the way Alice had been doing. It was understandable. Plus, Alice still had a fever, and everything in her fridge, from my last inspection, had gone bad and was giving out a noxious smell. She could be food poisoned.

Now that I had completely forgiven her, I thought that the right thing to do was to bring her some necessities. *No other work can be done at the moment,* I thought. So I turned off my laptop, shut the door behind me, and struck out down a windy street.

I did Alice's grocery shopping and deliberately avoided everything in the fast food aisles. I bought her toilet paper, fruits, rice and noodles, honey, milk, black chocolate, and arbitrarily added a pack of ground coffee as I assumed I would be visiting her often.

I stood at the door of Alice's apartment. She didn't answer until I tried the third time and yelled out her name. Then she opened it, still wearing the purple T-shirt, barefoot, face smeared with dirt.

"Is everything OK?" I asked.

"Oh, I am fine," she said, blinking her eyes incessantly, holding the door half opened, blocking my way to her room as if I were a salesman.

"I bought you some food and toilet paper," I said. "Are you hungry?"

"Oh, thank you, you don't have to do this." She was fumbling for words, "I owe you a lot of money, I will square up with you. Tomorrow! I will pay you back tomorrow."

Then it occurred to me that she was not alone in the room. I heard an impatient sigh in the apartment. I handed the shopping bags to her.

"I didn't know you had company," I said, "Then I'll see you later. But don't worry about the money."

"See you," she said as if she was not the person I had just brought back from Boston, as if she had lost her memory.

I guessed the person in the room was Vic. I had been seeing a lot of women act like demoralized puppets even in the presence of a male donkey. I wished I could have caught a glimpse of this lofty Vic. What an irresponsible, ridiculous jerk that guy was!

*I won't blame her,* I thought, riding the elevator down. *She's sick and lonely; you can't blame a sick and lonely woman for seeking company.* But I knew I hated her guts.

I walked past the dumpster, and blushed to think of throwing the books away. So I decided to rescue at least some of them to redeem my conscience. I stepped up on a ledge, stooped to look inside. To my surprise none of them were left except for one book named *About Alice*, by Calvin Trillin. Someone had salvaged those critical thinkers, taken them away, and now they must have been placed on another edgy bookshelf, carrying on the enlightenment mission.

I took the last book out, dusted it down, and walked away.

46

I missed Priscilla's wedding ceremony. She gave me the address of the church, and I went to one of its namesakes on the other side of the town. I sat in a pew until the time passed. No one came, and I thought it was a prank after all. "Is there a wedding here?"

"No, not as far as I know." A priest in robes told me amiably. I called her; she didn't answer. While I was waiting, she and her mysterious fiancé were exchanging vows at an altar, placing wedding rings, being declared man and wife, having themselves showered with rice and confetti. When I came around and made for the wedding reception held in the student union lounge, she was not Priscilla any more.

I caught up with the reception. I grabbed a glass of lemon water from the table outside the room. There, on the table, was a clutter of gift boxes wrapped in glossy, colorful cellophane and wrapping papers.

I sneaked in. The room was filled with mostly white folks and a few Asian people, polite and well mannered to a fault. However, they all seemed to have an opinion on the event, for when the Chinese music subsided on a small, temporary stage, they applauded as if they were attending an auction instead of a wedding reception, afraid of making themselves too distinct. There was no one in charge. A five-storey wedding cake was situated on a round table in the front. I saw her in a white gown, all made-up and in high heels. She was chatting with a Chinese couple. And as soon as she caught sight of me, she walked in my direction with a smile skewed by the make-up and a slightly uncoordinated gait.

"I never received your invitation card," I said.

"Really?!" She scowled. "Oh, it's a big mess," she said, bright confetti sparkled in her permed hair and on her dress.

"Getting married?" I muttered as if the whole ceremony was a big hoax and at any moment the guests would jump on their feet and shout, "Surprise, surprise!"

"Shouldn't I? I am thirty four," she whispered into my ear.

"So it's all true," I said. "Who did you marry?"

"He is a friend I met in Hawaii." She turned around, searching for the groom. Her eyes stopped in the direction of a man in a tuxedo sitting at a long table. He was a white man, tall, lean and young, as a matter of fact, so young and ruddy that I had the impression that he was still growing. And even from a distance I could see his doubtful eyes, typical for a young adult with an identity crisis.

I was about to say something when Priscilla was kidnapped by a sharp-voiced bridesmaid with long, pointy eye lashes.

"I'll talk to you later," Priscilla said.

I looked around. Rachel was not present. I would be a nuisance if I didn't pay some lip service to the groom, so I strolled up to the young man.

"Congratulations," I said.

"Thank you," he said, looking at me with a crisp grin, his blue bow tie setting off his blond hair and blue eyes.

"I am Alex," I said, "friend of Priscilla's."

"I am Michael. Cliff is my dad," he said.

"Oh," I was taken aback, and soon it dawned on me that I was actually not talking to the groom but Priscilla's step-son.

"Yes, congratulations on your dad; Priscilla is a very nice woman." I couldn't believe that I just said that.

"Thank you." The boy must have thought me a bore, for he turned back to the glass of wine in front of him.

"Excuse me," I said, left the table, re-orientating myself, and saw Priscilla standing beside a middle-aged man with a florid complexion and a receding hairline. Although short in stature and pouchy around the waist, he was fairly agile in his large-sized tuxedo. Even though I could not hear his voice, I could sense his energetic talk through a golden bow tie shifting up and down on his hairy throat.

Din, din, din, din. Someone was hammering a glass.

"Hello!" Everyone stopped, at the tables and alongside the wall, and turned to a Hispanic woman, middle-aged but in a good shape, wearing an expensive, green dress.

She was Priscilla's advisor. I knew her because countless times, Priscilla had mentioned her name in association with something evil, morally corrupt and intellectually challenged. She was an immigrant from Dominica. According to Priscilla, the woman cared about nothing but her bank account and two daughters, both in right-wing, private schools. She made every academic move count in order to get tenure by the time she was forty. After that, she went into wines and international tourism. Some undergraduates who had taken her classes rated her one out of five on their evaluation forms and made risqué, borderline racist comments. *"I have never met anyone so selfish and so pretentious,"* Priscilla used to say.

"Priscilla, come here." The professor waved to the bride.

Priscilla walked up to her; the professor grasped the bride's hand.

"I don't know if this is inappropriate, and I don't care," she said with real emotion, eyes almost brimming with tears, "but I feel I am giving away my own daughter today. Priscilla is a brilliant young scholar, and we've been working together for..." She turned to the bride.

"Six," the bride whispered.

"We have been working together for six years, and she has been teaching me..."

I couldn't bear this any longer. It was like watching a rape, and I couldn't do anything about it. I stole into a bathroom and stayed there until well after the phoney show must have been over, reading blasphemous, insulting remarks etched on the partition walls for a moment of vicarious joy.

I went back to the lounge just in time to catch the moment when the bride threw her bouquet. It bounced off a gaunt young woman in a floral patterned dress. A tiny blob of cake cream was still on her upper lip. As the bouquet hit the floor, she hesitated, quickly looked around and then picked it up like it was a dead animal. She earned a round of applause and smiled an awkward, blushing smile.

Then there were photographers, art students hired at twenty dollars an hour, and a videographer, a guy, I was casually acquainted with. And Pricilla's father and mother had flown in two days before from Hong Kong. They looked dazed, confused, awkward smiles frozen on their faces. After having been bombarded by camera flashes, Priscilla and her husband clambered into a limo. She was waving inside the window to the guests and friends desperately like a prisoner. If I had a car, an income and a US passport, I swear I would have snatched her away, thrown her into my car, and taken her to Cuba or Mexico or Indonesia. Then I would scrape up a music band for her, let her play for local restaurants at my expense, and one day, be killed by the local mafia. But the truth was that I had no car, no money, and no Visa to go to anywhere. So I had no means to rescue anyone or the privilege of dying a heroic death, just a slow and nameless one. When a simple mind hits a deadlock, it tends to believe that the opposite direction must be the right way. Having an abusive, drunkard father, the daughter would require teetotalism as the only crucial quality for her would-be husband. I knew a man whose father was a poet and murdered his mother in his poetic derangement and afterward saw poetry as the most disgusting nonsense in the world. Starvation generates money worship; Gay movements the New right. We tend to make something cheap and irrational to rationalize a trauma as if a cat has no other means to heal a gash except for lapping it with her tongue. It's easy to overrate conservatism after seeing the debacle of a rebellion, and to speak highly of slavish conformists when a coup has failed.

The limousine drove away. A just-married plaque was fixed onto the tail of the car; dragging a tin can along by a flimsy string, bumping along on the rugged street.

## 47

*Dear Alex:*

*I found this postcard in a gift shop of the Metropolitan Museum of Art. The picture on the cover is called living still life by Dali. It's interesting, isn't it? I am writing my dissertation in New York now. I like this city. Who doesn't? It's true that New York is not America. I'd like to invite you to visit us when I am more settled in.*

*Cheers!*
*Priscilla*

She never actually sent me an invitation. Our tenuous connection was maintained by liking pictures and leaving occasional cheerful comments on each other's Facebook pages. And she never finished her dissertation. She dropped out of the program, though, and managed to snatch a masters degree at the last moment. She got pregnant, gave birth to a boy, and then another one. But she rarely posted pictures or mentioned her family life to me. I knew that she had, during a brief period of time, tutored Mandarin and Chinese musical instruments to kids whose parents were either Chinese immigrants or who thought if their children had to learn a foreign language the most spoken one of this world was a safe bet. Then, one day, she stopped updating her Facebook page altogether and phased off my radar.

I didn't see Priscilla again until nearly three years after she had vanished.

At that time I had just started dating a young woman studying at the business school at University of Illinois in Chicago. She was an accountant who also read D.H. Lawrence and frequently visited the art institute of Chicago. I often asked her out to watch subtitled European films; she often dozed off, but woke up, when the credits were rolling, with rheumy eyes, asking me how the hero and the villain ended up, with her husky, sexy voice. In return, I also dozed off during quite a few business opportunity presentations and was often woken up by folks yelling about something inspirational or by her pinching my arm after everyone had left.

One time, at a relatively small gathering, a woman was sitting among a row of businessmen and women on the stage of an auditorium. She looked very familiar to me except that I had no friend who would dress like she did. She had permed hair and was in a low-cut black pencil skirt and five-inch, red, high heels.

When the emcee said, "Money will not be a problem for the rest of our lives," the woman nodded emphatically. And when the speaker reeled off, "If we plug into the system we can easily build a professional team and work like a team. The most important thing for teamwork is having faith, and believing that we can make it!" The woman in red heels leaned her body forward on the edge of her chair, and clapped as if she was about to jump up on her feet and hug the speaker and peers sitting beside her. Then the speaker opened the floor to candidates who had benefited from the system to share their stories of financial success. She was the first one, and as soon as she opened her mouth, I realized she was Priscilla.

She paced confidently on stage and said, "I have changed so much in the last year. Just one year ago I was anxious about my future, suffering from insomnia, and had black bags under my eyes all the time. Now I am completely transformed inside and outside. So much so that my family and friends keep asking me how I changed so much. Well, my answer is simple: if they ask about the outside, I sell them the skin care, retail; if they ask about the inside, I introduce them to the system, recruit." She smiled to the audience and the audience laughed and cheered her on.

Then the new version of Priscilla started to shout, "No hero, but team members! No special treatment, but equal work! No short term success, but persistence!" And at the end of her speech she introduced herself as Tracy.

"Are you bored?" my accountant girlfriend whispered to me.

"I think I know the lady who was just on the stage."

"Oh, really?" my girlfriend said, "she used to be a music student, a musicologist. And she was the youngest in the Million Dollar Members Club."

"What does that mean?"

"That means she had a million dollars, silly boy. And two and three and four, five more in the future," she said with a sweet voice, hands smoothing down her sleek business pantsuit.

I got a hold of Priscilla or Tracy after the presentation. I sat her down in a coffee shop. After having caught up on each other's news, I sprang the question I had always wanted to ask on her.

"Did you invite Rachel to your wedding? She said you didn't."

"Yes, of course."

"What happened?"

"I don't know. She might have had reservations about Cliff."

"Reservations about Cliff?"

"Yes." She sighed, "She said she didn't understand. Don't you think Rachel is too..." she paused and then said, "romantic sometimes?"

"Utopian is the word you are searching for."

"Yes, Utopian. She said she didn't understand why I was marrying Cliff, and we almost had a fight. I think that's why she didn't show up."

"So are you happy now?" I faltered.

"What kind of question is that?" She snorted. "How is your girlfriend? Is she an accountant student?"

"Agriculture finance and accounting."

"Good. If you ever want to start a business she could be handy." She laughed. She might have changed everything, lost the weight, found a new name, but she still had the same high-pitched, charming, wide-mouthed, bend-over-backwards laugh.

"You have changed a lot since the last time I saw you," I said.

"For better or for worse?" She sat straight pointedly as if she was kidding, but I saw her strained hands on the chair.

I looked at her. Her skin was tanned, and her eyes veiled behind ultra-thick eye lashes were light-strained.

"For better, of course, for better. What's the Million Dollar Club? Tell me about it."

48

Apparently I had nothing to hold against Alice. However, I decided not to contact her unless she contacted me first. What a proud and self-efficient individualist I was. I would soon pay the price for the false pride.

Just a week after she had turned me away at the door of her apartment, she sent me a text message, briefly asking if I was available in the evening. I didn't respond to her right away. I sensed trouble, yet there was this nagging temptation to find out what was going on with her. I left her messages unanswered in my inbox. My silence was meant to say I was not her servant and had my own business to mind. What a pretence. So she called me up; I even hung up on her twice, and after a while, she called again.

I picked up. "What's up?"

"Hi, I am calling to ask if you're free tonight," she said. "My mom came. She—we're wondering if we could have dinner together since…"

"Your mom came? When?" I asked.

"Yesterday."

"When? Where?" I asked impatiently.

She was confused and then told me they wanted me to meet them at a French restaurant. It was the most expensive restaurant in town. It was a nice gesture, but I was not looking forward to meeting her parents, not even under the right circumstances. A spoiled kid was almost surely the parents' fault and responsibility, so I would be forced to lie about Alice.

I met Alice's mother at the dark restaurant. I had never dined in a real French restaurant before, so I was wondering if all French restaurants were supposed to have inefficient lighting, and such simple decoration. I sat down facing the daughter and the mother, and before long, I realized that the choice of the place was Alice's. Her mother would have much preferred a Chinese restaurant serving normal-priced rice and beef noodle soup. Alice had insisted on this one, not despite, but because it was the most expensive one in town, and she seemed to be taking miniature revenge on her mother's long-standing negligence and the sudden appearance.

I was amused because Alice was dressed like a Japanese high school student at a beach resort during summer vacation. If Alice was neurotic, she was at least confident and comfortable in the clothes she chose for herself; this look must have been her mother's idea. She was in a black and white striped blouse with matching short, dark purple skirt. She wore a navy blue hair band, her hair cascading down onto her shoulders, and the whole juvenile look was completed with a pair of white canvas sneakers fidgeting under the table and a sulky and absentminded face hovering above the plates and cutlery. To jack up the price, she ordered a la carte.

"Thank you for looking after Alice," said her mother. The lady must have been in her fifties only her skin was oddly smooth and free of wrinkles. However, the effect didn't make her look any younger but somehow inhuman.

"He doesn't look after me," Alice interrupted, "We're friends."

"Yes, you're friends, you are good friends. It's so lucky that Alice has friends like you and Poppy."

The name reminded me of the woman spy whom I was not completely sure I had ever shaken off. And I thought this also diminished what I had done for Alice, so I said, "Never mind, anyone would do the same." It sounded awkward, so I added, "And what's more, we're friends."

The lady turned to Alice, two brocade yellow dragons perched on the lapels of her linen blouse worming their way out of a fold. She said, "See, everybody loves you. Should you feel beholden to us, too?"

"Everybody loves me?" Alice said mockingly, "Who am I? Jesus? What about him? Does he love me?"

I thought she meant me.

"Especially your brother," her mother said and clarified my confusion. "Do you know your brother cried when he knew you were sick."

"He cried? for me?!" Alice raised her voice sarcastically.

The lady turned back to me, "Speaking of Jesus, Alex, do you believe in Buddha?"

"Not really," I said. "My grandma was a Buddhist when she was... when she was alive. I used to go worshipping with her. But I'm not a Buddhist, not really."

"Mom, it's rude to ask people's religious beliefs in America?" Alice said to her mother accusingly.

"Alex is not a stranger," her mother said, smiling, "Alice is always an excellent student. All the teachers she has ever studied with bragged about her to the sky."

"Please don't embarrass me, Mom."

"Her nickname is Baby because she never caused any trouble to us."

"Can't you stop babbling?" Alice flew into a rage. "I'm leaving."

"OK, OK, I will stop," the lady said, "Alex, you're skinny, go on, dig in."

Then the lady remained quiet for the rest of the dinner. But she carefully saw to it that we finished up all the food in the dishes with the thoroughness of a responsible dentist. Alice put up a fight over it. I first sided with her mom, and finally with Alice after I ended up eating up not only what on my plate but Alice's leftovers.

I made myself amenable, as I respected her mother's flying halfway across the earth without speaking a word of English. Since the moment she landed in this country, she must have been picking up after her *Baby*, dressing her up so she could make a scene in public with an adorable face.

"Are you sure you want more?" Alice asked me with her eyes open wide as I kept eating.

"Why? I like it," I said.

Her mom expressed her appreciation with a nodding smile.

Alice must have felt betrayed, but I didn't care. Not being her ally in the presence of her mother was her punishment. My choking to death was her punishment.

After diner, her mother invited me to tea the following day. I accepted.

"Alex, what does your father do for living?" the lady asked me as we were about to part on the street corner.

"Oh, he has retried," I said. "He used to work in a coal-mining company."

"A manager?"

"Yes, he was a manager of sorts."

"I can tell," she said, "I can tell a person with good breeding from those with a low background at first sight."

"Then, you are a snob," Alice grunted.

"Well, Alice," The lady sighed. "In a perfect world, in the world perhaps my great grandchildren will be living in, people from different backgrounds are the same. But I definitely won't see that day, and I won't bother you if my great grandson has a black girlfriend."

"How do you know it will be a son?" Alice said, "how do you know he won't have a boyfriend?"

The lady turned to me, "Goodbye, Alex. See you tomorrow."

"Bye."

I never received a call about an actual arrangement for tea the next day. Alice must have thought I was indoctrinated, feeling it compulsory to act submissive and blindly respectful to a middle-aged parent. I didn't want to correct this misunderstanding. The last thing she needed, I thought, at least for the moment, was revolutionary ideas.

49

A Slovenian philosopher once said: "For Western leftists, Eastern dissidents were all too naïve in their belief in democracy — in their rejection of socialism, they unknowingly threw the baby out with the bathwater; but in the eyes of the dissident, the Western left played patronizing games with them, disavowing the true harshness of the totalitarian regime." In my opinion, it is not that either of them doesn't know the truth. In both cases, justice and integrity submit to urgent, self-serving needs.

Rachel's ruthlessness and the scathing, self-righteous nature of the newspaper stemmed from a refusal to be submissive to any urgent and self-serving need. The paper was by no means successful, but it was reputed to be incorruptible. For a Chinese institution, that was an achievement in and of itself. It is said that he who has no base desire, is invincible. The newspaper could have made more profit, or at least could have been more popular, if it had piped down and followed suit: a newspaper is supposed to be made of everyday clichés, and a diaspora newspaper should in particular celebrate the ethnic group that its readers belong to. That's what a newspaper is supposed to do. Rachel understood this more than anyone else. But she had been doing the opposite, continually using the newspaper as a weapon to disturb the comfortable, and piss a lot of local Chinese nationalists off. But in the same way, over the years, Corn-respondece did win a few diehard readers, making a lot noise, and attracting a fair deal of attention. When it became too noisy to ignore, the university gave Rachel the annual Feminist Activist Award for a series of investigative reports on the campus femicide case in which the Chinese student was killed and the murderer charged with a life sentence. Rachel invited me, and when I refused, simply ordered my presence at the ceremony, saying it would be a shame if she and I could not accept the award together. I had to agree.

I found the multi-purpose room 101 in Gregory Hall where the event was taking place. The suit I'd bought for Priscilla's wedding had another chance to see the world. A woman at the door handed me a pamphlet. The room was full of white students and professors sitting at round tables, looking overrated, leafing through the thin pamphlets with their biographies and accomplishments in them.

*"Rachel Wang is a Ph.D. candidate from the Institute of Communications Research (ICR). Originally from Guangzhou, China, she studied Chinese language and literature and is now writing her dissertation on the newspaper history of post-Mao Guangzhou. Before coming to the United States, she worked as a news editor. Her*

*interests in journalism have to do with the role it has played in domestic politics and its future possibilities towards a democratic culture in China.*

*"Back in 2003, Rachel introduced into China the first Chinese language Vagina Monologues and was involved in the performance (later the documentary) and other media advocacies for gender equality and social justice. The murder of the Chinese female student last year in the community and the silence that ensued triggered her former experiences into action. In a series of investigative reports, she worked with a few students to help bring the problems of gender culture especially within the international communities to the fore for public discussion."*

I found the table she was sitting at. It was already teeming with chatter and laughter, but she had no one to chat with. She had come alone.

I crept up on her, and threw down the pamphlet, giving her the start I had planned.

"I didn't know you brought *Vagina Monologues* into China," I said, putting one of my hands on her shoulder.

"They made a mistake; it's a shame, no, it's a lie; I have to tell them to fix it." She was about to stand up; I grabbed her, and made her sit down as I sat down. All the discomfort between us evaporated in the celebratory air.

"I'm very proud of you," I said.

"This is the problem with the system," she said nervously, "people who do so little gain so much."

I looked at her serious eyes and face all red. I grinned.

"See." She pointed at me with a flourish of her hand. "Even though I've won an award, I'm still not taken seriously."

"I'm sorry." I laughed. "Are you nervous? I've never seen you so nervous. That's all," I said.

"No, why? A little bit. How can you tell?"

"Your face is as red as a tomato."

"Really?" She felt her face with her hands. "Then I'm not going to give a speech. It's optional anyway," she said with a tremulous voice. Everybody had a weak point. For this iron lady, she had never practiced her social graces or public speech skills.

"Ladies and gentlemen!" the master of ceremony called out. The hubbub settled down. The audience sat up straight and heads cocked in the direction a podium up front. At that moment, a young woman in a black dress tiptoed across the room. She was a staff member from the East Asian Studies Center. Approaching, she lowered her head, grabbed a chair and sat down beside Rachel. She cast an affected smile at me and then turned back to Rachel-the-activist with a lowered voice, "Congratulations."

"Thank you," Rachel said.

"I have something to tell you after this, OK?" the woman said.

"What is it?"

"About the newspaper."

"What is it?" Rachel was nervous.

The woman paused, looked around and contrived another ugly expression.

"My boss said we could not sponsor the paper for the next semester."

"What?" Rachel muttered, "but we are not asking for any money. You know the paper can not print on campus without a co-sponsor."

"Yes, I know. But we have pressure from..." the woman said in an even lower voice and made up the loss of volume by forming her mouth in various shapes and pointing her finger up to the roof.

"What did they say?"

"Oh, always the same stuff. It is a load of bullshit, but they have been calling my boss all the time, complaining about your paper. The conservative Chinese community is more connected than ever. You know, China is rising." She made a gesture to mimic a lot of worms clawing out of a piece of fruit.

"The annual Feminist Activist Award goes to Rachel Wang!" the MC announced loudly. Multi-purpose room 101 resounded with cheers and applause. The honor went to the only Asian woman student who had ever won this award in the history of the university.

Rachel stood up, frightened, facing a room of admirers. She didn't move until I felt for her arm and accompanied her onto the stage.

## 50

Alice got married and dropped out of university. The wedding ceremony was postponed because the bride was not in good health. The groom was Vic as everyone expected. Though I had my doubt, I felt a rush of relief. I had seen many aspiring young women end up marrying and leaving the real world, though there were some fortunate cases. Before Alice, there was Priscilla. Before Priscilla, there was Echo, a competent and skilled journalist; harassed by her boss, who then quit her job and got married and quit everything. And before Echo, Jiaoxing, a promising artist, who'd graduated from probably the greatest art school in the country, and who could not afford her luxurious life, having no other skills to earn any money and spending like a burst water dam. She got married to a vegetable oil king, addicted to cats and dogs and basically became an animal tamer. And Elaine: we used to stay up all night discussing Socrates and Plato and Kant; she got married to a guy who was as dull as a church bell, because her mom died from breast cancer and her dad desperately wanted a grandson. And thousands of Chinese women who wanted to marry U.S. citizens to afford themselves another chance at prosperity. In this system, love seemed to be the least important element for marriage.

I got a chance to meet the husband and wife. It was at a housewarming at the apartment they moved into together. I brought a bottle of wine, a futile effort, for there was no shortage of wine, beer, sherry, and all sorts of alcohol. It was practically a wine cellar. Being a nuisance, I was punctual, and was the first who showed up. The door was left open to the outside. I hesitated at the door, hearing the TV broadcasting loudly inside. I walked in; there was a king-size mattress lying dominantly in the center of the living room, and Alice, whom I saw at an angle from behind, lounging on it, cross-legged, two arms propping her torso up, so she had a better vantage point to see the TV screen. It was a rerun of the summer Olympic Games.

"Hi," I said.

"Alex!" she called to me.

I waved. Then I saw Vic at last, the European, a tall Dutch man, emerging from a bedroom. He didn't come up to me, but said hello, and then went into the kitchen. When I was seated on a chair in the corner of the living room, he popped out from the kitchen, a beer bottle in his hand, and leaned on the door. He watched a diver who did a stunt in the air and plunged into the water. There was a self-satisfied smirk on his mouth as if he was a more seasoned athlete, judging the whole performance as silly.

I was ignored and left alone. There was nothing to do. I supposed that there might be something going on in the kitchen, but nothing except beers stacked on a fold-up table. In the living room, Alice and Vic hooted when a Netherlander popped his head out of the water. I had to join the audience. I watched the game half-heartedly; when they whooped, I whooped along for a few rounds, and soon my mind was elsewhere.

Vic asked me if I cared for a beer, and then brought one to me and Alice. He poked at Alice's head with the bottle mockingly. When she took it, he kissed her on her cheek. I was irritated.

A phone rang. Alice scrambled off the mattress and picked it up from a footstool.

"Hello, Poppy…"

I was startled. But another emergency stopped my reflections. The beer Alice had just put on the floor beside the mattress fell over and poured out on the damask cover. And when she snatched it up, it splattered all over the place.

"Fuck!" Alice yelled.

"Fuck you!" Vic yelled at her.

We pitched in, rescued the mattress from the sodden carpet, leaned it against the wall. While we were doing it, Vic and Alice squabbled, not exactly over this accident, but over something that had happened before. When it was all done, tissue paper covering the map of the stain, I thought I'd better leave before Poppy or whoever arrived. I made an excuse and made for the door. In the corridor behind, I heard the hassle, Vic yelling, "Would you calm down?!" And Alice retorting loudly, "I will calm down when I want to calm down. Don't you order me to calm down!"

The separation was also expected. For a whole month, I had not heard anything from Alice. Then Vic moved out of the apartment; she appeared, faintly drunk, bruises on her arms and calves. She obviously had not gotten her dowry yet. She had texted me asking if I was in town. I texted, "What's wrong?" So the meeting had the overture of me going through the motions. She must have also sensed my sufferance, for she brought a laptop with her and preceded my saying anything with an ambush. "Could you fix my software for me since you said you are a technician." I played along. But there was nothing to fix except her Word Office having no authentic license. Then she asked,

"Would you come to my place?" I said I'd rather not. She insisted. I refused.

"You can't treat me like this?" I said.

She was surprised. "Like what?"

"Seriously?"

"Yes, like what?"

"Well, let me walk you home."

"But like what?"

"Like I don't even exist when Vic is available?"

"But he's my husband."

"Sure, he is your husband. Never mind."

"What's wrong with you?"

"What's wrong with me?" I was about to give her a lecture, but she looked really confused. Perhaps I assumed too much, projected too much of my own assumption onto her. So I gave up.

"I'm suicidal," she said sheepishly.

"Please let me walk you home."

"But do you want to?"

"Yes, please."

Though I thought I had plenty of good reasons to simply dump her at the door, I wavered when she entered and held the door open for me. The living room was unexpectedly empty, despite a man's shirt and a large-sized sock in disarray. The mattress had been relocated to the kitchen, which seemed to have been out of operation eternally. The map of the stain had turned to brownish scum and appeared larger than what it was in the first place.

"Do you eat?" I paused, and then added, "regularly?"

She didn't answer.

"Have you had anything today?"

Her silence meant no.

"You have to eat," I said. And as I said it, I found rage within myself. I opened the fridge; it was empty. I opened all the cabinets; there was nothing except a paper bowl of instant noodles. I turned on the faucet; it coughed and burst out yellow sewage at first, and then water. Not in the mood for doing the shopping or taking her out for a meal, I boiled some water and prepared the noodles. When I laid it before her, she cuddled on the couch and refused to touch it.

"You have to eat, Alice!" I said.

"I want to go."

"Where?"

"Europe."

"Then you have to eat, or you will go nowhere. You have to have the strength to go, don't you?" I urged.

"I miss you, Alex."

"That's the thing. I can't believe it." I laughed drily.

"Don't you believe me?" she asked weakly.

"Prove it."

"Don't you think we had a great time in Boston?"

"Great time?" I was about to retort, but instead I said, "Well, I am happy that you thought it was fun." I found I couldn't stand it any longer, being drained down into her weakening whirlpool.

Then, I said what I wish I had never said, "You are a human being; if you want to stay alive, you have to eat." And I made for the door. "Is he coming back?"

"He... had only five plastic bags of stuff."

## 51

My advisor, a corpulent old Caucasian, was the least paid professor in our department. He didn't seem to care. There was an unsubstantiated rumor that he had inherited a *bank* after his old man passed away. He was well-educated enough not to flaunt his wealth, but on his parties, which he often invited me, delicacies and vintage wines imported from Italy, Japan and Australia were served on antique china and tableware. He was bald, but statuesque, liberally perfumed. His house was like a greenhouse, for he would never allow his guests to bring any gift save a bunch of flowers.

I was his only student at that time. He might have thought that having only one student wouldn't be that different from having no students. He had been treating me like a free range chicken, occasionally sending me a letter telling me he had been back from some European country, and in return me sending him a piece of writing on which he would comment: Good work, or I suppose so, or Keep at it.

The funding I had applied for turned out to be too competitive. The young scholar who actually got it had a resume with awards and academic achievements I could only imagine to possibly match if I had cut out all the entertainment and half of my sleep time for the last twenty years. Although I was anticipating this failing, once it was presented in black and white, panic still set in.

At the last minute, I applied for a job as a library assistant, responsible for checking out library materials, collecting fines and fees, answering general phone questions, and putting returned books back in their places. The position was to pay eight dollars an hour. Though I thought I was fully capable of these things, a more agile undergraduate trumped me. I also applied to work in a dining hall, to tutor American students in Chinese, and when all failed, doing sample tests for an interdisciplinary program initiated by the education department, for which I had to have my eyes and head scanned weekly by x-ray machines operated by students from the biology, education and psychology departments who may or may not be able to become real doctors in the future. In the last attempt, I scored. During that time, I constantly had dreams of myself spoon feeding pasta and French fries to pale-looking people in a nuclear power station where they spoke broken Chinese.

One day, my advisor shot me an email saying he was going to take a lucrative offer in Utah and wondered if I was willing to join him.

I replied to him at once, asking unceremoniously about the funding, and he replied, "funding larger than you have ever had is waiting for you." So I had no choice but to quickly accept it, although I soon had second thoughts.

I meant to discuss it with Rachel. But I thought I knew what she would say about it. For a few days, I had been turning it over in my mind while loitering on the campus. I couldn't do anything except for brood over the offer like a wistful Chinese concubine waiting for the husband to start her life.

One morning, when autumn officially ended and a severe Midwest winter was lurking behind trees with flaming leaves, Alice's mother called me, asking in a quivering voice whether I could come to the hospital because Alice was in surgery and Vic could not translate into Chinese.

"OK, OK. I'll be there in about twenty minutes," I told her.

She thanked me many times and handed the phone to a man whose voice was grave and husky.

"Hello." Vic gave me an address.

I met the mother and Alice's husband in the waiting room. Vic seemed older and calmer than the last time I'd seen him. He was not as tall as I'd thought. As a matter of fact, he was a plain-looking western European of average height with deep eye sockets and thin, blond, straggly hair.

"Thank you for coming, Alex," Alice's mother said.

"Sure, sure," I said. "What happened?"

"The doctor has given her a liver test," she said with a tremulous voice.

Vic came in, "She has been drinking too much alcohol. She was diagnosed with alcohol hepatitis and cirrhosis. They did a biopsy because her liver has scars…"

"Sorry, I am not medically savvy, what does this mean?" I asked.

He paused and then said, "She has the most serious type of alcohol-related liver disease. Her liver is scarring. They removed a piece of tissue from her liver; then it didn't stop bleeding."

"Didn't stop? I mean, the bleeding didn't stop?" I said hesitantly wondering if I was asking the right question.

"It didn't stop automatically. They had to cut her abdomen open."

I flinched inwardly at what he was saying.

"But at least it has stopped now, hasn't it?" I stammered.

He didn't answer my question, so I turned to the mother.

"Has he told you what happened? She hasn't woken up yet," her mother said anxiously.

I said, "Yes, I think she will be fine. She is..., very athletic. She is a strong woman."

"Yes, she is," Alice's mother said. "She used to be a track-and-field team member in high school."

"Yes, then I bet she will be well soon."

There was another family in the waiting room. They were in a relatively joyful mood. Around dinner time, they had large-sized boxes of fried chicken legs and wings delivered.

"Are you hungry? I can get us some food." I had to say it twice in both Chinese and English.

"A friend said he was coming," said Vic. "He's supposed to bring us some food."

"Good. Any of you want a coffee?" I saw a coffee machine in the corner.

"I am fine," said Vic.

When I asked again in Chinese, Alice's mother didn't seem to understand my question. She wore an expression that suggested she had never been asked a question like this before. Suddenly the memory of Chinese customs came over my half-baked, Westernized mind. She belonged to a generation of women who would rather have a cup of tea served authoritatively, rather than being asked for an opinion of her own.

I made each of us a coffee. As I was balancing two paper cups across the room, a circus stormed in. They were Alice's friends. Some of them claimed that they just came from Indiana and Iowa. They brought with them a dozen or so get-well balloons and many cards filled with cheerful writing and cartoon characters. They even had recorded a cheer-her-up video in which eight of her best friends — none of them could make it — had contributed. Alice's mother accepted the gifts on Alice's behalf and had her cheeks kissed many times. Sandwiches came and went around, except amongst two young women who said they were both on a diet. The friends waited for half an hour, and a nurse came and said they were not to see Alice. Then, they said their multitude of goodbyes and left. And for the rest of the evening, Alice's mother had to carry the balloons and cards wherever she went.

I checked Alice's mother into a hotel, and kept wondering why Alice's father and brother had not come. But afraid of inflicting any more pain on her mother, I didn't ask. I returned to the hospital. Vic said he was desperate for a cigarette and asked me if I wanted to join him.

"Yes, I'd like to." Maybe he had pent-up emotions and needed someone to talk to.

After lighting a cigarette on the pavement, he poured out to me. He complained about how unreasonable Alice had been acting and how terrible her parents were. "They are just so awful, so awful," he said emphatically.

"Alice is not easy." I consoled him.

"I told her she had to do something," he said. "I said, 'If you don't like your major, change your major. If you don't like your family, cut them off.' The problem is, she doesn't seem interested in anything. Every day she locks herself in the damned bedroom and fights to keep me from coming in, bringing her food. She just refused to give in."

I paused, and then I asked him a question boldly as if we were already old friends, "Then why did you marry her?"

He stubbed the cigarette out against the railing and threw it into a flowering shrub. He said, "Sometimes she is very cute. When she's not acting ridiculous, she's very cute. Don't you think she's cute?"

"Oh, I think so. She's cute," I said. "I understand."

The next morning in the ward, Vic, Alice's mother and I were waiting at her bedside to see her wake up. She had been transferred from a post-anesthesia care unit to a regular ward. Nurses with an antiseptic smell and consoling smiles on their faces came and went. Multiple electronic screens were monitoring what was going on in the crucial areas of Alice's body.

Once in a while, one of Alice's fingers, clamped shut, and the electrical wires connected to her hands, would move spasmodically. It took a long time for her to wake up, and when she did, she fidgeted like a newborn baby. She neither spoke nor opened her eyes. She had no expression on her face except when her body was fidgeting. Then, she screwed up her face as if she was in a good deal of pain.

Toward noon, six Buddhist monks in black and brown robes came in. Vic and I were astounded and then embarrassed as they walked around the ward bed, chanting prayers, drumming wooden and metal bowls. Unlike Vic and me, who had been paralyzed in the face of all the modern and complicated medical contraptions, her mother thought she still could do something for her baby daughter.

## 52

Alice was allowed to go home after two weeks in the hospital. The operation and the two week stay cost the family half a million dollars as she had dropped out and had no health insurance. She was lucky that she was from a rich family.

After that, I didn't hear anything from her. I was getting ready to leave for Utah, selling my vacuum cleaner for ten dollars, a TV screen for twenty, a chair for five, and a heap of novels for one dollar each or seven dollars for ten pieces. When it came to throwing away a pile of old issues of the newspaper one day, I had a pang of nostalgia. Rachel was now planning to hold a fourth year anniversary party for the newspaper. She persisted at trying to drum up more attention and attract sponsors. She had no idea at all about my leaving and appointed me the chief of the party planning committee, which consisted of me and three other interns. Desperate measures.

I found myself standing beside a dumpster, flipping through a bunch of sheets of paper weighing down my arm, and then chucked them in.

On my way back from the recycling mission, coming around a street corner, I saw a very skinny young woman clutching two plastic bags in each hand and walking away with a clumsy gait.

"Do you need a help?" I said, flirtatiously.

She turned around, "I'm OK. Thank you," said she in a low voice.

"Alice?!" I exclaimed.

She raised her head slowly and squinted her sun-strained eyes in my direction like an old person having a hard time getting around with withering bones. She smiled at me, "Oh, Alex. I didn't recognize you."

I was fighting back tears as I walked up to her, and my eyes were all wet. She was like a survivor of a severe famine. I had never seen anyone so thin in real life.

"He let you do the shopping alone?" I asked accusingly.

"Oh, no, it is good for me to walk around. It's not heavy," she said with a hoarse voice that didn't seem to belong to her at all.

"Do you need my help?"

"No, thank you, really, it's not heavy. It is supposed to be good for me to do some light housework."

"Then…" I didn't know what to say.

"How are you?" she asked.

"I'm…I'm leaving for Utah," I told her.

"Utah?" She smiled mildly as if any larger expression or body movement would inflict the pain of her wounds. "It's warmer there," she said.

"Yes, it's warmer and everything is supposed to be bigger," I said.

"Good luck. I have to keep walking; it is good for me."

"OK, good luck to you too. Bye-bye."

She turned around and went on walking.

"Alice," I called out and caught up to her. "We're having an anniversary party for the newspaper. I hope you can come. Do you still use email? I'll send you an email if you don't mind."

"Yes, please. Congratulations." She nodded. Her eyes looked oddly large on her emaciated face.

She walked away, clothes hanging loosely on her skeletal body. This image would haunt me for years to come. Though I was always confident that I was in the right, now I had such doubt. She looked like a dead woman now, a sterilized, declawed pet animal good for nothing except being fondled or harassed. She was disturbingly calm. Was she finally cured of her schizophrenia because she had been literally rent apart? I couldn't think straight, or I refused to; it was too soon and too cold to rationalize it. But I knew from the bottom that even though I could have helped her, I failed her. I should have done more. I should at least have told her earlier that the certificates and diplomas she had been collecting to decorate her parents' living room backfired on her. She had been driven by her vanity to gun for one academic achievement after another, until everything she learned from those liberal arts classes and critical thinking professors was aimed to deconstruct her drive and pride and, even worse, make a fool of her wealthy family. I should have told her, though she seemed to despise academia. Nobody took school more seriously than she did. Nobody was more self-absorbed. She was a student of genius. What other identities did she have? But the only requirement for being a genius was giving up life. And I should have done more to stop her indulging in her downfall: live like you will die tomorrow! Start and exhaust a whim in just one day, went on an escapade without telling anyone, acting out all sorts of emotional turbulence, and pouring out her heart vehemently until her friends could not bear to be with her, shunned her, kept her at a distance. She desperately wanted love but was unable to offer any. In every romantic relationship she was like a greedy sponge, absorbing love and patience from her partner, asking him to forgive her, until the poor guy was worn out and wanted out. What was worse, once she thought she had been ditched, she had a good excuse to assume all the bad things she had been taking on along the journey. She drank, had sex promiscuously, and swore at whoever happened to cross her, until she had no home to go back to, if home means unconditional love. She had no future to look forward to either, for future meant simply repeating what had happened. She tried to care about things larger than her own life and people who were needier than herself. But she neither had expertise in social services nor was she sophisticated enough to make friends with people who were not as rich or as careless as she was. In the end, she became her own enemy; she became the tragic heroine of her and her family's wrong dream. I should have told her earlier.

## 53

I didn't expect Alice to come to the anniversary party, which took place in a spacious auditorium. Rachel finished her opening speech. A big screen was showing a video bragging about the past glories of the newspaper. One of the exuberant undergraduate interns had done a good job on it. According to the narrative, the paper was a smooth, glamorous path from one victory to another. Everything seemed to have been planned out beforehand by a mastermind, and the achievement was mystified. I enjoyed the show as I also played a part in the masterminding, as if an American boss rejoiced in the background while the young and beautiful maintained the facade.

Spoiler alert. After the ceremony, the revolutionary newspaper would survive another two years of financial insecurity and administrative turbulence, until it eventually turned into a newsletter for mainly gastronomic reports in the hands of a few young Chinese undergraduates.

Alice came in late just as the video was ending, and still caught the tail end of it. When the lights went on, she stood up with the rest of the audience, clapping weakly, and she was drowned out by a room of thunderous applause. I went up to her as the audience dispersed, forming small groups.

"I am glad you came," I said warmly.

"You guys are doing great!" she said.

"Yes, things are looking up."

"It was a great video."

"The student who made it is a film major," I said. "We're expanding. Actually, they're expanding; I'm leaving."

"That's sad, but this is great!" She exclaimed again.

"You know what?" I said, "Rachel has always been fond of your writing. If you're interested in writing for the paper, we can still have a talk about it, all together."

"Really?" she seemed excited. "Because that's what I can do. I can."

"Certainly you can," I said, "I'll tell Rachel."

Alice smiled. Her smile was again imbued with innocent hope like a little girl dreaming of her birthday gift.

"I will," I promised her.

Then she told me that she couldn't stay; she'd come by taxi, and a driver was supposed to pick her up a half an hour after he dropped her off. So she had to head out, though she should talk to Rachel, who was then surrounded by a clamorous crowd.

Outside the auditorium, I saw her off. She got into the taxi, and rolled down the window.

"Do you miss me? Alex?" she said suddenly.

"Yes, I do," I said as earnestly as I could.

But the truth was that I didn't. There was nothing about her I could miss, only the worry. Then the taxi drove away, and I never saw her again.

I went back to the auditorium, grabbed Rachel out of the crowd.

"What's up?" she said. "Who's the girl you were talking with?"

"That's Alice!" I muttered.

"Alice?" she muttered. "Are you kidding me? Wait, which Alice?"

"How many Alices do you know? The Alice."

"Oh, my God. You said she was sick. I didn't know she was... She looked so..."

"I know. She needs help. She wants to write for the paper. Will you talk to her?"

"Now?"

"Later." I shrugged my shoulders, gesticulating. "Will you?"

"I don't know. Things are running differently now. But she's a good writer."

"Great! Great!" I muttered rejoicing.

## 54

One month later, Alice died. I'd brought up the subject of Alice's writing for the paper to Rachel a few times. Each time, Rachel had said she would work in an appointment in her watertight schedule and then never did it. Then, I stopped bringing it up, for the semester was ending and the holiday season was coming around. The stores were decorating their windows, ineffectively though, because Chicago was about to have the coldest winter since the records began in 1872. A large pocket of very cold air, called a polar vortex, had just visited the university town; we were snowed in for two days, and the campus was dotted with cars with dead engines, and was torn apart with racist remarks, because the Asian woman chancellor had decided that it was not too cold for the undergraduates to show up for exams. I had renewed the document for my student Visa, getting ready to go back to China for the Chinese New Year. I had sent a message to Alice, asking whether she needed anything from the mainland. She didn't reply right away. Then, she replied, "Oh, thank you, Alex. I'm OK."

Nobody knew when she died. By the time they found her, she was lying on her bed, long gone. An empty bottle of vodka was lying on the floor. Vic couldn't get through to her for many days and finally called the police. They'd been getting a divorce.

Then, a bunch of young critical scholars in her previous department, feminists, Marxists and a Chinese young woman who could not talk for five minutes without mentioning Michel Foucault and Judith Butler, all popped up and completely took over Alice's posthumous affairs. A slender young woman who had never met Alice even suggested an award in her name. Alice's Facebook page was suddenly bombarded by condolences, eulogies and prayers, all in praise of her. Almost none of it was remotely true.

I was not even invited to her funeral. But I went anyway. Vic, her mother, a few strangers, and her former advisor were there. It was the most excruciating funeral I ever attended. According to her mother, her brother and father were both too sad to come. I doubted it. And there were more praying monks. At one point, nobody knew what should be done next, nobody was in charge, and her mother kept wailing. For the whole time, I couldn't stop thinking about what I should have done to help her more. Finally, I got a hold of Vic. "I am so sorry," I said, and then I burst out crying. He looked at me for a while. "You can't force somebody to live, can you?" he said at length.

Rachel called me up a week later. She sounded stupefied and demanded to see me immediately in her new office. They had moved into a newly decorated one with three brand new iMac desktops as well as ultra-high speed Internet. The idea of the anniversary party worked; a wealthy Chinese businessman cried after watching the video, saying his father was a persecuted journalist during the Cultural Revolution.

"You're leaving? Why didn't you tell me?" she sounded really agitated.

"Oh, it is not official. I don't want to make a big fuss about it. And you're busy, aren't you?" I said coldly.

She brushed my attitude aside. She continued, "Alice died? When? How did it happen?"

"A week ago." I sighed, "You know what? We could have helped her."

"Helped her?"

"I told you she wanted to write for the paper, didn't I?" I said.

"Oh, that was about helping her!" she said as if it finally dawned on her. "Then why didn't you tell me?"

"Now, you're blaming me?"

"I mean it was so unforeseen," she said. "What did happen to her? I heard that she died from drinking alcohol."

"It's not just that. It's complicated." I was about to explain it to her, but I found I couldn't. Rachel had just managed to shake off a few pounds on her waist and arms over the last few months by working out in the gym two times a day. Now she didn't look a day older than when I first met her. And she was sort of a star now. Some aspiring Chinese undergraduates looked up to her and spread rumors about her, saying she was actually from a high-ranking party leader's family.

"I'm sorry, I still can't; I'll tell you some other time; I still can't," I said, knowing that she would not mention it ever again. I had learned that great passion and sympathy were for those who have been refused, shunned and depreciated. When things like career or whatever prospect one was going after were looking up, seeking compassion and sentimentality would only be seen as childish, hysterical or as pathological dysfunction. That's why I never sought emotional shelter. I was one of those people who would rather heal in absolute privacy.

Soon, Rachel would get a job offer at a university in San Francisco. She would accept it because there were a good many international Chinese students. She would be able to start up a Chinese newspaper as soon as she settled in. And later, her dissertation would be published. She would send me a postcard saying she was now living in a two-bedroom apartment, and she couldn't believe it, but she even had had a dog. She was not an animal person. She would say she was very happy with her life, maybe because she was still single.

She would also write on the card, "I am very happy with my life. I go to sleep every night with one hand choking my dog and the other gripping my book. Ha, ha, ha, ha." In a word, she would completely forget that there was once a young woman whose writing she'd admired.

## 55

I never went to Utah. I backed out at the last minute. My final year I was at the university, all my friends and enemies had left. The town had turned into a big construction site. Hotels, new residence halls, and restaurants were being built or renovated. The town was making major economic strides with more disoriented students coming in. This was the year when everybody was talking about the wealthiest one percent of Americans, who earned more than nineteen percent of the entire country's household income.

Having no friends left and tired of making new ones, I hung out with the autobiographer more often, listening to his complaints. He had been converted to Christianity but still was not content with his wife, who was now expecting their third child. I asked him if he still wrote. He told me that going to church, doing Bible studies, and hanging out with his Christian friends had been taking up most of his spare time. Plus, his second baby was already two years old but could speak neither Chinese nor English, and was smaller than eighty percent of the babies her age. "Really? What's the matter?" I asked him. His answer was, "I don't know. I guess genes. My mother came to take care of her, but she and my wife couldn't live under the same roof for a day without complaining about each other to me." His story could not be verified, so I reserved all my advice and judgment. I just lent a sympathetic ear and heard him out. I had learned how to be more patient with people who felt helpless.

Alice and her tragic death had soon been reduced to Vic being a feeble husband. Once the community had a scapegoat, it was easy to understand and to forget. One day, a middle-aged man added me on Facebook and soon introduced himself as Alice's father. I was imagining an old man who must have been locking himself up in a dark dungeon, mourning, and who finally decided to get it over with, ready to come to

America, vowing revenge for his daughter's death. I was fazed when he sent me a message.

"How are you?"

"I'm fine. How are you?" I wrote back to him.

"How are your studies? When will you graduate?"

"I am taking it very slow," I typed. "I don't really know."

Then he sent me a few photos of a graduation ceremony.

"I just got a masters degree myself," he wrote.

My first instinct was that this poor man must have been suffering too much mental affliction and must be insane. But when I looked at those photos closely, I found that he was indeed standing among a row of people, all smiling, wearing graduation gowns, holding diplomas over their chests. *So it's all true.*

I typed, "Congratulations on your graduation."

Then he sent me more photos, and one of them was him standing behind a podium addressing a big classroom of students.

*So this is not about Alice at all, I thought. Her father has moved on?*

I chatted with the tycoon for another ten minutes. The whole time, what Alice used to say about her boorish father kept flashing back to me. I couldn't believe they were the same person. This man seemed humble and sounded even a little intimidated, picking words carefully and, at last, ended the conversation as sensibly as a sophisticated ambassador.

Maybe the accusations Alice made against her father were not exactly genuine. Maybe she was not sincere, and actually looked up to him and wanted to copy his vain life, only she went too far, and way beyond what he could understand and appreciate. But none of these hypotheses could ever mature. Her father never contacted me again.

Then, I thought I should have told Priscilla about Alice's death. She was astounded on the phone and then asked a few quick questions, and the subject branched off. When I was certain that there was no one who would care, I stopped bringing it up in conversations. One day on campus, I came across the young woman who had warned me to stay away from Alice. She was in a hurry with her school bag on her shoulder and books in her arm. I called to her, "Excuse me."

She stopped, startled.

"I thought you were good friends with Alice; I didn't see you at her funeral," I said.

"What?" she asked, confused.

"The funeral."

"What funeral?"

"Come off it."

"What are you talking about?" She scowled at me.

Then, I realized that she really had not known.

I got a job offer at a teaching college. It was not exactly what I had been dreaming of, but I had learned the difference between an egoistic dream and a dream that could co-exist with other people's dreams. I was quite satisfied with it.

Moving day. I was packing and selling what was left in my apartment. Early on, two quick-eyed graduate students, both good bargainers, had made a raid and left a few dollars on my kitchen table.

Taking books out of my bookshelf, I found the book I'd salvaged outside Alice's apartment the night we were back from Boston — *About Alice*, by Calvin Trillin. I was holding it, leafing through the pages back and forth, letting the memory come back to me. All of a sudden, I found that on the last few intentionally-left-blank pages were some sketches and scribbles. I turned the pages and read them carefully. Among a good deal of nonsensical and illegible scrawls and drawings, there was a paragraph of neat and small writing.

> *To Alice five years from now:*
> *Cheers! Because I have finished my dissertation and become a doctor. I have completed forty-one of the one-hundred-things-to-do-before-you-die list because forty percent of my life has passed. I have read all the novels on my book list and have finished my first draft of my own novel. I sent it to a book publisher, and they haven't called me back! I also have made a short film and acted in it. I have made up with my brother and his girlfriend or wife and now we respect each other like grownups. I have been to forty different countries and made one thousand friends. I just finished another full marathon. My allergic nose has been cured. And...*

The paragraph was never finished. I closed the book carefully and put it into one of my moving boxes.

## More books from
## Harvard Square Editions: